# SKYBLUE

M.P. HALLIDAY

MONSTER IVY PUBLISHING

*To David.*

*(Okay, you can read it now.)*

*Dear Reader,*

*This book contains difficult subject matter, namely: inferences to sexual assault and abusive situations. Please listen to your body and seek help if you need it. You can call RAINN at 800-656-4673 or visit online.rainn.org. Remember, you are loved. I believe you.*

# CHAPTER I
# POACHER

I can only pretend to listen. The pastor's remarks are longer than Papa would have liked, woody tones vibrating from his cords as if he had a cello caught in his throat. He speaks of death as a door, the Will of Fate unlocking it to usher us in. Fate, he says, is a map, and God is the master cartographer. Mamma hangs on his words like rope, her knuckles tight with grief around her twisted handkerchief.

If death is a door, then it's too easily opened.

The cemetery is stifling, its headstones crammed, leaning with the centuries. Stone angels droop toward the graves in poses meant to venerate and bless the dead, but seem instead to pity them. Amidst the crumbling fieldstone, my brothers assist the undertaker in lowering our father's casket into the earth, which had frozen in the night, taking several hours to dig. Byron grunts, the weight of our father dragging down his shoulders. A droplet of sweat courses Simon's temple, proof to me that my brothers have rarely experienced such back-breaking labor. At harvest, when our orchard was ripe and hands were few, Papa elected to hire the sons of widows or the odd vagrant passing through to haul away the apple crates. To his sons he taught that a proper work ethic was rooted in the intellectual mind rather than physical labor. As such, Simon and Byron have hardly worked a spade, let alone the new military muskets strapped to their backs.

They step back from the grave, their chins pointed to their chests and their new cavalry uniforms of yellow-gold and black. They look like targets.

"Don't worry," they've said, as if such an inane comfort could possibly ever help. India is not war-torn, but the Crown has lent troops to protect the interests of the East India Company, our country's monopoly on global trade. My brothers also neglected to mention the tigers and cholera, either of which could kill without remorse. Just thinking of it spins worry in my mind, and tears press against my eyes. I clench my jaw to hold them back.

My sister's tears are enough for the both of us. At my side, Anna sobs into her hands, her breaths pitching like a ship's sail torn loose. She looks at me and I can barely contain myself, though not just out of grief at losing our father. No, it's much worse than that. Much worse because I'm a selfish creature, the truth of my situation a yoke of burden—fear pressing on my neck. If my brothers leave, then *I* must stay, and all my dreams with me. I don't think I'll get the chance to see the world as Papa saw it.

Reverend Moody's black eyes lift from his Bible, cutting Anna a glance of distaste as she cries. He is shrewd and bigoted, believing women have no place at a gravesite or even in the world. I despise his callousness, his patronizing tone as he implies my father's life was one lacking in heavenly fortitude. His business called him away on too many Sundays, too many sermons missed. Well, he's present for this one now, and us girls—who don't belong in this scene by the angels—all we want is to look at Papa one last time and say goodbye, cursing Death's doors for ever opening.

The morning breeze lifts, a crow flitting over the pastor's black-brimmed hat. For one blinding moment I wonder if Papa opened Death's door on his own, welcoming the other side with his arms outstretched, the wounds at his wrists weeping out his life instead of saving him. Bloodletting, our physician said, would kill the consumption, so Papa lifted his hands and he looked at me, saying, "Take care of your heart, Beatrice." And then his eyes went to Anna and to Mamma, and I realized what his words really meant. Once he passed, I would be their keeper.

My fists shake against my sides. I take a breath and the smell of wet earth sticks to my lungs. My brothers, their chests broad and yet so breakable, set sail for India tomorrow. At dawn, I'll be left to care for our mother and sister alone.

The sky commences to drizzle out a misty English rain, muddying the open grave. My chest seizes, petrified that if we don't bury Papa soon his body will decay before my eyes and then I'll really have lost him. Already the worms—awakened by the rude disruptions of the undertaker's spade—drag their intestinal bodies across the casket.

As if revived, a beetle breaks through the mud at the grave's edge, climbing into the air. It hovers in front of my nose, wings blurred, colors shifting from black to gold to iridescent blue. My heart flitters as the insect zips through the sky across the cemetery where the crow dives for it in the air, crushing it in its mouth and devouring it. The bird alights on the headstone of an Irish cross, beyond which stands a man at an open grave, burying his dead alone.

It is Monsieur Dumas.

Intrigue, one of my cleverest and most incessant companions, settles my rampant heartbeats. I've never seen M. Dumas in the flesh before, though I know his broad figure from the titillations of drawing room gossip. Very little is known about the Frenchman, except that he's an aristocrat with lineage extending back to *Madame la Guillotine* and that bloody war. One can easily see his arcane and gothic manor house atop Shakespeare Cliff, overlooking the harbor, but few have been inside it. Like some fox in the hedgerow, M. Dumas shows himself only when he wants to be seen.

His head isn't bent in misery like mine, though his shoulders have the curve of someone unalterably depressed. News of his wife's death rushed about town like a hurricane, obscuring Papa's passing as if he were a transient who died in the outskirts—close to home but not close enough to pity him. The townsfolk have quickly forgotten their best merchant and tradesman.

I wonder what she was like, M. Dumas's wife. I wonder if his love for her was more sincere than for the wives who came before her. There have been several of them, or so I've heard.

The crow squawks from its perch, and M. Dumas lifts his head in my direction. My gaze darts away before our eyes can meet, so I glimpse only a quarter of him: an eye, black as space, and one dark, arched brow.

Little shivers prick at my spine like witchcraft.

An umbrella appears overhead, the piney odor of gin accompanying it. An oily voice invades my ear.

"Black is not your best color," Mr. Haskell says. The man I despise most above all others.

"And pandering for my interest isn't yours," I say, raising my sleeve to shield my nose from the smell. "You're late."

"I was mourning."

"You were drinking."

"Is that not the same?"

We're hushed as Reverend Moody reads his final lines, commending Papa's soul to God. He nods to the undertaker, who lifts his spade for the final time.

I don't expect the thud that comes from earth hitting pine or the hollow sound it makes in my chest.

Other hollow sounds, like the words *I'm ready*, rope themselves around me. Final words are empty things, deficient promises and senseless comforts. Papa's last words seemed illogical—how can one ever be ready for death? The idea is like a plunge into a river of ice when the plunge is not a plunge but a *push*. You see your end—*there*—on the bank of your life, but never expect to feel so bitterly the weight of water. It's usually then when a hand breaches the void and pulls you out, saving you.

Papa's fight was brief and defenseless. He gave up too readily, and that, more than anything, is what makes me mourn.

The pastor leaves us without further comment or comfort. Mamma, trailing her fingers across her pale mouth, repeats Papa's name like a mantra, as if worshipping a gilded idol with six arms and two faces. *Charlie, Charlie.* His last kiss haunts her. She feels it still, the grooves of Papa's lips, the pucker of a marriage sweet but severed too soon.

"Mamma, let's leave this place," Anna says, taking our mother's arm to pull her away. She goes willingly, *Charlie* still on her breath.

"Such a pity."

I startle, remembering Mr. Haskell standing behind me, sheltering me from the downpour. He lays an unscrupulous hand on my back, veiling it as consolation. It lingers too long and too low.

Everything about Papa's business partner is thin: his face, his fingers, his pocketbook, his ethics. A drip of rain slides down his narrow nose, notched in the middle with a scar, which my father gave him. Papa caught him in their office one night, drunk, with all their documents dangerously close to the hearth. One lick of flame and their whole business would have burned. As his partner, Papa couldn't fire Mr. Haskell. But he *could* break his nose.

"I gave Charles my word," Haskell says, his voice smug. "His family will receive every care and comfort they stand in need of." His hand vexes, creeping greedily around to my hip. I nudge him off, stepping backward to my father's grave. I've a pressing need to join him there, just to be rid of this despicable man before me.

"Your words are worthless," I spit. "You can barely take care of yourself. You look like a vagabond and smell like a tavern."

His face contorts. He grabs my arm, and the umbrella drops to the mud, soaking us instantly in rain. My brothers are on him in a blink, wrenching him backward.

"Touch her again and you'll find my musket widening your navel," says Byron, Simon moving to his side, cautioning him against recklessness.

Mr. Haskell stops wriggling, wincing under my brother's grip. An amused, wolfish smile spreads his lips. "Do it," he says, spittle foaming in the corners of his mouth. "See what victories you achieve from within a prison cell."

"Leave him, Byron." Simon's prudence irritates his twin, though he's never ignored him. Just this once, I wish he would.

Byron lets go with a shove. "Mark me, cur. You'll not lay a hand on this family so long as I am alive."

Steadying himself, Mr. Haskell picks up the umbrella, shielding me with it once again. Behind his eyes, I see a lion prowling, pacing its den. "You forget, boy. The contract I signed with your father is binding. You forfeited your right to his business the moment you pissed your inheritance away on that whore." He laughs, the sound keeping strange time with the undertaker's shoveling behind us. "You should have known the second she sat in your lap she was a charlatan. And you thought you were in love."

Byron lunges, but Simon is on him, holding him back. I throw out my hand.

"That's enough, Byron," I hiss. "Go home. You're disgracing us."

"*He's* the disgrace!" Byron cries.

"She's right, brother." A melting sort of weariness pulls at Simon's mouth. "This isn't the place. My will is spent, and I no longer have the patience to defend you."

Byron recoils in disbelief, his fists like stones, heavy

and enduring. "Defense is worthless when the defender is a coward." His regret flushes over him as soon as the words leave his mouth. Simon hides his hurt well, but never well enough. It's true he's cautious, but not gutless. He'd follow Byron to the ends of the earth—and he *is*, and all because of Byron's carelessness with the women he thinks he loves.

I've had enough of this. "Bryon, please go. Let me mourn our father in peace."

His anger slips from his shoulders, and he plods away from us with his musket thumping against his back. Simon, loyal to a fault , makes to go, but hesitates when he realizes I'll be left alone with Mr. Haskell. The glances they exchange are full of disdain.

"Byron needs you," I say, speaking *I'll be fine* with my eyes. "Be sure he doesn't do anything rash."

He goes, if only because he's seen me handle Haskell's impertinence on several previous occasions. He looks back at us twice.

Driven by the deluge, the undertaker finishes his task with unearthly speed. I watch him unceremoniously shovel the last of the mud over Papa, the cemetery gates clashing behind him as he takes his leave, unfeeling and indifferent, just like the pastor.

I search for M. Dumas—the last living body in this boneyard—but he, too, has gone, his wife lorn, already forgotten. At least she has the protection of the grave, while I have none at all.

But this isn't the first time I've had to fend off the prurient interests of a man, and I hardly doubt it will be my last.

I feel Haskell's presence like a snake, slithering about me. He meets my eyes, and it's hard to look away, the umbrella over my head a snare as well as a shield. He's silent a moment. Then says, "My word is honorable, Miss Tilney. But words are weak without incentives to bolster them." He scans my face. Then the rest of me.

Anxiety chews at my stomach, but I refuse to show it. I make myself stone, projecting power, control, a belief I have both.

"The contract I signed with your father is legally binding," he says. "The law now recognizes me as your guardian. I hold all stock in the business. By all intents and purposes, the survival of your family now rests with me." He pauses, lengthening my pain and his pleasure. In the breath he takes, I hear the tightening of noose around a neck. *My neck.* He rolls his hand through the air, nonchalant in his predation. "Why not sweeten the pot?"

I stiffen. "What are you proposing?"

"Exactly."

I fire my insult at him with the force of a flintlock. "You are a despicable cad. I'd never marry you."

I expect him to lash out, as before, but he only grins that slick, malicious grin. "*Never* is a word easily altered, Miss Tilney. Do not be so quick to reject me."

"And don't be so quick to mishear me," I say, swallowing the lump of disgust building in my throat. "When I say never, I mean it."

"You're in no position to refuse."

"All the same, I do."

Frustration tightens his jaw, but he smothers it. The advantage is his, and he knows it.

I know it, too.

"It would be cliché of me, dear girl, to say your passionate—nay, *impertinent*—spirit only adds fuel to my fire. Nevertheless, I'd be cheating myself out of the pleasure I feel *not* to say it." Mr. Haskell's slick grin spreads a little wider, sickening me.

Spurring me to run.

I run until my lungs ignite with fire and my legs break away from me, extensions of an incredible fear propelling me down the pebbled streets of town and onto the dirt footpath of the orchard, where I trip on the twisted root of a tree and skid to my knees. I rip off my bonnet, tear my constrictive cloak away. I can't breathe. Clouds of foggy breath whirl about my face as I take in great gulps of air. My heart will burst out of me if I don't cool it, and my head, my head is high, up in the treetops.

A laugh gusts from my mouth. How comical, running from Haskell as if he were a poacher, intent on catching sweet game. What a game, this running. This chase.

I've scraped my hands, shreds of skin and dirt and clotting blood; they sting. What a game, this game of fear.

A poacher. That is exactly what Mr. Haskell is.

I sicken, not from the sight of my bloodied hands, but from how narrow my escape really was. I don't want the attentions, the wanton desires, of any man. I don't want to be wanted in that way.

The fire in my lungs intensifies, eating up all my air. My body leaps up of its own accord, and my legs begin again to run, back to the path, to the road, but not to the cemetery and the man who thinks he has a claim on me.

*But what if he does?*

The thought lances, terrifying. If the poacher takes the shot, he may strike true. My running is defenseless. I'm too panicked to see a way out of this nightmare.

My lungs feel too small to breathe, and I stall out in the middle of the road. Black spots flash across my vision, the world darkening with every failed inhalation. Running is useless and my body knows it, so it freezes. Arms, legs, knees—they atrophy, and I collapse once more, the world too much and too big, an incessant roar of blood and fear and pain.

And as I go down, fighting against the dark of unconsciousness, I hear the wheels of a carriage grinding upon stone.

## CHAPTER 2
# SHELTER

Pebbles jump and skitter as if enchanted. An ebony coach reels forward, pulled by four black Hackneys with feather plumes. It is M. Dumas in his funeral coach. His cortege is that single crow from the graveyard, attracted to the musk of the horses whose proud gait seem slower, more somber, than what fits their pedigree.

The driver shouts, reins snapping against the horses' muscled necks as they grind their hooves into the dirt. The coach stops alongside me, a coatless girl collapsed in the middle of the road, soaked under this torrential rain. The coach door is thrown open, and two black boots with silver buckles splash into the muddy road. I keep my eyes down, failing to think what it might mean for a middle-aged man to scoop a semi-conscious girl in his arms and carry her into his carriage. But the carriage is shelter, and my lips shiver, my wet hair clinging to my neck in ratty strings.

He sets me carefully on the bench, sitting in the seat opposite me—for that, at least, is proper. Though propriety seems largely immaterial to M. Dumas, as his first words to me prove.

"Your clothes grip you like a second skin," he says, removing his coat and throwing it over me. The anxiety roaring in my ears dulls a little with the new warmth. I take deep, steady breaths to bring my heart back under control.

"*Détendez-vous, belle fille*," he says, and it is like a croon. "You are safe."

"*Oui. Mais suis-je vivant?*" His brow shoots up, surprised how the French language pours from my mouth with ease. It was the one language Papa insisted I learn, as French seafarers frequently dock in our township's ports. *Yes*, I said. *But am I alive?*

M. Dumas peers at me curiously, unsure if I'm serious. I glance around the coach's interior, horse musk mingling with the scents of leather and something else. Something floral, yet heady and exotic. A man's cologne. The dim light obscures the Frenchman's finer features, though I can make out a strong nose and a furred jaw, and it's funny: in all my imaginings of him, I never imagined M. Dumas with a beard.

My skin needles with an emotion that's not quite fear and not quite pleasure. I knew he was a foreigner, but now I've had it confirmed to me. He's curiously out of place here, every rumor I've heard cloaking him in an air of salacious adventure—of *newness*—as if he's not only seen the world but actually been a part of it. A hero *and* a villain, depending on the story.

Intrigue arouses in me, a blush speeding to my cheeks. My heart flitters with a sudden, maddening desire to know *all* of this stranger's secrets, all his mysteries, even if they turn out to be dangerous.

"What happened?" he says in English, his voice like honey oozing from a dipper. Sweet enough to compel me to respond.

"I was running," I say.

"From what?"

"From—" My throat tightens, fear threatening to return. I swallow it down. "From everything."

His brow creases. M. Dumas retrieves a handkerchief from his breast pocket, taking one of my bloodied hands and bandaging it, not looking at me as he says, "Fear is just a feeling. Release your hold on it, and it will fall to the wind." He says this as if reciting a Psalm he'd memorized, as if sympathy for another human being came only occasionally, and this occasion felt imperative enough to lend comfort.

It works. Whatever fear molested me escapes like a servant through a side door, and it's like I can breathe again.

"Thank you," I say.

He nods. "Please, let me take you home. This rain is ice, and I fear for your health. Your family cannot afford to lose another loved one."

"Nor can you," I say, with more surprise than embarrassment. Even with the loss of his wife, M. Dumas hasn't forgotten the death of the town's best merchant, my father. I clear my throat of tears before speaking again. "Thank you, *monsieur*. But if you would oblige me, I'd like to be left here."

This situation is strange—he is, after all, a stranger. I shouldn't feel so at ease sitting with him alone inside his coach, where the windows are shut to the road and there is very little light. With a bit of work, I summon discomfort, scooting away from him to the door.

"Wait," he says. I pause, fingers on the door-latch. "Your eyes, what color are they?"

I blink at him, confused by the random question. "They're lapis."

"Like the stone?" I nod, and he settles back into his seat, returning to the point in our conversation before the non sequitur. "Very well. You know your mind, it seems, and I should not like to dispute it."

Mercifully, the rain has turned to a fine mist. I step down from the coach and shrug out of the Frenchman's coat to return it to him.

"Keep it," he says.

I smile, the first in weeks. "No, *monsieur*. *Merci*. As you've said, I know my mind." I set the coat next to him on the seat. Dipping into a curtsy, I glance at him just quickly enough to catch the upturn of an eyebrow, the exhale of a humored breath. The driver snaps the horses into a trot, the coach vanishing around the bend in the road.

Another shiver streaks through me, and I hug myself, feeling as if I were under a spell, and it has just broken.

By the time I return home to our yellow-brick manor house, our bulldog Quincy yipping at my heels as I track mud through the door, the winter deluge has ebbed. I'm no less wet than I was in the cemetery, only now I have no coat, and my brothers are furious with me.

"You gave us a bloody fright! Where were you? Whose kerchief is that?" Byron jiggles my bandaged hand in front of my face.

I wriggle out from his grip. "No one's. It's mine." They follow me to the drawing room, where I slouch on the rug next to the fireplace. I unpin my hair, chestnut waves dripping into the flames, sizzling. "Where's Mamma?"

"In bed," says Simon, a concerned line tugging at his brow.

"She'll be there for days," adds Byron, his own brow sullen.

"Don't be cold, brother. She's just lost her husband."

"And have we not lost a father?" I say. "She should mourn with her children, not alone in her room."

"Be kind," Simon chides, though gently. "Both of you. Until you have buried a spouse, you shouldn't judge her so harshly."

"I'll not marry," I say.

"Neither shall I," says Byron, smirking. "But only because women are looser in their scruples before marriage than after."

I snatch a pillow from the sofa and throw it at him. It bounces off his shoulder, and he laughs.

"What a terrible thing to say, Byron."

"It's true," he teases, "for the most part. Except in your case, Birdy, destined for the holy spinsterhood."

"Spinsterhood? No. I seek something far more sacred."

"Which would be?"

*Independence.*

I pull my lips together, shame beating double-time in my chest. Though Papa would have clucked his tongue in disapproval, I've dreamed of being the free and uninhibited young woman I've read about only in books. I've imagined myself, after a youth exhausted on travel and delicious adventure, renting the ivy-veiled cottage bordering our orchard, where a spinster called Ami Rose lives with her collie and her garden, her existence uninterrupted by the fast and persistent peregrination of time. I imagine, with her books and her snapping hearth, that time has altogether stopped, forever halting her age and suspending her blush of hope and innocence. She is virtuous. Independent. She is happy being alone.

I shudder, the chill not escaping my brothers' keen eyes. Byron stokes the fire, adding another split log, while Simon finds me a stole for my shoulders.

From beyond our small drawing room, the dulcet, melancholy tones of Chopin's Prelude Opus 28 No. 4 sound from the piano in the adjoining room. The exquisite E-minor key gives me a sense of dwindling, of release into an ether of stars. I drift with it, into those stars of diamond light and silver. And for once, I have no thoughts. Just feelings, pertinacious in their need to be felt. When the music ends, I'm left feeling cold.

Lately, Anna has become a taciturn creature, preferring to speak only through song. The house weeps from the keys of her piano, saying everything I could never even begin to express. Yet Anna says everything without ever parting her lips.

My brothers and I say nothing as we listen. We hear the cover drawn over the keys with a careful yet final *thunk*, and Anna enters the drawing room. Quincy is flush at her heels, bounding into my lap. I bury my face between the wrinkles of his neck.

"Beatrice, you're shivering," says Anna. "Are—are you unwell?" She fears my answer. She couldn't stand to lose another family member, after Papa, and now our brothers.

"I'm fine. Thank you."

A smile blooms across her face. She kneels to the floor, far more gracefully than I could have, settling next to me at the fireplace. Quincy, fickle pup that he is, leaps from my lap into hers, and a twinge of jealousy pricks at my chest.

The clock above the mantel chimes a quarter to eight, the ticking of its hands like the gradual rise of a guillotine's blade. The evening is lengthening into midnight, stealing away my minutes of postponement.

A bubble of anger—of sudden, vicious rage—blurts out of me. "How could you?" I yell, bolting to my feet. My siblings all stare at me, mouths open, but I can't—I won't—stop myself. "How could you leave us now? *Now*, of all times? Papa has just *died*!"

My brothers' eyes cut to one another, Simon's expression guilty, Byron's irritated.

"We know what we're doing," he says.

"Our time for reconsideration is past," Simon adds. "We took the Queen's shilling. It's done." He shrugs his shoulders, and I want to scream. I want to make them *stay*.

"We wouldn't reconsider even if we did have more time," says Byron. "You are prudent, Beatrice. You know we need the money."

Holding myself, I scrub at my chin in angry motions. I hate Byron for his truth. I hate him for his choice. But most of all, I hate that he will experience the world, away from the pain of scraping life from the bottom of an empty food tin. For I'm certain, with Haskell's patronage, that's exactly what will happen. While Anna and Mamma and I struggle, my brothers will survive, because they are men.

"How much?" I ask it angrily, never having thought money mattered all that much until now, when I feel it drifting from my grasp. Now I understand how money is life.

"A penny each per day."

I laugh, incredulous. Scant wages for the cost of suffering.

"We wouldn't do this if we didn't think it was right." Simon's voice contains all the softness and caution of a parent. He takes up my bandaged hand, gently rubbing warmth back into my cold fingers, and the affection of it is too much. I close my eyes to keep from spilling over. "Out of all of us, Beatrice, it was always *you* Papa trusted to take care of them."

Anna's cheeks are pink, her shoulders close to her ears as she recognizes herself at the center of our words. She shrinks whenever she's talked about, as if to make herself invisible. And she is talked about often as of late. *She is our pearl*, Papa would say. *She must be protected.*

But what about *my* protection? Who will ward off the threats of poverty and danger when men like Horace Haskell are set to be our guardians? My bravery can only keep for so long before it's whittled down to desperation. And desperation makes sinners of us all, doesn't it?

My brothers are young, only twenty-one. I am younger still at just nineteen. How can I let them go?

Byron rises from his seat in what was Papa's favorite armchair and casually announces his retirement to bed. As if this were just another late-night soirée among siblings. "Sleep well, Birdy," he says, smiling, a divot notched in his chin. "And dream of the habits of nuns."

My jaw aches from holding everything in, but his levity nearly breaks me. No matter what I say, I won't convince him.

Tightening my jaw, my heart, I say, "And you. Dream of women with loose scruples." It's the closest I can come to saying how much I love him.

## CHAPTER 3
# PREMONITION

My brothers leave for India the next morning, and life begins again, moving at a monotonous pace, our fatherless weeks stacked upon one another like book towers, precarious and cluttered. Already, we feel the noose of indigence tightening around our throats. We have to sell Papa's writing desk, Mamma's jewelry case with most of its contents, and the bookshelf Papa surprised me with on his return from Spain. Along one of its sides is a switch disguised as a moonbeam, which opens a clandestine compartment. Inside, he hid a single rose, picked from the Spanish queen's own garden. I hung it upside-down in my windowsill to dry, trying to save it, but its petals cracked, crumbling just like my hopes for the future.

Just last week we let our servants, Molly and Archibald, go. Not only do our appetites suffer in consequence of their departure but also the state of our house. Dust floats down from the ceiling, spreading itself along the shelves and floors and furniture, dulling the colors of Mamma's once-fine burgundy velvets and hand-woven rugs.

Mr. Haskell has neglected us, as I knew he would. For all my father's goodness, he was hopeless at reading people, letting his humanistic ideals obscure the reality. He believed the good in a man always won out in the end. *A mortal warrants mercy*, he would say. But what good is mercy when that mortal ruins the happiness of an entire family, jeopardizing its health and safety? No, I don't share Papa's sentiments about the good in people. I have read too many novels to know the villain's heart never changes. He is always calamitous and vile, and in the end, he is vanquished knowing his cruelty and loving it. Mr. Haskell has left us to suffer, relishing our pain.

To escape our dreary house, Anna and I have adopted daily strolls through our family's orchard. Eden, we call it, because when we were young it was paradise. My clearest memory of this place is when Papa and I would play hide-and-seek among the brambles. My blood would vibrate as I kept low, close to the cowslips hemming the trees, as a nearby shrew dug its nose into the roots of some bluebells, snuffling for earthworms.

The game would change into an autumn hunt as I crept forward on my hands and knees, my buttocks raised like the haunches of the tiger I imitated. My chestnut hair did well for stripes, mottled orange by the sun cast through the orchard's canopy.

The shrew sensed me, pausing. Sniffing the air. I readied my leap, muscles bunched to spring—when Papa slung me over his shoulder like a stag, chortling even as a cough impinged his lungs.

I remember asking if he was well. He told me I worried just like my mother. *Too much.*

But, oh, Papa. I didn't worry enough.

Now, Eden is withered and frostbitten. We take lazy steps, lifting our hems above the stratum of rimy mud and leaves, vast columns of skeletal branches reaching skyward to an indifferent sun. Buntings chitter to each other overhead. A redwing thrush pecks at the flesh of a frozen apple, and the smell of my family's prized fruit carries to my nose. I develop an urgent craving for apple tarts.

Papa said I was like an apple. The third offspring of four, I was the fruit of an exquisite love, sweeter and more sublime than the first fruits of man. That's how he described it, anyway, and I seldom argued with him.

"Remember how Papa said he and Mamma met?" asks Anna, her cheeks dimpling.

"Remind me," I say, and she dives into a narrative, a skip to her step.

"Like every respectable couple," she begins, "they met at a private ball. After being introduced by the Master of Ceremonies himself, Papa asked Mamma for a dance, and then another, and yet *another*—stirring up grievances among the other gentlemen in attendance. Their courtship was long with poetic words, bridled passions, and just a *touch* of handholding." She giggles at her pun. I smile at her. "It culminated in the immaculate chapel of St. Paul's church, resonant with a carillon of golden bells." She sighs, her hands brought under her chin like a woman posing for a fashion plate.

Yet Anna is no woman. She's a girl of fifteen. Her rendition of our parents' love story is charming, but completely fictional, a version Papa liked to feed people he'd newly met. The truth is, Papa met Mamma at a *public* dance, where they'll let any sort of riffraff in, and introduced himself by spilling his punch on her white muslin gown. His manners were so ill executed he even tried to clean it for her with the hot lemon water normally reserved for the tea. Nevertheless, their fortuitous meeting (a fluke, really) actually did bring them to St. Paul's, though the church's bell had split, producing a horrendous clang when rung.

Still, if only to humor Anna, I laugh with her, our breaths spooling above the branches.

She sighs against the gnarled trunk of a Bramley. "Their love was exquisite."

"It was," I say, humoring her again. "How they survived the derisive horde of highbrows, I'll never fathom."

My sister looks at me appalled, as if I've squashed a

baby bird that fell from its nest. "How can you say that? Our parents were well respected. Mamma was properly out in society, and Papa was a gentleman."

"He was ten years her senior. Even by today's standards, that's quite the gap. At least Mamma was twenty before she said *'I do'*."

"Their ages hardly mattered. They were in love. Love trumps all."

Fighting the urge to roll my eyes, I suck in a swill of air and hold it, feeling how my lungs stretch and tighten, then exhale dramatically. Anna knows about as much of love as I do, which is to say nothing at all. She's naïve, and I'm just as innocent, though I hate to admit it.

"Love didn't trump Papa's death," I say. "Mamma barely speaks to anyone anymore."

I glance at Anna, her head down, shoulders quaking as she begins to cry. I've been too harsh with her, and my guilt is like the pain of an empty stomach. Papa would never have allowed me to speak this way to her. It's time to be the sister she needs, the mother I don't want to be.

Tucking a wispy strand of blond into the braid of her hair, I say to her, "I will always take care of you," but I can't keep the chill of memory from frosting the edges of the sentiment.

When Anna was eleven and I fifteen, we were playing near the pond behind the gardens. Winter was crisp and new and the pond had formed a silvery sheet of ice across its surface—a rarity in our coastal climate. I was goading her, teasing that she was too much of a mouse to brave even a foot across the ice, while I danced recklessly across its surface. I did a pirouette on the air, spinning once, barely making a quarter turn before I slipped on the landing. The ice split—the noise like cracking glass—and Anna vanished before my mind understood what was happening. She'd watched me fall and rushed to my aid, but two bodies were too heavy for the pond and it broke, swallowing her whole while I stood frozen on the narrow shelf of ice. I should have dived in after her, but I was too scared to even scream for help. Having heard the ice break, Papa took to the rescue.

When he pulled her out, her lips were blue. So blue.

I couldn't save my sister then. How could Papa have thought I can save her now?

It's late. Dusk blushes pink to violet, giving in to the night's advances. In the east, palatial gray-white clouds usher in a winter storm we shouldn't get caught in. I brush the tears from my sister's cheeks, and we start for home along the road that runs parallel to the orchard, the road where I'd met the Frenchman.

We hear a carriage clambering over the dirt behind us and move aside to let it pass. The carriage slows by command of its passengers, whom I recognize as Felicity Crane and her cousin Georgiana Field. Both girls flaunt the wealth of their fathers—Felicity the progeny of a banker, and Georgiana the daughter of the town physician—by wearing the most expensive, flounced taffetas they can find. Felicity waves me over, but I stay where I am. I find them incredibly dull and am in no mood to pretend otherwise.

“Beatrice!” she calls. “I’d wondered why we’d not seen you at Lady Lambeth’s party last night, but then Georgiana remembered you’re now the ward of that buffoonish man—what’s his name? Mr. Haskell? My cousin tells me he’s viciously jealous and keeps you locked away in that dingy house of yours. But now I see she’s mistaken—it appears he lets you out for air.”

If I were a tiger, I’d growl at her, though insults are an equal defense. I won’t be the grist in the town’s rumor mill. “Gossip is a vapid lady with no creativity,” I tell her. “Truly, Felicity, you’re as unoriginal as you are empty-headed.”

Felicity looks at Georgiana, and the girls burst into laughter, unaffected. They eat up my reaction like cake, sweet validation for the vicious lies they spread.

“Has he asked for your hand, yet?” says Georgiana, clucking like a hen in a roost. “You’ve no other prospects. Only last night I heard Mr. Haskell boast to Lord Lambeth that he’ll have you in his bed come St. Valentine’s Day!”

Pitching into a fit of laughter, the cousins frantically wave their driver on to escape the wrath I’d throw at them.

But I’ve no wrath at all, save the cold, creeping terror at the thought of filling any man’s bed.

As each Sunday comes, Anna and I sit in church to honor Papa's memory (absent Mamma, who's labeled herself an invalid and must remain indoors). Papa's faith was strong, and I long to feel close to him there in the invisible world, if such a kingdom exists.

Perhaps it's only in my forsaken state when I feel doubt replacing my faith, but as I try to believe that Papa sees me here and knows my prayers, I'm only skeptical. I want to believe that the dead hear us, that they feel us reaching blindly for them.

Hunger grinds at my ribs. We aren't totally emaciated, though we will be soon. Haskell gives us little money for bread, never fresh, and meat, always meager. I've supplemented our pantry as best I can from the pittance of my dowry, which was far less than I had expected it to be. It was like I'd found a hole in my pocket, kept secret from me until it was all but empty. When I asked Mr. Haskell about it, he played ignorant. It was then I realized what he meant when he'd said, "*Never* is a word easily altered." He means to drive us to starvation in the hopes that I'll crawl to his door and plead for his mercy. His words to me at the cemetery, slippery and sly with insinuation, rattle about my brain with intensity. It's only a matter of time before he propositions me again, forcing my hand in marriage.

My neck feels flush and fiery, my thoughts in a tizzy. *I*

*don't want to be wanted in that way.* I smooth down the now wrinkled crepe of my black mourning dress, bunched in my hands since the start of Reverend Moody's tedious sermon, another grating diatribe of death and doors and fated choices.

Anna clutches her handkerchief in her small hands, her eyes red, straining to be tearless. She's as desperate to feel Papa's presence as I am, inspiring her soul with more grace than she could ever find in a chapel so cold and staid, so lightless. I've struggled against the fog of my own suffering so long that I've forgotten she loved him too.

Pierced by a tendril of sympathy, I take Anna's hand and give it a squeeze. She looks into my face, smiling weakly into hers, and turns up a corner of her mouth.

Something whirs past my vision—a smudge of azure scuttling beneath the pew into the aisle, as if marching in a wedding. A queer beetle, the same I saw in the cemetery. I don't think it's native to our region; I'm not sure how it came to be in England at all. Its iridescent back shimmers blue to gold to blue again, in constant contrast to its surroundings. Blurred wings break from its shell, sending it airborne and whizzing over heads unseen, unfelt, disappearing in a blip. There one second, fading the next.

A portentous quiver crawls down my back, sharp and tactile like hands. I feel eyes on me. In a slow pivot, I turn my head to look behind me. Far in the back, by the door, sits M. Dumas like a drapery of shadow and cold air.

In all my suppositions of him, I never supposed him to be religious. He has never come to church before now.

He sees me watching him watching me, and he bows his head. The congregation of sober faces stymies my view so it's again only those dark eyes, and a portion of off-colored beard that I see. My heart beats erratically, a sudden, palpitating mass of expectancy and what I think must be dread. *Lord, those eyes!* Veiled and unfathomable, their awareness of me turns me skinless, all barren and bone and open like a wound.

*Look away.*

I try, but I'm caught, reeled in by those penetrating eyes. His stare is eternity, stretching onward into a forever void of midnight and ash, undoing me. In his coach, I'd been curious being so close to him, but now I find myself afraid. Fresh swatches of color come to my cheeks, piquing his interest as his eyebrows raise, and the sinewy drawstrings of my nerves unravel. To stare back at him as boldly—as *foolishly*—as this, is an invitation I don't want to give, yet I feel as if I'm caught under a spell.

I force my gaze away, clamping my eyes shut to pray with more fervid religiosity than I've ever prayed before. In my communion, I beg to be invisible, to never be looked at by such eyes again. Because to be caught in their centers is exactly that: a capture. An abduction. My mind has awakened with an understanding, like it did with Mr. Haskell. In the sights of this widower is a dangerous place to be.

"Beatrice? Beatrice, you're pale."

The muscles in my hand spasm around Anna's fingers, and I release her hand.

"I'm all right," I say, but it's a lie. I'm not all right at all.

"Who is it?" She starts to turn, but I stop her.

"No one. It's no one." Inhaling a breath, I brave a look back.

He's gone. The door brushes closed, icy wind gusting into the chapel. I clutch my coat around me, the buttons all done up, though it hardly settles the erratic dance of my nerves. This is not the bleak and pressing cold of winter.

This is premonition.

## CHAPTER 4

# Unhappy News

Anna and I haul our underthings to the side of the house, where we had sometimes helped Molly on washdays. I scrub the clothes against the washboard, blowing suds into the air with vigorous breath, and rinse them in a basin of hot water. Pulling the linens out with wooden tongs, Anna wrings and secures them on a clothesline with dolly pegs. She hums as she works, steam spooling about her pretty face. The work does us good, keeping us fit, occupying our minds. We haven't yet forgotten what it means to wear black, but we can pretend we have.

"You can go once you've hung the stockings," I say. "Tell Mamma I'll be in for tea."

"I'll put the kettle on," Anna says. She unties her apron, entering the house through a side door, and within a few minutes, I hear the jaunty notes of a Mozart concerto. She seems happier. Maybe because she senses winter is taking its exit from the stage, and she's helping it along with her musical direction.

The river Dour dithers in the background, rousing me. There's work left to do. As I go to lift the basin to drain the soiled water, my slight frame strains with the effort, and I end up sloshing half of it onto my feet.

Quincy, who's been dozing in the flowerbeds, lurches into a territorial stance, growling low.

"Allow me!"

A man garbed head-to-toe in black jogs to my aid, and without any preamble, takes the basin from my arms to toss its brownish muck into the bushes. The short acts of hastening and heaving produce a bead of sweat, which plows into the man's sideburn.

Even in those stygian hues, he's handsome. His light hair has been fashionably trimmed, swept backward at the sides of his beardless face. His frock coat looks expensive, expertly pressed with a high collar.

And here I stand in a fraying work dress, my hands chapped and my hem dripping with suds. I can hear Mamma now, mortified that her daughter looks so disheveled before a gentleman.

He dabs at his face with a handkerchief monogrammed with the letters S. M., Esq. "Forgive me for disturbing your work, miss," he says, "but seeing as no one answered with the bell, I thought I might locate the servants' entrance."

He must have rung while Anna was playing. "I'm sorry for the inconvenience," I say, stuffing flustered hands into apron pockets. "But we don't receive visitors anymore."

I pull a damp sock from the line, making like I'm going to wash it again. But one glance at the man's sympathetic stare and I swing the sock back onto the clothesline. I won't be felt sorry for.

A bit cross, I say, "I'm pleased to make your acquaintance, Mr.—"

"Mitchell. Silas Mitchell. I come on errand from Mitchell, Crane and Company." He fumbles uncomfortably with his handkerchief, and I feel the color trickle from my face. "I have, I'm afraid, some unhappy news with regards to your late father's finances."

My heart plummets. He's a creditor. Come to collect what we don't have.

I brace myself against the house, my hair tangling in the barren wisteria vine scaling the brick. My legs want to move, to run as far as possible from this merciless life. Must everything be taken from me? What else is left but my virtue, or must that be taken from me, too?

The thought gores a hole in my chest and packs it with fear. Without a word, I push off the wall and dash into the house, a flummoxed Mr. Mitchell in pursuit of me.

The kettle skirls angrily in the kitchen. Anna is nowhere, neglecting the task. In my haste to remove it I burn my hand on the iron grate, gasping out a sound that's too much like an expletive.

"Can I help?"

"I'm capable," I snap. Ignoring the pulsing sting, I throw the tea things onto a tray and hurry through the house into the drawing room.

Anna sits at the piano, which I had helped her drag into the room to fill it. We sold the rest of our furniture, save for the velvet armchair, which is arguably the last dignified object we own. I smack the tray down onto a sidebar with more intensity than I intend to, and Anna jumps from her bench, curtsying for Mr. Mitchell, who bows lopsidedly in return.

"I've, uh, upset you," he says, tugging at his collar, now rimmed with sweat.

I steep and pour the tea, guilt tingling up my neck. How horrid I'm being. The first guest we've received since Papa's death, and I'm distressing him.

"You haven't," I say, feigning civility. I sit on a cushioned chair displaced from its set in the dining room, a signal to Anna to return to her bench and for Mr. Mitchell to sit in the armchair. I pass him a saucer and cup, which he promptly sets down. A deliberate gesture. I flinch, dreading whatever disagreeable thing he's sure to say next.

"Will your mother join us?" he asks.

I sip my tea, wincing as it scalds my lips. "No, I'm afraid not. She's...indisposed." And by that, I mean she's in bed, lying in the dark with the curtains drawn and the door closed. She's threatened to lock us out if we don't leave her alone. I saw her emerge once, early in the morning, with her cloak around her shoulders and her boots laced up. She wouldn't tell me where she was going, and I wasn't awake enough to press her.

"Ah." The creditor clears his throat. "Miss Tilney, I wouldn't have called if I'd already found success with your benefactor, Mr. Haskell."

*Benefactor.* Hardly. Haskell has ruined us.

"Mr. Haskell has neglected my family for two months now, Mr. Mitchell," I say, not bothering to disguise my bitterness. "Honestly, I'm surprised we've lasted this long. He's drained our money as if we had a vault full of it to begin with. I don't understand where it's been or where it's gone, only that there isn't enough of it to feed us. It's only been *two months*, sir! How is this possible?"

The man looks away like I've shamed him. "I have no idea, miss. I'm deeply sorry to hear about your predicament." Then, bolstered by a remembered sense of duty: "But the fact remains that your family is in debt to the mortgage owed to the bank. I've been instructed by my superiors to collect immediate repayment."

My brow wrinkles. "What mortgage is that, sir? I haven't heard of it."

"Why, the mortgage on the orchard, of course."

My heart clenches. I shake my head, dumbly. "You're mistaken, sir. We own the land outright."

Mr. Mitchell's expression dampens with some realization. He reaches into the breast pocket of his suitcoat and hands me a document bound in leathers. It's the mortgage deed for one apple orchard, measured fifty acres, recorded June 23, 1856, more than one and a half years ago. Papa's signature survives on the page in bold, black letters.

The deed trembles in my hands. "I don't understand," I say, my heart squeezing tight. It's getting hard to breathe. "Why would he have done this?"

Mr. Mitchell clears his throat, and the sound, delicate and cautious, irks me. "Over a year ago, Mr. Tilney came to Mr. Crane and my father in need of a loan, the reason for which he would not disclose to us. Nevertheless, my father, trusting yours, granted the loan and the orchard secured it. Since your father's passing, however, the bank has taken a great loss as payments have not been made. I'm afraid foreclosure alone is not enough to settle the debt. So now you see, Miss Tilney, why I am here."

I do see. I understand Mr. Mitchell's words, but I can't comprehend why Papa kept this secret from us—from *me*. What's more, I can't understand why he didn't tell us all this the night he lay dying, choosing instead to leave us in the feckless hands of Mr. Haskell. More than the shock of the debt itself, it's this lack of honesty that confuses me, that distorts the image I've kept so carefully of my father. This was not the behavior of the man I idolized.

Mr. Mitchell wears impatience like a cravat, heavily starched. Folding up the document, he says, "I do not wish to add to your distress, but I have been ordered to attain payment in one form or another."

I look at him through wet, blazing eyes. "And what else do you suggest we give up, Mr. Mitchell?"

He shrugs. "Surely your family has managed to keep a few things of value. Your horse, I hear, would cover a quarter of the sum, at least."

I stand, as does the creditor. "Hastings is not for sale," I say. The horse isn't mine, anyway, but Simon's. The morning he left, he made me promise I'd take care of Hastings, a Dale with a silky black mane and a jaunty trot wonderful for riding. At 14 hands, he's easy to mount, and by far the gentlest equestrian I've ever met. With my brothers gone, he's been my best support.

"Do you have another choice in the matter?"

I bite my lip hard enough to hurt. The piano bench creaks as Anna adjusts herself, nervously tugging on the splitting ends of her hair. I'd forgotten she was there.

So did Mr. Mitchell.

Her movement draws the creditor's attention, and his eyes, glinting with purpose and newfound authority, look to the instrument.

He wouldn't.

*He can't.*

"Mr. Mitchell—"

"I'm sorry, Miss Anna," he says, ignoring me, "but under the terms of a contract signed with Mitchell, Crane and Company—effective immediately—I must seize this instrument."

Anna won't look at him, frightened by the severity in his voice. She cants her head in that birdish way our father was so fond of, saying faintly, "Beatrice?"

What can I say to her, except that I'd rather Mr. Mitchell take her piano than Simon's horse?

I don't have to say anything. She reads my preference in the guilty glancing away of my eyes.

"Anna, wait," I say, but she's already fled the room, a sob breaking. I turn on Mr. Mitchell. "How could you?"

"Sacrifices must be made, Miss Tilney."

I step back, disbelieving. "Sacrifice? The word is an *offense*, sir! An excuse to divest people of the things they love most. How can you say such a thing after what has just happened to us?"

I see the remorse pinching up his forehead and my pulse spikes. This is not petty wroth, but indignant, seething anger such as I've never felt before. I desire suddenly to twist his lapels in my hands and scream at him how he can wear black for us but he will *never* know the constricting fear I feel that my mother will be next to die, and Anna soon after her, if I can't find a way to take care of them. *Sacrifice* is a weak word to describe whatever I must do to keep them alive.

The burn from the stove cries out as I clench my fists. The urge to apologize presses on me, but I tamp it down. I motion to the piano. "I trust you won't need assistance carting it out."

I've never been so hateful to a guest before, slamming the door, leaving him alone in the drawing room while I sprint from the house. Outrage has heated up my blood, and I need to expel it through exercise. I need to think, to breathe. I need Papa.

*Papa.*

Papa's dead.

I drop to my knees at the riverbank. Is *this* what my life is, silt on the river Styx, that river of decay? I feel the urge to plunge into the water and let the weight of my grief crush me. I feel broken. Irrelevant. Incapable of fulfilling the promise I made to my father. I can't stop Mr. Mitchell from performing his duty, nor any other creditors who are certain to come calling. We're going to lose everything.

The realization is slow, but it comes. It's *not* my fault. Not really. Mr. Haskell made a promise, too, one my father should have forced him to sign in his own wretched blood. Our suffering is by *his* hand, a deathly orchestration of malice and coercion. This—my torment—was his plan, and this—my desperation—is his achievement.

Never *is a word easily altered, Miss Tilney.*

Fistfuls of mud and sediment squeeze through my fingers as I relax into a resolve I haven't felt in ages. I unlace my apron and bunch it into a grubby wad to hurl into the river.

I've made a decision.

I don't bother washing. Where I'm going, it won't matter.

## CHAPTER 5

# FEATHERWEIGHT LIFE

The rain begins as a drizzle then comes pelting down in huge, stinging droplets. The road is a river of mud and gravel, spattering my boots as I trundle toward the port town. From this height, I have a clear view of Dover below: chimneys steaming, coaches lumbering along the Sea Front, and ships, moored in the harbor, breathing with the tide. On the coast the castle looms, our bastion from the time of the Roman occupation; and in the Heights, our militia safeguard the redoubt, weathered forts erected at the height of the Little Corporal's second reign of terror. Napoleon is dead, but his nephew has now taken on our suspicions.

The road steepens through the valley, where heifers graze on clover and short, calcareous grasses, into the woods flanking the Dour. In the summer, my brothers would hunt rabbits while Anna and I chased the cerulean

Adonis butterfly, homemade nets flapping over our heads. The sun, it seemed, was in a perpetual state of beatitude, never covered, never cold, and I never felt even the remotest sense of peril. Or of darkness overshadowing me.

Now the valley is gray and misted o'er, and my heart pumps my blood madly through my veins. The distant caterwaul of the train charging from London to the coast redoubles my dread. I'm walking too quickly. Even though I'm thrice soaked through, I deliberately slow. *Twice* I reconsider confronting Mr. Haskell. He's dangerous. Adulterous. Undoubtedly, he will try to have his way with me.

The idea makes me squirm. Not for obvious reasons—his slipperiness, his snake-like appearance—but by reason of his apparent hubris, his insinuation that he can take what he wants and that, as if by taking, I'll somehow be different. Changed. Emptied. Like I won't be *me* anymore, but someone of his shaping.

*Never.*

I walk too slowly now. The rain absorbs into my stockings and dress, to my very core. Everything wet with hesitancy.

*Anna and Mamma—I'm failing them.*

Steeling myself, I quicken to a horse's lope. The sky thunders like a cannonade, the storm refusing to wave the flag of surrender. Like the rain, I will not yield.

I turn onto Snargate Street, stopping below a sign

reading in elaborate, scrolled letters, *Tilney and Haskell Mercantile.* Heart skidding, I grab hold of the iron knocker, and before allowing myself to think any more about it, pound it to the door.

I wait.

My knees quiver.

*From the cold,* I tell myself.

No one comes. I try again, but still, no one. I try the handle next, and, finding it unlatched, ease open the door.

The tight entrance hall reeks of vacancy and musty neglect. Two offices stand to either side, Papa's forsaken one on the right, a wasteland of his belongings I haven't had the heart to rummage through, and Mr. Haskell's on the left, an uncertain peril. His door is shut. He could be on the other side of it, the lion in his den, anticipating the careless wandering in of his prey. Why hunt, when you can wait?

I swallow the bile clawing up my throat. If I can't convince him to make good on his promise, we'll be lost. I push open the door, watching it swing inward, and without further doubt, step into the bedlam that is Horace Haskell's office.

THE PUNGENT, crinkling odor of stale alcohol assaults my nose. Dust lies everywhere. Musty curtains trap shadows, and scattered candle flame, melted down to dim, day-old nubs, casts everything in bluish hues. Haskell has always been averse to the light—*sensitive eyes*, he says—but he's really a vampire. One needn't siphon only blood to qualify.

Lightning flashes through slats in the shuttered windows, wanting sanctuary, the bellows of thunder shuddering the panes. It's in this burst of light I see the evidence of his desertion: Haskell's desk, once littered with unread books and crumpled parchment, has been cleared.

He left in haste, not even bothering to douse the fire, smoldering near extinction in its hearth. Paper remnants, and what looks to be the flame-warped binding of a leather journal, lie blackened and charred to ash. He took his every vice with him, save for the scattered tobacco leaves that crunch under my touch, and the decanter of gin on the sidebar without even a drop of liquid left.

He has abandoned us.

My relief at his absence mingles with a rage that I can't confront him. He was a cad, but I thought at least he was a predictable one, who'd linger on the fringes of our lives so he could glean pleasure from watching us suffer. But Haskell was a *coward*, as well as a cad. He couldn't stuff down his guilt far enough into his heartless body to face his victims, to watch us waste away under his carelessness. How easily he gave in to his impatience, his boredom. Apparently, the victory of my consent to marry him wasn't even worth the wait.

*Would I really have consented?*

The idea of being a wife sets my skin shivering—the idea of being *Haskell's wife* stilling my body cold. Now that he's gone, I should be grateful to have escaped such a fate.

I slump against the edge of the desk, grasping my hair by its roots. Am I really so desperate, so naïve? Surely marriage isn't all a young woman can do. It can't be! I've seen women dedicating themselves to work as a governess or a shop girl or even a mill laborer. They make cotton up north, where some women have wages. *And smoke and soot and strikes*...but never mind all that. From the beginning, I should have quit my grief and my moaning and been more resourceful like Papa would have expected me to be.

A swelling pride, like hope, overwhelms me, though it's precarious, lacking any sort of foundation. Yes, Papa had expectations for me, but he never trained me to fulfill those expectations. I have only those pretty, quaint talents deemed appropriate for women in my class—like embroidering tea towels or reciting poetry from memory—yet absolutely no connections or practical skills. I lack the patience required of a governess and the strength necessary for a laborer. Not to mention I've never sold a thing in my life—that was a task for our servants—and wouldn't even know how to go about it. If it ever came to it, would I even be brave enough to sell myself, my body? This is desperation in its oldest form: bartering bliss for coin. For survival.

I scorn myself for even thinking it. Acid terror scalds my throat, and my eyes burn with the pressure of tears. Months, even days ago, I wouldn't have understood how anyone could ever do such a sinful thing. But now, I think I know. The stress to survive creates burdens only the destitute understand.

A leaf of parchment pokes out from a gap in Haskell's desk, catching my eye. The drawer sticks when I pull, tearing the paper, though it looks already as if it's been hastily ripped from a book. Crisp lines of ink crisscross the page in the fashion of a chart, indicating that it came from a ledger.

It's an account of goods purchased and exchanged: figs from Ibiza, wine from Corsica, and other exotics to be sold in shops across England. Papa told me much about his business, how it was a competitive struggle, what with the East India Company's monopoly on foreign imports. Money had to be well managed and records accurately kept. These records appear inexact, written in the hand of the lesser business partner.

Mr. Haskell's writing is much like the rest of him, thin and sloping, teetering on the paper like a ladder abutting a house. What words I can make out are few and careless, the mathematical figures inconsistent. Even with the government's unconscionable taxes, the price of imported tea should have brought the company more revenue than what was written here.

Suddenly a thought pricks my reason, and blood rings in my ears.

"Embezzlement." Mr. Haskell has been gradually, cripplingly bleeding money from us.

He really is a vampire.

The ledger is dated January 6, 1855. Two years. For two years, he has been leading us to bankruptcy. And when it came, he fled like a deserter.

I understand Papa's secrecy now. He bargained our lands and our futures in his fool efforts to save us from the disgrace and scandal that would result by turning Haskell over to the law. *Right under his nose*, the rumors would have said. *His own business partner.* Papa, in denial or disbelief, justified Haskell's actions on his behalf. *A mortal warrants mercy*, he would have said.

But what mercy is there when there is first no justice?

The truth stitches me with anguish and hate, and I crush a hand to my chest. Why did I come here? Did I, in my ludicrous self-confidence, really think I could convince a bad man to alter his ways, to become *good*? It was folly! Some men are in love with their wickedness, chasing after it like light.

And now Haskell is gone, and I feel, more than ever, how forsaken we truly are.

The paper drops from my hands as everything around me numbs, and I watch it waft to the floor, landing with the featherweight of a life in ruins.

## CHAPTER 6
# In All Things Honesty

I walk home, a floating specter along the lanes, misty rain suspended in my hair, my cloak, capturing light from the sunset. Mamma has finally left her room. She sits by the window in the velvet armchair, watching my approach with a skein of thread and a tatting shuttle in her lap. The patterned lace is hardly any longer than when she first started the project, before Papa's death. I'm not sure it will grow any more, or if it does, how quickly.

"It rains?" she asks me, as if surprised. Water slips down the windowpanes next to her, yet she doesn't turn to look, instead relying on my report.

"It appears to have stopped now," I say. She absently rubs her neck, itchy from the crape trimming on her sable dress. Mourning has never been comfortable, made even more miserable when combined with bombazine. Hesitantly, I note, "You're still not eating." A smattering of clotted cream, dolloped onto a scone, sits untouched on her tea plate. She starves by choice, despite the repeated coaxing from my sister and I. Ghosts don't eat, and a ghost is what she has become. If I don't take care, I'll become a ghost, too.

"I haven't an appetite," she says, her voice floating away from her. She fixes her eyes on the mantle clock, hypnotized by the pendulum's oscillations. Unlike Ami Rose, for whom time has stopped, time has merely slowed for Mamma. I read it in her face, densely glazed: she wishes her own time would hasten. The sooner to reunite with her beloved husband.

He's there, on her lips. *Charlie, Charlie.*

*Marjorie, Marjorie.*

I remember him entreating her as he lay dying. His breath brushed her face as he struggled to speak: *Each day I have loved you, and I will continue to love you every day forever.* He kissed her mouth then, never kissing her again.

"The door," Mamma says, startled into life. "Anna, dear."

My sister materializes in the drawing room like a dedicated servant—hardly seen but always listening, a ghost in her own right. She obeys Mamma's command, though I heard no knock, no bell. My ears have begun to ring again, keeping time with the rainwater dripping from my dress onto the hardwood.

Anna returns to the drawing room paler than when

she left it. Behind her, a man lords over the threshold, his shoulders breaching the small width of the doorframe. Unnerved, the candles dim, casting the papered walls in purple shadow.

A shiver bolts down my spine as I recognize him.

M. Dumas's kohl-colored eyes roll listlessly under bushy brows, boring into the room, but it's his beard—pepper gray with an otherworldly, sky-blue tint—that intimidates. It limns the sharp contours of his face, which as a youth must have been handsome, but now, in middle age, waxes austere and stoic. Finally seeing him in full, and here in my home, does little to unriddle his mystery.

He tips his top hat to Mamma, though she doesn't look at him. She didn't even stand at his entrance. "I thank you, *madame*," he says, his voice leonine with the subtle lilt of a French accent, "for extending the invitation to come into your lovely home, and for again allowing me to speak with you."

I sway uneasily on my feet. *Invitation? Again?* Has my mother been conspiring with our neighbor? To what end?

"I realize how mistimed my visit is," he continues, "but it could not be put off any longer. I'm sure you understand." At this, Mamma nods—a quick, fractional movement.

He hasn't looked at me, hasn't acknowledged my presence in the room. I simultaneously do and don't want him to, and it has me all fidgety, a bit unhinged. I work my damp sleeves over my wrists, trying to build up the courage to speak.

What, exactly, has M. Dumas come here to say? And *again*?

"Would you sit, sir?" I finally manage, though my voice is hardly a voice at all. More like air piped through a reed. As he looks my way, I instantly regret saying anything.

His stare is eternity.

Midnight. Ash.

Undoing me.

He glances at the humble chair, the one from our dining set, behind me. "*No, merci.* In a moment, I'll have no need for a seat."

A dreadful feeling creeps between my shoulders, prickling skin. This man doesn't pay social calls. M. Dumas's *rôle* in our town theatrical is as the wealthy recluse, venturing from his minacious home only to board his three-masted barque for business excursions. He's a merchant, like Papa was, trading for the East India Company. He doesn't have time to bring baskets to the poor.

He turns back to Mamma. "I was grieved, *madame*, to hear of your husband's passing. I, too, have recently lost a spouse, and have the deepest empathy for you."

Mamma's mouth, a vacant line, has gone mute in her grief. But her eyes blear with a film of tears, saying everything.

"Please, pardon my mother," I quietly say to him. "She's not well. I'm afraid none of us is since...since Papa." I pull my lips together, blushing at my honesty. Such personal things, like pain, shouldn't be shared with a stranger. Mamma says there's no room for sympathy in polite society, and as my embarrassment grows, I'm wont to believe her.

M. Dumas's mouth, musing, pulls into a frown. "Then please allow me to lift your burdens."

The jangle of coins cuts the air. Anna gasps, and my impulsive, greedy hand reaches to snatch up the little purse from the floor—but I stay it. Very few are charitable with their money, even to the church. It's reasonable—no, *necessary*—to assume M. Dumas desires something in return.

"What do you want for it? If you don't think it discourteous of me to ask," I add quickly. I mustn't be rude when a miracle has stepped freely through our door.

Tension twists through the room as we await his answer. He grips his cane, a gorgeous polished mahogany with a strange handle—two hands, clasping each other. He's nervous.

No. Impatient.

"Of course," he says. "You are right to question me, a righteous judge, indeed. You see, *mademoiselle,* I have been admiring your grace and resilience for some time now. As your family grieved for your loss, I ached for mine. But when I saw you that day on the road, I felt assuredly I could again gain reprieve." He steps forward, and my body is thrown into disharmony, paradoxically cresting hot and cold and hot again. "Your eyes," he says. "They are the purest blue I have ever seen, as if I could dive into them and find myself in paradise."

I try to take a breath but find I can't. Those were Papa's words. *Your eyes are a gift from heaven,* he said to me often, searching them. *An interminable day of lapis and sunlight, one has only to gaze into them and will see into eternity.* Never before had Papa been so earnest for this paradise than on his deathbed. Nor M. Dumas, now, as he bends to his knee.

The floor is wet, puddled from where I've dripped, bleeding into his trousers. "Beatrice," he says, and my pulse jumps at his use of my Christian name, all formality tossed aside like a weed, wilted. I am. *Wilted.* Withering as he speaks. "I would be more blessed than a sinner redeemed if you would say yes to becoming my wife."

His proposal is rushed, as if he's waited long to say these words and can't even abide the time it takes to speak them. A leaf swept up by the wind, I fall hard into the vacant chair. M. Dumas catches and releases my shoulders, hands loitering just over them.

He spoke of an ache, a reprieve. I feel his ache to touch me, and I shudder to allow it.

How could he even ask it? His wife—*God rest her soul*—has been dead barely a season! At the very least another year is required before a man wishes to court another woman. And not to mention his age, which is *well* beyond my own years. Although he's aged gracefully, he can't be less than thirty-six...thirty-seven...thirty-*eight*. The scandal alone prevents me from accepting him.

My heart pummels my ribs, and it's all so loud, so glaringly loud. Only Mamma breaks through. "Do you mean it, sir?"

There's a note in her voice I must have misheard, for it sounded like...*hope*.

"I do," he answers. "I mean it most passionately."

Both look to me.

I look to the purse, crammed with money. Not an hour before, I endeavored to work for our salvation, in a mill or a shop. Society would frown upon me as a vagrant, lacking respectability, but at least I'd be an honest vagrant. An industrious woman, independent from men and their expectations. M. Dumas's money is easy and would easily save us from starvation. But his proposal is hard.

Besides, I have nothing to offer him in return.

"Monsieur Dumas, my dowry is gone," I say. "My family is in debt. We could not afford a suitable wedding. We—*I*—would be a burden to you."

In a bold maneuver, he takes my hand. His touch is firm, though not cold like I expected it to be. "I desire only your companionship. Your faithfulness. Caring for you would hardly burden me, for my wealth stretches far beyond the borders of this country. I have carriages, stables of thoroughbreds, a home filled with wonders. You will want for nothing. You will have the world, Beatrice."

*The world.*

The idea excites me: the vastness of it, the *freedom*. But just how far would we journey into this world of his—for in truth, that is what it must be? *His* world, so very, very different from mine.

"Beatrice." Mamma again. In silence she pleads with me, reaching out with her brown eyes, soft like earth freshly turned. She anticipated this. M. Dumas implied it himself—they have spoken before. I think she has known his intentions for many days, and yet she said nothing to me, gave me no warning. I didn't think she ever left her room, let alone sat with visitors. But like Papa, she has been keeping secrets.

Papa, a romantic like the Cavalier poets, was against arranged marriages. *Our daughter will not be auctioned off to the first punter who bids*, I'd heard him say to her. *She will be battled for—and won, at great peril to self—as is proper. No less than the most gallant of men is worth her companionship. Nor yours, my dear.* Papa took up Mamma's hand and kissed her palm, tempering her passions. She softened for him like butter, and his expression colored like a starburst in the heavens.

Like a simpleton, I once dreamed of a love as real as theirs, as real as sky. But that is too far to reach.

I feel it keenly, my parents' betrayal. Papa betrayed me

first by hiding the truth of our ruin, and now Mamma has displayed me like a mare in some silent auction, all pedigree and broken spirits. Have there been other bids, besides the monsieur's? If the King of Swine, Mr. Haskell, had made her an offer for my hand, would she have accepted him without hesitation?

The sun has set, leaving only candle flame for our light, which must be playing a trick on me. Concealed near the fireplace, Anna's face is colorless, her lips tinged with blue like on the day she slid through the ice, into the arctic depths of the Reaper's skeletal hands. But then I blink, and she's staring at me with Mamma's identical eyes, with anticipation and encouragement, delicate posies abloom on her cheeks.

Anna has always spoken of love and marriage like they're fairy stories with blissful endings. But those kings and queens, those knights and ladies, when their books are closed, their lives are not always happy. Just look at Mamma, forlorn, and Papa, dead.

But M. Dumas's proposal could save Anna's life, as well as Mamma's. This is a fact I can't ignore, no matter how selfishly I want to. And it would be. Selfish.

Throughout my silent apprehension, he has yet to remove his hand from mine. Deftly, I take it back. I find my voice, wedged beneath my ribs. "If you would, spare me a day to consider your offer. I promise you'll have my answer by tomorrow evening. Sunset."

His expression hardly changes, and I wonder if he

even considers I might decline him. "Of course," he says. "Until tomorrow. Sunset." Before he rises, he retakes the hand I extracted and bestows a kiss. Below his breath and mouth and beard, my skin burns.

I CAN'T GET WARM. I prod the fire until it snaps at me, refusing to blaze any hotter. It's all embers and ash left-over from its peak of exploded glory. I toss on another log, but it lies there, lank, smoldering. Hardly a flame. It needs oxygen. It needs to breathe.

In our stable, I take down Hasting's bridle. The bit is cold and he objects to having it in his mouth, but after I warm it in my hands and slip him a cube of sugar, he submits. We ride east to the cliffs and the sea, the sky a gray lid. If I peeled it back, I might find the sun, a golden ball dropped into a well of blue water. And at the bottom of this well, a frog, asking to be kissed.

The tale is Anna's favorite. She pines for her own accursed prince to disenchant. Never once did she stop to think why the prince was transfigured in the first place. Maybe it was punishment for kissing a King's daughter, or for calling an old hag ugly. What if, in his human state, he wasn't a good man? At least the princess of the fable took her time about it, resisting till the very end when her upright father demanded she keep her promises. That's the lesson of the tale, I suppose. Honesty, in all things.

M. Dumas's house lies ahead, on Shakespeare Cliff. I slide from Hastings's saddle to let him graze on the frost-bitten samphire and grass, while I sit on the knobby stump of a felled chestnut tree. I gather my skirts around my boots, sitting on my hands to keep them from the brittle cold.

I study the building's sharp architectural lines, its dips and shadows, its balconies and balustrades. Chimney flues puncture the sky, in symmetry with its gables and diamond-paned windows. Gargoyle creatures perch on buttresses carved from weathered bath stone, streaked black with age. It's exactly the image conjured when I read Mrs. Gaskell's creepy ghost stories, or Brontë's descriptions of Thornfield Hall. I don't know the name of M. Dumas's estate. As with the bath stone, it's been weathered down and covered up, forgotten forever by those who no longer care for its history or see its importance. Some parts of the manor have been neglected, new wings built around the old, the decayed, the forbidden. For some elusive reason, it makes me sad.

It's not fair, saying yes to him only for his money. M. Dumas *is* rich. As he said, my family would want for nothing, and right now, *nothing* is what we are on the verge of becoming. His money would solve everything.

I still have the handkerchief he used to bandage my hand. The material is thin and fine, little *fleurs-des-lis* embroidered in a silk-thread border. I couldn't quite get the blood from it, and dark reddish pinpricks are now a permanent feature of the cloth, as if my fate were decided for me. As if, even now, I'm already a part of him.

I blink against a savagery of tears.

*Protect your heart, Beatrice.*

I don't want to do this.

I don't, I don't.

It grows dark. My thoughts grow darker. I have the urge to rise, to run, to scream *you cannot make me* at the sky. Reseal the lid on that well of fables and make-believe happiness. You cannot make me.

I say it aloud, whisper it to his silhouetted manor house. "You cannot make me."

Hastings chuffs against my face, and I cry into his mane. I ride him home.

I don't wait for sunset or even midday. Using a quill and a pot of Papa's ink I'd managed to save, I write my reply to M. Dumas.

*Dear Monsieur—*

*I appreciate your proposal and am obliged to inform you of my answer at this time.*

*My answer is yes.*

*Yours,*

*Beatrice Tilney*

Folding M. Dumas's handkerchief neatly into a square, I pin it to the note.

*Meerut, India*

*28 February 1857*

*Dear Beatrice,*

*What a comfort it was to receive your letter as we arrived at the cantonment. After the trials of seamanship, and the worst seasickness I've ever experienced in my life, your words were a reprieve, though I must admit I was disappointed you didn't elaborate on mother's condition. Is she truly well, or are you fibbing to ease my worry? You were always expert with a lie, though it might be considered a transgression on my part to compliment you on such.*

*India throngs with life. Do you remember the stories Father told us of his journeys here? In my small mind, I could scarcely imagine them as being true—that people rode on the backs of elephants? That leopards lived alongside people, strolling down their market places? I didn't believe it until I saw it: sauntering right down the cantonment's parade path, a spotted cat, huge and shadowy! The officers, when they saw him, fired shots to frighten him off, for though magnificent, leopards can be a deadly nuisance.*

*It behooves our brother Byron that I ask you what gossip there is from home, particularly concerning Miss Lilly Coons. I've suggested he write to her, but being the stubborn prat that he is, he refuses on the grounds that such an act would be taken as a proposal, which he—quote—"Is not inclined to consider at this time." He fears having a wife might actually be agreeable to him. Or perhaps it's his fear of disappointment, called up by past experiences, that stops him. A hundred times I've reassured Byron that Father forgave him his past mistakes, but to listen to me would mean I'm right. God forbid Byron ever admit to being the humbler twin.*

*India suits him. Thanks to his affable (or foolhardy) nature, Byron has become a favorite among our comrades, but a bane to the officers, who must discipline him with frequent chores. Not once can I recall having so many pots to wash, or socks to darn, or drills to run. I'm ashamed to say that for the twenty-one-years of my life I've taken our dear Molly for granted. Please give her a good word for me, and tell her that I miss her Sunday roast.*

*There's no doubt Molly would appall at the hygiene of us soldiers, though we can hardly help it when the sun brutalizes us with its heat, sending its infantry of flies to bathe in our sweat, which we attempt to mask with incenses of sandalwood and frankincense. The sepoys, our counterparts of Indian birth, say we'll get used to being dirty. I think the comment was more to slur our origin than it was to provide encouragement. I feel keenly the resentment most of the natives bear at us being here. I hope it won't prevent me from making friends among them, for though our faces, tongues, and gods be different, I am in great need of a friend. Byron hardly counts.*

*We miss our sisters, and our mother, and pray for your happiness and health. I pray, also, for the health of my horse. How is he? Are you taking great care of him? I look forward to your reply on the matter. Until then, I remain,*

*Your affectionate brother,*
*Simon Tilney*
*Cornet, Bengal Light Cavalry*

## CHAPTER 7
# PORCELAIN

Our engagement lasts a mere thirteen days. M. Dumas didn't want to wait any longer than needed to make arrangements, and I didn't counter him. After all, my family couldn't afford to wait. Mr. Mitchell would have returned for another payment, maybe this time to seize the house. I suspect Mamma had realized this and informed M. Dumas during one of their clandestine meetings. At first, I wondered who had approached the other, but then realized it hardly mattered. My fate was set the moment they met.

Anna cinches my corset up tight, knotting the ribbons twice. The whalebone ribbing hoists up my bust and straightens my posture. She powders my décolletage and pinches my cheeks for color as I study myself in the vanity mirror. I'm pale today, my blue eyes stark against my skin.

Listless, they stare, portholes to my own eternity. I see no gift in them. Not since M. Dumas's stolen compliment.

In those rare moments when my mind wandered onto the topic of weddings, I imagined it was spring. My bouquet was a weave of white lilies and apple blossoms, and my complexion, incarnadine, was effulgent with optimism. I can't bring myself to smile now. Not when my stomach froths with something sour.

I had a dream last night. I stood at a precipice, a lake of clouds before me, rippling and writhing like snakes. And in their midst, M. Dumas, his hand extended. He spoke to me, imploring me to come to him, his feverish voice enwreathing me, studding my skin with ice and effervescence. The urgency of his tone compelled my feet —but when I demanded them back into submission, they defied me. They'd found a new master, and each step toward the precipice burned like a path of coals.

*Come to me.*

"You cannot make me," I said.

*Come to me.*

"You can't, you can't," but my foot lifted. The precipice swam black and misted, and it looked solid though I knew it wasn't.

*Come to me.*

I did.

I did, and I fell.

"Step in." Anna pulls me from the dream world, adjusting the petticoats around my waist, which add volume to the skirt of white rolling over my hips. The organdy gown spools to the floor in a gauzy train, which she arranges in a perfect arc of lace and ruffles. Smoothing the diaphanous fabric, and taking care that each wrinkle is subdued, she says, "I'm sorry."

I peek at her over my shoulder. "For what?"

Her voice tightens with emotion. "When that man took my piano, I blamed you for it. I wished you would lose something, too. But I didn't think it would be this."

I turn, reversing her careful work. "This?"

"Your happiness."

Dismayed, my lips part. My happiness was lost when Papa died. What I lose now is my sovereignty. Because after today, I'll no longer be ruler over myself, but will be the acquisition of M. Dumas. My husband. It's a sacrifice I make for *her*, for Anna. How do I make her understand this?

I kneel before my sister, holding her hands in mine. I took away her voice by allowing Mr. Mitchell to take her piano, yet she has managed to find another way to speak, which speaks of *strength*. I've always treated Anna like some breakable thing, a string of pearls instead of the pearls themselves. Looking into her eyes, I see now how wrong I was. She is infrangible and full of hope, far more hope than I could even imagine.

Her eyes shine lachrymose, like dew on petals. I kiss them each. "*You* are my happiness," I say. "You and Mamma, Simon and Byron. So long as you laugh and are merry and glad, so shall I be. Nothing can make me sad if you're smiling."

"But Monsieur Dumas," she says. "You don't love him."

I smile, and I make her believe it's real. "Not all of us can be like Papa and Mamma. We can't see someone and know immediately we'll love them."

There's a burning sensation under the bridge of my nose, tears forming in their ducts. I flutter my eyelids to make them leave.

"Here," I say, plucking a snowdrop from my bridal bouquet of ivy and purple hellebores. I weave the stem into Anna's hair. She hugs me to her, holding fast, and I squeeze her tightly, wishing my embrace alone could be enough to keep her safe from the cruelties of this world.

She pulls away. "Your hair."

I brush a few harried strands from my face. "I'll do it. You've done enough. Besides, you have your own dress to put on."

The change in her mood is swift. Anna bites her lip with glee, bouncing giddily on her toes. She chose her dress herself, a white muslin with pouf sleeves and a delicate pink ribbon tied about the waist. Though I refused to wear a crinoline—rings of steel stacked and riveted into a bell-shaped petticoat—Anna insisted on one for herself. As if the corset weren't cage enough, the modistes of Paris say we must wear an entire *oubliette*, and I've never seen a girl so excited to wear one as Anna.

I hustle her to the door, the ghost of a laugh on my lips. It drifts to the air, lingering over me for just a moment until it fades into an exhale. I close the door, pressing my forehead to it. And I sigh into the first sob. No tears, just whimpers. Gasps of empty chest swells. If I cried, he'd know. He'd see the tracks on my cheeks, and he'd ask me what's wrong, and I'd tell him. I'd tell him...*tears of joy.* I'd lie to him, because it's easier than telling the truth.

There's a rap on the door.

Panic leaps to my throat. The ceremony isn't until ten o'clock, and it's not yet nine. It's bad luck—*isn't it?*—for the groom to see the bride before the wedding?

Another rap. Sharp. Persistent.

I don't think M. Dumas is concerned with luck, or any other play kismet would make. He's waiting, and the consequences could be grave if I don't let him in.

The face I open to is aged, though neither rough nor forbidding. It's heart-shaped, riven with laugh lines around bright blue eyes, veins of silver in satiny auburn hair.

The face of a friend.

"Ami Rose!" I throw my arms around her, gushing relief.

"Beatrice," she chimes, her smile deepening those symbols of prosperity and gladness. "How beautiful you look! Like Aphrodite's omitted twin—except more glorious." I laugh as she twirls me around, my train tangling in my ankles. She steadies me before I tear the hem, then purses her lips. "Your hair could use some work, however. Let me assist you."

She ushers me to the dressing table and begins to coif my chestnut hair into a high chignon. And just like that, every crumb of fear I had is swept away by her elegant fingers. Since the last day I saw her, the day before Papa's funeral, I've longed to see her again. But she's almost always just out of reach, travelling to London or Vienna or wherever she pleases. She has the freedom of a bird and never takes it for granted. With every storm, her wings have only grown stronger.

"I'm so happy you're here," I say, and I sigh as if drunk on wine. In Ami's presence, I've never felt anything but safe. "I was afraid you wouldn't come."

"I wouldn't have missed it even if my house were sinking into the Dour." She skims my cheek, the backs of her fingers coming away with the tears I couldn't hold back. "But you look so pale. Porcelain, as if you'll break."

I am breaking. Crack by crack, I'm slowly shattering. I'm frightened, but I don't tell her this. I've made my choice. Nothing will change it.

Ami looks at me through the mirror, her mouth turned into a thoughtful expression. "He courted me, too, you know. Many years ago. But I declined him."

My eyes widen, my voice leaping an octave. "What? When? Did he propose marriage?"

"I was young," she says, "though not nearly as young

as you. The fire had just consumed my parents' home. You remember."

I was seven. I remember Papa tearing across the field in the middle of a raw October night, my brothers sloughing buckets of water behind him to help stanch the blaze. I remember how the flames clawed their way into the sky, garish in their frenzy. If I close my eyes, I can still see imprints of the house, a charred cadaver smoking in the ash-gray morning, on my eyelids. That hellfire claimed Ami Rose's parents, and the remaining two of her three brothers, the third having disappeared a few years prior. Benjamin, I think his name was.

"I was heartbroken," she says. "Homeless, penniless, alone. Then came M. Dumas, riding up in his black chariot."

Right in step with her narrative, we hear horses' hooves clop along the road beside the house. A coach, approaching. It's his.

It's nearly time.

Unlike Ami Rose, I have a craven heart, weak and cowardly. I couldn't have refused M. Dumas so readily as she did. "Was he angry?" I whisper, as if even now I could be overheard.

"I believe he was." Then, with urgency, "But he veiled his emotions like a gentleman. Beatrice"—she grips my hands and my heart skitters—"I came today not just to see you, but to warn you. Be *vigilant*, Beatrice, always looking about you. Do not be fooled by him. Though his words are soft, their meanings are false. He is a *wolf*."

"It's time, my love."

I startle, swiveling around on the dressing stool. I didn't hear his knock, nor see the door open. Like some specter, he emerged from the air.

My neck creeps with heat as I take in his attire. His top hat tucked under one arm, M. Dumas wears a slate frock coat and breeches with a white paisley waistcoat and cravat. His beard has been combed and trimmed, though still maintains its length, and a white rosebud sticks from the flower-hole on his lapel. He looks...

Well, he looks like a groom.

His mouth, at first beaming with youthful excitement, now pulls lower as he recognizes Ami Rose. "Amelia," he says tightly.

"Gaston," she returns, equally rigid. "Are you well?"

Even when cross, M. Dumas exudes cordiality. "Very well, for today I wed the loveliest creature I've ever beheld." He requests my hand, and I give it to him, standing breathlessly still as he regards me. I've never been so self-conscious as when I'm under his gaze. Nor felt as stark.

"Bewitching," he says. He cants forward as if to kiss me, and in that minor thrust I freeze—helpless to stop it as his mouth creeps ever nearer to mine.

Ami throws out her arm. "You will have to wait until

*after* the ceremony, Gaston, before you may embrace your bride."

"Shouldn't you be making your way to the church, Amelia?" he retorts. "Though I thank you for attending to my bride, I should dislike it if you were late to see us march the aisle."

Her lips tighten. She's been dismissed, and to disobey would be impertinent. She is a woman of scruples through and through, and though her contempt seethes behind her teeth, she has learned to compose herself. So must I learn. And quickly.

"Thank you, Ami Rose," I say. "You've made this day all the more special for us." I say it because M. Dumas will take pleasure from it. Because I don't want him to suspect how much I've dreaded this.

I kiss Ami's cheek in parting. She looks me over a final time—*like porcelain, as if you'll break*—before veiling me. *I won't run from him,* I want to say to her. I won't run, even if he is a wolf. I want to convince her this is the only way, that I'm making the right choice. I want her to tell me that, even though I'm marrying him, I can still be like her. A woman with wings.

M. Dumas impatiently drums his fingers on the silk plush rim of his hat. He opens the door for Ami Rose, shutting it behind her. The click of the handle lifts my breath, filches it right from my lungs. "Are you familiar with matrimonial traditions?" he asks, turning back to me.

The room shrinks, and he's close, close to me. I struggle to meet his eyes. "Some of them, yes."

"The lucky ones, I hope?" He smiles. It's warm, and I'm eased, just a little. "Let us list them, to be sure we miss nothing that would spoil this day of bliss. Firstly, something old."

I touch the brooch at my neck, mother of pearl, an heirloom passed through my maternal line. I hoarded many items when Mr. Mitchell was on his errand to collect our debt. This was one of them. "Will it do?" I ask, and M. Dumas touches it, touches my throat. I swallow.

"Perfect. Now, something new."

He paid for my gown, the newest thing I own.

"Something borrowed."

I wear the same lace veil and beaded coronet Mamma wore to her wedding—another hoarded item, though I'd thought Anna would be the one to wear it. I saved it for her, never suspecting that life intended it for me. The paste flowers dig into my scalp without mercy.

"Something blue, for fidelity. Ah, I think your eyes will do fine." M. Dumas gives them a lengthy gander, sending blood to my face.

"And the sixpence for my shoe?" I say, swiftly curbing any romantic advance he might have thought to make.

"Ha," he says. "Wealth is something I've plenty of. Never again need you fear poverty."

At that, I smile. And for the first time since Papa's leaving me, I feel comforted.

A LIGHT RAIN spills through the shafts of morning sunlight, illuminated like fire.

"*Le diable bat sa femme et marie sa fille*," says M. Dumas from the stoop, catching the rain in his hand. *The devil beats his wife and marries his daughter.* It's a proverb for when it rains while the sun still shines, though I'm uncertain about its etymology. "It means good luck for us. Our union is blessed."

He gathers up my train, and I step into his coach. We ride to St. Paul's pulled by two gray horses, the bells and that one cacophonous chime ringing out our arrival, expelling any nefarious, waylaying spirits who would seek to plague us. M. Dumas is well rehearsed in the nuptial proceedings, having endured them four times previously. With my hand set gingerly atop his, we march the length of the chapel on a carpet of white rose petals, stopping before the iron communion rails.

At his insistence, the ceremony is strictly a family affair. I'm glad for it. I wouldn't be able to bear it if any of the townsfolk were here to witness this. The only person of non-blood relation permitted to come was Ami Rose, and that was because I lied, claiming her as my aunt. In truth, I have no living relatives. No one whom, from the goodness of their Christian hearts, could have taken us in. Thus making this marriage imperative.

Ami Rose sits next to Mamma, who doesn't smile and

wears her mourning clothes, but appears, from this angle, to be content. She sees I wear her veil, and I think that makes her happy. As it should me. But all I feel is numb uncertainty coupling with resignation. This is happening whether I want it to or not.

*You chose this,* I remind myself. As if it were any comfort.

Anna, our ring bearer, stands to the side of Reverend Moody. She looks radiant in her dress and her ringlets of gold, like an angelic depiction from the Romantics, haloed and bathed in light. I hate to turn from her to face M. Dumas, whose smile is gone, replaced with alert impatience.

At the word of Reverend Moody, the chapel stills, the air thins, and my heart tumbles in my chest. He drones his lines from the Book of Common Prayer as my stomach roils like the sea. Like M. Dumas, I'm impatient. I want this done and finished before I realize how binding it is, how permanent. From this time on, I will be his wife. His *wife*. The title should be celebrated. I should be in raptures to marry a strong man, an able man. Able to protect and care, not just for my family, but for *me*. It should be an honor.

But it won't be. Not when I'm the fifth to wear this distinction.

"My love?"

I didn't realize my eyes were closed, hidden beneath

the safety of my veil. They cut to M. Dumas, his thick brows pinching together disapprovingly.

"The vows," he says.

The vows.

*The vows.*

The words stick in my throat like gruel. I memorized them, of course, but it scarcely occurred to me I'd actually have to say them. My voice quivers as I stumble through, cursory in my recitation. "I, Beatrice, take thee...Gaston... to be my wedded husband. To have and to hold from this day forward. For better, for worse. For richer, for poorer. In sickness and in health. To love, cherish, and to..." I swallow, the final phrase a needle in my throat. "And to obey till death do us part."

Satisfied, albeit annoyed by my slaughter of the solemn verse, Reverend Moody asks for the ring, which Anna passes to him. He gives the gold band, engraved with ivy vines, to M. Dumas. As he slides it onto my finger, his dark timbre ripples through me.

"With this ring," he says, "I thee wed. With my body, I thee worship. And with all my worldly goods, I thee endow."

Whatever Reverend Moody says next I don't hear. My ears are lost to the sense of my eyes, large with the ring on my finger. I feel its weight and girth and how it repels the fingers around it, an uncomfortable band, a manacle. His hand to my chin, M. Dumas lifts my eyes to his. He would have me look at my new husband.

There's no husband-and-wife kiss as the French and the Romans do. Such intimacy isn't permissible in an English vestry. Therefore, M. Dumas—

No. He's my husband now. I can call him Gaston.

Gaston will have to wait, as Ami Rose put it, to embrace me.

As we exit the church, we're showered with a profusion of rice and birdseed, blessings for fertility. The seeds strike my face and catch in my hair, and I shield my eyes from them, ill at ease. I failed to contemplate the possibility of bearing children, or even conceiving them.

The gray horses have been exchanged for white ones. We start forward, the boisterous church bells fading into humdrum trotting. Gaston sits next to me on the bench, close, his fingers moving along the air like a spider on a string to find my veil, unveil my face, and guide it towards his for the immersive, passionate kiss he's been waiting ages for.

"Where are we honeymooning?" I ask, thwarting it.

Disappointment flashes in his eyes for no more than a second, his mustache obscuring a little moue of chagrin. But when I smile guiltily, regretfully, it seems to charm him.

A canty smile springs to his lips, and he drops his hand, sitting back.

"Paris," he says.

## CHAPTER 8

# PARIS

I once made a list of all the places I'd visit as soon as my parents were convinced I was old enough to travel long distances. Paris, with all its romance and revolution, was number two, after Egypt's Valley of the Kings, and before China's Great Wall. On the night Papa died, I set a corner of that list to a candle's flame and watched those dreams ignite and curl inward. I swept the ashes into my hands, the soot marking them black, and blew them to the wind. I thought my dreams were done. But maybe they hadn't even begun.

After changing into our travel clothes, we board a ferry to Calais, crossing the channel within an hour and a half. Two hours more on the French Northern Railway and we step from the train onto a smoky platform. The station teems with businessmen and bourgeoisie setting out to visit relatives in Dijon, Toulouse, or Marseille.

Gaston comes from Lourmarin, a village in the Provence region he describes as charming, ivy-cloaked, and perfumed with lavender. Well. As pretty as that sounds, it's not the City of Light.

Paris is a potpourri of odors. Burnt coal gas from the former night's lamps and fresh, succulent pastries mingle with the mephitis of sewage from the street drains. The rush and clatter of people promenading between the shops excites my nerves, filling me with a giddiness I knew only as a child at harvest time, when the encumbered apple trees were ready for plucking. It was more my anticipation for the coming pies and puddings, than for the fruit itself, which thrilled me. Similarly, it's not so much the city making my body thrum, but all its delights.

Linked by the arms, Gaston parades me through the streets. As per the Emperor's directives, most of the medieval alleyways and structures have been replaced with wide avenues and striking monuments to modernization. The Old World is razed to rubble and swept away for all things New as if never having come into existence. This is innovation, almost cruel in its abasement of the past.

We dine like socialites in Paris's most prestigious restaurants. I try snail for the first time, though the French have a more appealing name for it. I expect some slimy, unsavory thing, but what I taste is salt. And garlic. Lots of it.

With our bellies full, we shop. Smelling money, dress

and millenary, boutiques throw open their doors to us, the salesmen and women exhausting in their enthusiasm. Gaston insists I sit down to rest—"As the city can tend to overwhelm"—while he orders the modiste to show me every bolt of fabric available in the shop. If I'm overwhelmed, it's not by the city, but by Gaston's constant doting. He must feel immortal in his affluence. His pockets run deeper than Papa's ever did, and spending it hardly seems to lessen its weight. If anything, it springs forth like a fountain of everlasting waters.

"Do you like it?" he asks, as I model a silk hat embroidered with pearl beads.

"It's exquisite," I say. "But I have a bonnet."

"Not this one,"—and before I can refuse him, he's paid the shopkeeper a full twenty francs for it. We exit the store, leaving the shopkeeper with mouth agape, the money in his open palm.

We float lazily down the Seine in a *bateau*, supping cordials under wafting clouds like swaths of cotton. Sunlight spirals down, warming my neck, my face. I wear the new hat, and although it *is* exquisite, and exceedingly more comfortable than my other, I want to take it off. I want to feel the sun's fingers in my hair, endowing me with peace and positivity. I crane my face toward the sky, sighing contentedly, because right now, I'm happy.

"What goddess lies here before me?" I open my eyes and squint at Gaston. He faces me in the boat, leaning semi-recumbent on his elbows. His look isn't hot, as expected, but admiring.

Flattered for once, I offer a smile. "A goddess, sir? I think not. What would you know of goddesses, anyway?"

"I know everything," he says. "From Athena to Diana, Isis to Sati. And do you know what they each have in common?" I shake my head, feeling flush. "They are each breathless in their beauty. As are you."

A warning triggers in my mind. I break our gaze to the river lapping at the boat. His words give no hint at being injurious, though they're precisely the words a wolf might say.

I skim my fingers along the water's surface. "How do you know these things," I say, impassive, cool. *Be vigilant, Beatrice, always looking about you.* I had almost let my guard down.

"I was an archaeologist as a younger man."

I bounce up in my seat, accidentally flinging water onto his trousers. "A treasure hunter?"

Gaston laughs. "In a word, yes. *History* was my treasure, the wisdom I could glean from the ancient world." He sits forward, elbows on his knees. Absorbed, I come closer. "When just a lad, I toured the East with my parents, traveling to Abyssinia and Egypt. And when I saw those pyramids at Giza—those sovereign testaments to time and power—I knew no greater love would pierce me so thoroughly as my love for them." He pauses for breath, eyes narrowing satirically. "But a man cannot marry a pyramid."

I laugh—a moment of girlishness that seems to inspire him to plunge even deeper. "At eight years old, I joined Salt's excavation team in Thebes. By eighteen, I was with Vyse in Giza, unearthing—for the first time in millennia—Pharaoh Khufu's tomb, the very *builder* of the Great Pyramids."

"It sounds like every adventure I've dreamed of having." My voice seeps with adolescent wistfulness, but I don't hide it. Let him hear. Let him know what I ache for. "But what made you stop?"

Gaston fingers the knob of his cane, a bulb of golden amber entrapping some hapless black beetle, round and round in circles. It looks, for a moment, like the bugs from my visions—until the light changes, morphing the blue-gold sheen into a matte black. Wealthy men and their eccentricities were discussed at every party Mamma forced me to attend growing up, so it hardly surprises me to learn that collecting canes, rarely accessorizing with the same one twice, is Gaston's particular proclivity.

His voice drops, lukewarm with something like sadness. Or bitterness. "Most of the artifacts we recovered were sold to the British Museum or la Louvre. When they demanded more at the expense of the people whose culture they plundered, I decided I'd had enough of the avarice of men."

I've never met a man who's felt as affectionately for the past and its people as Gaston. Indeed, as he loomed over me in my drawing room, blackening the candlelight with his steps, I'd questioned if such humanity was thoroughly out of his breadth. I see now that I was wrong—I hardly know anything about this man, and as I sit here, commiserating with him under a clear Parisian sky, the desire to know *everything* wholly envelopes me.

I scoot forward, my dress draping over his knee, and he runs his knuckles over its smooth silk. "Will you take me there," I ask, "to the Louvre? Show me your discoveries?"

He smiles, kneading my dress between his fingers. "I will show you everything. But let us go. The sun is setting, and we have an opera to dress for."

THE SALLE VENTADOUR swarms with people. Monocled men flirt with mink-furred women, the sexes mingling in the immense foyer of the opera house, all of them impatient for the production to begin. They stare at us as we pass, the women masking their mouths with their gloved hands, intimating to one another while the men smirk knowingly. Next to Gaston, I don't look young; I look like a child. I turn my face from them, hiding my embarrassment in Gaston's shoulder.

We ascend the carpeted stairs to the upper levels of

the theatre, where we have box seats directly left of the stage. The mezzanines hum under the brilliancy of a chandelier, a giantess drawing our eyes to the stage and its velvet, wine-colored curtain.

"Madame Brambilla is a celebrated soprano," says Gaston as the house-lights flicker and dim, their gas siphoning. "I saw her at the Odessa, in Russia, an age ago. She was younger then. As was I." He looks to his veined and roughened hands. "How fickle time is. How rushed."

"How fleeting," I agree. Nostalgia, that longing for the past and its simplicity, is something we have in common. We share a look—his adoring and mine compassionate—and he takes my hand to hold throughout the night. It surprises me, how my small fingers lace comfortably with his own.

As the curtains rise, I lift a pair of Galilean binoculars to my eyes. The opera sings of an amorous duke who boasts he can woo any woman. Rigoletto, the Duke's jester, plays accomplice while keeping his own daughter, Gilda, well out of the Duke's sights.

"But he has already seen her in church," Gaston explains, translating the Italian verse. And as an aside, "Rigoletto thought he could keep her safe from him. But look—Count Monterone has wished a curse on them for seducing his daughter."

The threat of a curse pierces Rigoletto to his very soul. "Horror!" he cries. "What horror!" And all at once he realizes the great lust and villainy of his master. His daughter is imperiled!

Gaston edges forward on his seat, seemingly unconscious of the action. He's so immersed in the tale that he forgets to translate, and with each swelling note, he takes a breath, prolonging it as the actors do. At one point, he mutters Rigoletto's curious, introspective line along with him. *Pari siamo.*

"We are alike." Remembering himself, he looks to me, the first blush I've seen on him disappearing instantly. But I saw it. He couldn't hide it from me.

I find I don't need his translation. The actors render the story with such vivacity it's like I'm *within* it. The set has changed now to a courtyard enclosed by a low, stone wall, where we behold the virtuous Gilda—*Madame Brambilla*—sitting with her duenna Giovanna under a weeping willow. As Rigoletto pleads with the governess to keep his flower safe, and pure, he's startled by a noise. *Someone is outside!* He exits the courtyard while the Duke, silent as the night, slips in.

The Duke tosses a purse at Giovanna's feet for her silence. "My name is Walter Maldè," he lies. And the beguiled Gilda falls immediately in love with him, for he is handsome, and she is gravely tempted to be charmed by him.

When the opera ends, I'm left terribly depressed. Only a ridiculous woman would sacrifice her life for a man who held no true affection for her, especially when she knew it.

The curtain drops and the theatre erupts with applause, Rigoletto's final exclamation resounding in our ears. *La maledizione!*

"The curse," says Gaston, with an air of grave finality. "What did you think of it, Beatrice?"

"It was tragic."

"Ah, but all the best stories are."

My eyebrows rise up contrarily. Gaston laughs, and then escorts me out of our box, our fingers still entwined.

# CHAPTER 9
# ALL FRUIT

Our suite overlooks the Seine. Moonlight glimmers on the water, a million scintillations of stars like a parallel sky. Boats clank against the docks, bobbing with the current. There are people still out: a late-night fisherman dragging in his final net of perch and trout; a vigilant gendarme trotting his pony over the Pont Neuf; and two indiscreet lovers, embracing under a gas-lamp. I flush, espying the intricacy and depth of their kiss. I turn away, painted with heat.

"Are you unwell, my love?"

"Fatigued, is all."

His eyes sweep to the couple, percipient. "Let us retire," he says, offering his arm. Afraid to look back, down into that gas-lit street, I let him guide me away from the window.

Gold and Venetian red inundate my eyes. The suite

has been done in the opulent, overabundant style of Napoleon III. It is a mélange of mirrors, tortoiseshell furnishings, and caryatid candlesticks. The draped women support their flames, burdened as the wax dribbles down their upraised arms. *Dazzled,* I believe is the appropriate sense to be felt, but instead I feel dizzy. I'm too prudish, it seems, to suitably admire the Emperor's taste in fashion.

A gauzy nightgown with layers of lacy trim hangs on the dressing screen. Gaston nods to it. "For you," he says.

I take it cautiously, as if it will sting.

Behind the screen, I take my time undressing, my hands fumbling with the grommets and ties of my corset. Anna fortified it well; I can barely get the knots undone. I suppose she thought I'd have help unlacing it, but Gaston brought no servants. When I inquired as to why, he said that he values his privacy and cannot abide the pernicious gossip between footmen and scullery maids. On that much I agreed with him. He keeps a cook, a butler, a driver doubling as the stable master, and one housemaid, paying them all double to take their sleeping quarters at the inn near the center of town. They keep their hours from breakfast to supper, and at all other times Gaston remains self-sufficient.

I slip into the nightgown, which is thin and vapory, too spare for proper modesty. Like wearing mist. My gut flutters, heat rushing down my neck in a wave of apprehension.

"I hope it fits," he calls, his voice lush with hot anticipation.

*Be brave, Beatrice.*

I step out from behind the screen.

While I fidgeted, Gaston changed into a nightshirt and turned down the bedcovers. His eyes lift to mine, and he surveys me like an artifact, the way my arms conceal my stomach, how my feet overlap. The moment is long, his assessment painstaking as I stand, nearly bare.

"Lovely," he finally says.

He extends his hand to me.

*Déjà vu.*

Suffused with heat, I quake. His hand, this scene—I've been here before. In a dream. On a precipice. I know what happens next.

Gaston slides into the bed, but I'm fixed to the floor, each rapid pulse of my rabbit heart knocking against my chest.

His voice honeys with concern. "Is something wrong, my love?"

*Yes*—everything. This isn't my life. This is a dream, a nightmare. Wake up, Beatrice. Wake up!

I shake my head, and he laughs breathily. "Your innocence is refreshing. Do not worry, my love. I'll be gentle."

Gaston pulls me to the bed, and I sink into it like quicksand. His arms enwrap me, reminding me of the snakes that slunk between the apple trees in the orchard.

How I hated them, detested them and their pernicious, flicking tongues.

His mouth meets mine.

His lips melt into me hot and purposeful, and it's strange, this pressing. It's terrifying. His beard repulses, chafing my skin. It gets in my mouth, and his kisses deepen, serpents tightening-constricting-suffocating—I arch away—to the bed—to the quicksand—deeper and deeper *away*.

I whimper. He pulls back, short of breath. And he says into my ear, "I will wait until you are ready," and I hate it. I hate the way his breath sets my skin afire, churns a crucible within my stomach. "All fruit requires time to ripen. Even days."

Gaston rolls to his side and turns down the light.

I weep silently in the dark.

## CHAPTER 10
# BOTTLED CHAOS

Light breaks through the parting in the curtains, shimmery motes dancing like flecks of fairy dust. I roll onto my back, spreading my arms, feeling the bed half-empty as I make an angel in the sheets.

Sitting up, I scan the room. Red, gold, mirrors. The dressing screen. A table garnished with more food than I've ever seen: cakes and croissants, marmalade, hearty slabs of Brie and Gruyère, soft-boiled eggs, fresh butter and cream, *pâté en croute*, cold meats, and a basket of the choicest fruits. The teapot steams.

I heard none of the hotel staff enter the room as I slept. Neither did I sense any presence, as sometimes happens in the lucid dreams of early morning. Stranger still is that the table has only been set for one.

I'm alone.

The thought gives me a jolt of energy. I leap out of

bed, sweeping a peignoir around my shoulders, and pad across the room, the carpets plush and irresistible on my bare feet. Pouring myself a cup of tea, I admire the floral enameling on the bone china as the liquid faintly glugs. Between bites of pastry, I let my thoughts wander from the delights of Paris to the tragedy of *Rigoletto*, coming finally to rest on the event of last night. Serpentine arms and viselike embraces. Hot breath and flicking tongues.

I denied him.

I feel no relief in it. No victory. Instead, I feel...bothered.

My appetite scampers away from me. I go to the dressing screen, where a gown of Chantilly lace and silk faille hangs from a gold inlaid hook. Pinned to the bodice of the gown is a note. *For a goddess*, it reads.

Embarrassment at being desired by him creeps up my neck, uncomfortable and mortifying. Mamma always admonished me to be pure but pretty, chaste but inviting. She couldn't have known how it'd paralyze me, that in the moments when a man's expectations rose, I wouldn't know how to respond or even act. She didn't prepare me for this.

I hook the busk of my corset and ease into the black-and-burgundy-striped dress, my arms straining as I feel for the buttons.

"Let me."

I startle, Gaston at my back, already doing them up.

How softly he came in. Stealthily. Like a wolf through the trees.

How long has he been standing there, observing me?

My blush is deep, his hands near and gentle as he works. He ties the ribbon at my back into a neat bow. "There," he says, turning me around to face him. "In this dress, you'll not fear coming undone."

"It's beautiful," I say, diffident. What could he have meant by that? Is he upset that I spurned him? Yet there's nothing in his aspect or posture to suggest offense. His demeanor is cool, genial, as always.

"It is my pleasure. *Humph...*" He combs through the hair at my temple, a nest of weedy snarls. "Something must be done about this before we go out."

My lip curls into a mug of annoyance—*must everyone comment on how bad my hair looks?*—but I pull it back into place. I nudge Gaston's hand away, a move he isn't pleased with. "It will be decent before we leave, I assure you."

His lips purse at this show of insolence, yet he says nothing.

He goes to the breakfast table. Plucking an orange from the basket of fruit, he begins peeling it. Fine mist sprays from segmented flesh, juice streaming over fingers. The saccharine scent reaches me across the room, where, brushing out my long hair, I watch him, intrigued by his careful methods. Choosing another citrus, Gaston rolls it between his hands and slices it, squeezing its juice into a crystal-cut goblet.

The goblet halts at his lips. "How intently you study me, Beatrice. As if I were a man not of this world."

Cold in my hands, I set down the brush. "Not at all. I was just thinking how..." *Human*, is the thought, but I don't say it for fear it'd snub him. I diminish to a whisper, embarrassed. "Handsome you are."

It's not a lie. Incandescent with sunrise, the room glimmers about him as reflections from the Seine shimmer off his eyes, softened to umber. In the prime of youth, Gaston must have kept a whole parcel of women's hearts tucked into his vest. It would surprise me if those women, surely married now with a mess of children crawling about their ankles, don't often think back on the suave adventurer with the uncanny beard. I wonder, though, has his beard always been tinted blue?

With that, he's pleased. "When you're ready," he says, "I will take you to la Louvre."

THE GREAT SPHINX OF TANIS, sculpted in granite, riddles me with its esoteric smile as we approach the Louvre's wing of Egyptian Antiquities.

"This piece was purchased in 1826," Gaston curates, his voice resounding crisply throughout the room. "It dates to the Old Kingdom." Excited, he pulls me to an exhibit of a wooden tablet, stuccoed and brilliantly painted with two figures, one of them kneeling before the other. "A stele," he says, "a grave marker. Here is the deceased, a harpist, hymning to Ra-Horakhty. God of the Rising Sun. Stunning, don't you agree?"

"I do," I say, awed as he is. Gaston looks at each artifact with reverence and devotion, like the harpist as he plays before his god. Gaston lives because the sun rises, though it has set on his career as an archaeologist. I can see, by the fading of the gaiety in his eyes, how greatly he misses that past. All that's left now is his future, and that future is me, his fifth wife.

I worry it will be a dismal future.

He guides me through the exhibition, narrating facts about the shocking statuettes of nude men and women, the lank and haughty cat symbols of the goddess Bastet, and the ram-headed falcon pendant inlaid with the vivid oranges and blues of carnelian and lapis lazuli stones.

"What's this one?" I ask, pausing at a case containing what appears to be a turquoise carving of an insect set into a gold plate. The plaque identifies it as a scarab beetle, and all at once the mystery is solved. The beetle of my imaginings—it's this one.

"A wadj amulet," says Gaston, "hewed of amazonite. It belonged to the vizier Paser, high priest of Amon under Ramesses II, and buried with him for protection in the afterlife."

"Would he need protection? Did the Egyptians not believe they rested in death?"

"Certainly, they did. But to achieve that rest, you must first pass through the trials of *Duat*, the netherworld, where you'll be faced with the terrors of spirits, and if you survive them, your heart will be weighed for its righteousness. The final test." His eyebrows bridge upwards, inveigling a smile from me. Soon after, his tone sedates, doomful. "Of course, an amulet's ensorcelled properties applied to the living, as well as the dead, though not all were a blessing."

I look at him directly. "Spells, you mean."

"*Prisons*. For the gods themselves. For the sanity of man, some chaos must be bottled." He stares at me, long and close, and I feel his breath on my face, my mouth, where his lips want to touch. I turn to ice.

A gentleman behind us clears his throat. Gaston scowls at him while I turn to the artifact, grasping at my squeamish middle. How close, how close. How close we were.

Too close.

I take a cooling breath, turning back to him. "What do you mean, 'some chaos must be bottled'?"

A mischievous glint in his eye. "Come," he says. "I will tell you exactly what I mean." Gaston guides me to a viewing bench, where we sit. With both hands gripping his cane—a roaring lion's head with emerald eyes—lain across his lap, he begins.

KHEPRI, the sun god, grunted mightily as he rolled the blazing sphere toward the edge of the world, straining as he pushed it above the horizon and into the sky. Every day he did this, and every day the scarab imitated his work. Glinting in the early sun, the beetle's convex body reeled the camel dung into a tight ball across the desert sand, never stopping, never slowing, racing onward till the source of its life grew in triplicate to its size.

It stilled, antennae quivering, tasting the air. A falcon rode the wind, swooping over the pyramidal summit of Al-Qurn. Silent. Searching. Its keen eyes espied a speck of jet among the tawny valley floor. Patient, it circled twice.

And dove.

The scarab shot for the tombs, skittering through an entryway and plunging down steep corridors with painted walls. The Litany of Ra looked on, reliefs of antelope, toothy crocodiles, and ram-headed men etched into the limestone. The scarab paused atop a carving of its kin and then scuttled onward through a gateway into the ever-descending darkness.

In the burial chamber, an archaeologist scratched at a sand-encrusted *ushabti*, a funerary figurine, with his pick. Behind him lay a sarcophagus of purest alabaster, inlaid with the vibrant blue of copper sulphate. A cartouche had been inscribed at its feet, the hieroglyphics reading: THE

JUSTICE OF RA IS ETERNAL. SON OF RA, HE WHO BELONGS TO SET, BELOVED OF PTAH.

"As fortunate a day as when Belzoni discovered it," said the man to himself. He smiled, his teeth glowing in the torchlight, which blackened the crusted walls in soot. Crouched among a scattering of rock and chert, he used a horsehair brush to sweep away the sand from a miniature Pharaoh, setting it aside with the rest of its battalion canvassing the floor.

He stood, knees cracking. A reminder of his aging limbs. Although he was still in the robust prime of youth, and the features of his face—scarab-black eyes and a strong jaw, thickly furred—were aging beautifully, the rest of him was in protest. He sighed, aggrieved, for when a man is required to squeeze his body through belly-tight passageways and crawl snake-wise over roughened floors of sandstone, he is nostalgic for his previous self. But despite the closeness of the chamber, and the sand, sand, everywhere sand—in his shirt, his boots, the little flaps and pockets of his ears—the archaeologist was content with his careful work. He took to whistling a merry little French tune he'd learned as a boy from his Romani grandmother.

His falsetto rapped the walls, converting the underground into an echo chamber of a thousand voices whistling back to him. At the song's end, he straightway began another, stringing the two together as if they had been matrimonially joined. In a way, they had. This tune was Indian, subdued and sleepy and low, and it teased a thought from his mind. *His wife would be missing him.*

He rubbed at the skin above his heart, as if to push out the homesickness. He could still hear her tremulous voice imploring him not to go, not to leave her all alone in that country so foreign to her. But the valley had called to him.

Oh, the relics to be dug there, the history! He thirsted for a drink only the Nile could satisfy. The Valley quenched him, and the Pharaohs threw out their arms to him in their tombs. *Honor us,* they cried. *See how we lived, and loved, and died!* The archaeologist had never experienced such ecstasy as when he was prostrate in the dust, chipping at shale with a chisel.

And yet, in the dampness of the chamber, whistling now with strange breezes, he yearned for his beloved wife. And he wondered... if only they were able to bear a child, she might not feel so forsaken.

He plumbed his trouser pocket for the daguerreotype, a silver plate set into an alabaster case, which he unfolded. Sultry eyes peered back at him under a veil of black lace, a Bindi stamped between the brows, and he recalled, with a laugh, his wife's objections to having her image captured.

*It is vanity,* she'd said. *Ganesh will smite me!*

*No, my love,* he'd rejoined. *It is beauty. And he will worship you as I do.*

A scarab dashed over the man's boot. The daguerreotype flew from his hand, and he lost purchase, smashing into the brittle wall of decorated limestone. The foundation cracked, air hissing through the new fissure. The torchlight twisted toward it, its flame enticed by the darkness.

The archaeologist paused, listening.

His blood fluxed with excitement. A chamber, undiscovered for over a millennium, lay behind this wall. And *he* had just unearthed it.

He reached for his torch—but before the *huzzah!* could leave his lips, an uncanny thought came to him. If all the chambers of the tomb had entrances, why had this one been secreted, *sealed*, behind a wall? A shiver climbed his spine, the myth of Pandora's jar surfacing in his mind. It felt as if something...*someone*...were waiting for him.

"Pah!" The archaeologist laughed, chastening himself. He was a scholar! Not some superstitious fool. Whatever lay behind that wall was most assuredly put there for protection against raiders—an antechamber, perhaps, glutted with the Pharaoh's wealth of gold and jewels.

His fingers tingled in their eager anticipation to touch it all.

Spurred to action, he fetched a crowbar and carefully jimmied open the wall, chunks of rock and dust showering down on him, slipping into his thin cotton shirt. Holding his torch aloft, he stepped into the antechamber.

The low ceiling forced him into a hunch, and the posture reflected his disappointment. Except for an unadorned sarcophagus, resting at the center of the room, the chamber was empty. No gold. No jewels. Not even an *ushabti* or canopic jar. Just a coffin, devoid of markings.

An unmarked tomb, it was speculated, meant the person inside it had shamed his king, died dishonorably, or worse, been cursed. But only the antiquated believed such rubbish. It was more likely this fellow's body had been snuck in by laborers desiring to give their friend as close to a royal burial as they could. The archaeologist admired their loyalty.

As he turned to quit the disappointing room, his name, in whisper, reached out to him.

*Had it been a whisper?* He wasn't sure. He was tired, having risen from his sleep well before the brutal desert sun. The dull lighting spotted his vision with greenish afterimages of the sarcophagus, yet he saw nothing sentient within the room. No colleague whose clomping footsteps he would have heard approaching. His throat dried, and when he swallowed, his saliva had the mouth-feel of sand.

Again, he heard his name, a sibilant whisper reaching for him from the sarcophagus. An inclination to see inside that lonely coffin beset him—or perhaps it was the fatigue, the unforeseen heaviness of his mind. He yawned, and in that yawn a voice crept up from his throat, speaking in his own utterance.

*Regardes à l'intérieur,* it said. *Look inside.*

Bent like an ape, the archaeologist stalked to the coffin and slid back the heavy stone with nary a flinch as it clamored to the ground. He batted down the cloud of dust, blinking. Inside, a stale mummy lay supine, arms shriveled and crossed, its skin taut with resin.

His hands gripping the sarcophagus, a sound escaped the archaeologist like a gasp, a plea for air. An amulet of carved lapis lazuli, the Persian sky stone, was anchored by a leather chord and threaded through the mummy's arms. It was a falcon. Horus's symbol. God of the Sky.

The man fell to his knees. The amulet was neither large nor incredibly rare, and although the vibrant blue appeared to be riven with gold, its veins were really pyrite, *fools' gold.* What held the archaeologist was its *glow*. The amulet pulsed like a heart with a blue-white light. It whispered to him, *sang* to him, a provocative chant of heavy drums and bamboo flutes. Louder and faster and harder and *harder* they beat and they beat and they beat and his chest tightened with the pounding, the blood, and the rapture.

And then it all stopped. Even his heart. His heart held its breath and refused to let go until the archaeologist had stretched forth his hand to touch the sublime relic.

As he did so, the puckish laughter of hyenas gusted through the room, but he was deaf to it. No other sound but the frantic heart-thumping of the amulet affected him. His hand, moving thick and slow through a miasma of greenish fog, felt for it, *fought* for it. This was a gift to him from Horus, the sky god. And it was *his*.

The room hushed its whispers. An oppressive silence

constricted his lungs, but he couldn't feel it. He felt nothing but the cool fire in his hands as he caressed the amulet to his cheek, sighing a moan of ecstasy.

In the burial chamber, the scarab hovered over the relief of a chimerical beast with the body of a canine, the head of a jackal, and the tail of a scorpion. *Set.* The God of Chaos.

"AND SO YOU SEE, my love, some jars must never be opened. And some chaos must remain bottled."

My blood runs with heat, my heart fast with his words. There were so many of them, I thought I'd have to machete myself out of their thickets. That mischievous glint in Gaston's eye remains, yet the emotion in his voice is deathly serious, as if he believes every word he's spoken to be true.

"Nonsense!" The gentleman who'd saved us from public impropriety looks reprovingly at Gaston. He'd been eavesdropping. "A woman's head should not be filled with such fantastical ideas and falsehoods. It is the highest degree of indecency."

Gaston's grip on his cane has gone white. Without thinking, I cover his hand with mine. "What do you think of it, my love?" he says to me, his composure holding. He meets my eyes. "Do you believe such a 'fantastical' thing could really happen?"

I take back my hand, answering truthfully. "I think you have a remarkable talent for embellishing stories."

He doesn't laugh or smile, the playful eye-glint vanishes. He gets to his feet. "Come along. You are pale and must be in need of some nourishment."

As if in obedience, my stomach makes a woebegone noise, increasing my unease that I've said the wrong thing.

## CHAPTER 11

# A WOLF THROUGH THE TREES

Gaston holds a profiterole to my mouth. "Try this, my love."

I take a timid bite, and he catches the cream dribbling down my chin. As he licks his finger, I pinken, aware of the pastry chef behind the counter watching us.

The chef's thin black mustache twerks with a disconcerting grin. "How do you like it, *mademoiselle*?" he says.

*"Il est délicieux. Merci."*

The chef continues to leer at me with that ribald, uncomfortable curve passing for a smile. I find myself inching closer to Gaston, whose face has darkened. Slamming two francs onto the counter, he slurs something low and in rapid French at the man, who reels backward, stunned and equally furious. Hooking my arm, Gaston steers me out.

"What did you say to him?" I ask, struggling for breath. His strides are fast and fuming, and I'm tugged along, nearly tripping over my skirts, as my words.

"Nothing significant," he says, but I hear him hiss curses under his breath.

We step from the *pâtisserie* onto the street, where a coterie of young ladies swallows us whole, blinking behind their fans at a gathering of gentlemen opposite the thoroughfare. The distance is too great a span to hold the men's interests for long, and so they tip their hats, going into the *club messieurs* behind them. Pretty faces or no, the girls are quickly forgotten, left alone to pout and feel sorry for themselves. I'd pity them if I didn't wish I were them. They have a freedom they've not yet realized. But they will, soon enough.

Having collected himself, Gaston slows his pace. His temper still brews beneath the surface, but for now it has lulled. I battle an odd smile tugging on the corner of my mouth. I've never had a man defend my honor as Gaston just did—swooping in and rescuing me—if only from the pastry chef's slatternly imaginings. He protected me.

The same wouldn't have been true of Mr. Haskell, had he been the one I wedded. I hope he's hunched in some gutter somewhere, miserable with guilt and empty pockets.

Gaston hasn't slackened his husbandly duties. He's spoiled me, given me far more than I ever expected or even dreamed. But with his every offering my guilt builds, as I've given him very little in return, besides my companionship, though even that is held in reserve.

Our week in Paris has sailed by like a lark in the wind, each day more luxurious and diverting than the last, and each night, more easy. True to his word, he's hardly touched me. In truth, he doesn't have to touch me at all. It's his eyes—those orbs of blackest black—that feel me, watching everything I do.

What have I given him? Very, very little.

I should thank him, at least.

As I open my mouth to do so, he says, "Your dress is lacking. We must purchase something to liven it."

Gaston conducts me to the jeweler's shop across the road. With a clangor of door chimes announcing our entrance, the shopkeeper and his assistant, a gangly boy of no more than fourteen, paste on their most congenial faces.

"Choose something," Gaston says, ushering me to the jeweler's case.

I protest. He's given me too much already, and I'm beginning to suspect it's more to please himself than to please me. He sips the air, annoyed but trying not to show it.

Mamma's complaints enter my mind like unbidden telepathy: *You err, Beatrice. It's you he wants to please, but in your pride, you refuse him. You must be meek yet agreeable.*

Little by little, I weaken. "All right," I say.

Alit with the prospect of an expensive sale, the shopkeeper mines a necklace from the case, simultaneously swatting the air for his assistant to retrieve a mirror. Though the size and luster of the diamonds might tempt most women, I find them gaudy and overbearing.

"What about that one, there?"

The shopkeeper holds a lorgnette to his eyes to better see where I'm pointing.

Gaston speaks quickly. "I would advise against the opal, my love. Ever since reading Sir Scott's novel, I've highly disfavored the stone. Baroness or no, I'll not risk my new bride encountering the same malignant fate."

I know the book he's referring to, as I've read it myself. Sir Scott's *Anne of Geierstein.* On its pages lives the enchanting Baroness of Arnheim, a Persian, who wears an opal in her hair said to be a talisman of supernatural power. But when the opal is spritzed with holy water for her christening, it loses its color, and the lady falls into a swoon. Upon the morn, she's discovered in her bedchamber, a pile of ash in her sheets.

It was not, as a careful reading of the text will reveal, the opal that killed her, but the result of a poison administered by the viperine Baroness Steinfeldt. It bemuses me to think Gaston would shy away from the stone when its superstition is clearly derived from fiction. But rather than spar with him, I demur, choosing instead a ruby that's been set into a wreath of gold.

As Gaston secures it around my neck, the shop boy returns with a cheval glass. Gaston hasn't noticed him. He turns unawares, knocking the boy over, and the mirror slips, shattering in a hundred silver shards.

In swift movements I never thought possible from him, Gaston strikes the boy with his cane, shouting, *"Stupide garçon! Essayez-vous de nous maudire tous les?"*

*Are you trying to curse us all?*

"Gaston!" I throw myself between him and the boy, narrowly blocking a second strike. His chest pumps savagely, the cane still raised.

The red and the rage drain from his face, and he looks at the stupefied shopkeeper, the boy immobilized on the floor with a welt swelling on his brow. It's my fear that finally lowers his cane. Wide-eyed, shaking below him.

He straightens his waistcoat, smoothing it over his heaving chest. "I'll wait for you outside."

The shop bells sunder the tension, a chipper mockery to the furor of violence. Though his body is gone, Gaston's presence remains heavy. And I realize: this is what Ami Rose meant.

The wolf has shown himself.

## CHAPTER 12
# THRESHOLD

Saying *au revoir* to Paris is harder than saying "I will" to a man I don't love. But I miss Anna and Mamma, so I follow Gaston up the gangplank to the ferry. He hasn't said anything of his outburst in the jeweler's shop but has again donned his innocuous sheep's clothing. If he senses my apprehension to be near him, he doesn't show it. He's more respectful, more reserved, than he's ever been before, as if some semblance of guilt has made birth in his conscience.

Perhaps he *is* sorry.

I just wish he'd say it.

The journey is rough and wind-tossed. Sea mist sprays my face as I listen to the skawing of seabirds and the *shuh-shuh* of waves plashing against the paddle steamer's wooden hull. England expands, approaching quickly. *There is a cliff whose high and bending head looks fearfully in the confined deep.* That cliff is Shakespeare, and, waiting atop it, Gaston's estate, turrets and chimney flues penetrating the milky, cloud-cast sky.

Imminent.

"My home has missed having a mistress," Gaston says, emerging at my side. "I hope you will be its last."

My heartbeat quickens. Does some sickness fester within the bulwark of that mansion, claiming every female life that enters it?

I say nothing to him. Only work the stern's taffrail in my hands.

"PLEASE—I beg you—don't make me."

"I insist upon it." Gaston's stubbornness outweighs my own. No matter how long or loud my protestations, he won't be undermined.

"It's tradition," he says, but the true reason is that he's superstitious and worried I'll stumble upon the threshold, ruining us all and especially our marriage.

I glower at the Tudor archway and large ironwork door, which he intends to carry me through.

*Tradition.* It's the silliest, most ridiculous tradition I've ever heard. Why carry a girl when she has two perfectly functional feet capable of walking *herself* through the door? If a man is worried she'll stumble, then he shouldn't demand she wear so many petticoats!

I could explain all this to Gaston—rail and gnash my teeth at him—but it would hardly benefit me. He's already miffed I insisted on carrying my own travel bag. *You'll strain yourself.* Well, I haven't strained myself *yet*, and I *won't*. The only strain on my person is from the butterflies in my gut, aflutter with uncertainty.

I don't bother stifling my moan. "Fine," I grumble, and before I can change my mind, I'm swooped into Gaston's arms, clinging to his neck in terror that he'll drop me.

"Get the door for us, Crawley," he instructs his grave-faced butler in coattails. "Ready, my love?" There's a waggish charm about the way he says it, and although I'm unhappy with him, my grin fights for complaisance.

With cheek, I say, "Proceed."

His black boots thump the floor, trefoil patterns laid out in marble before us. The commodious foyer glows, lambent with soft, colored lights scattered by stained glass windows. An ornate grandfather clock stands sentry at the far end of the room, near twisting stairs of rich walnut parquetry, dutifully ticking away the hours.

"How lovely," I breathe. If I weren't already in Gaston's arms, I might swoon with the resplendency of it all. So different from what I expected or imagined.

The only feature the room could do without is the garish sword—of Arabian smithery, I think—bracketed to the wall. The crescent blade grins balefully, shooting shivers down my back.

"Do you think you could call this home, Beatrice?" Gaston's breath on my face turns my head, and, nose to nose, I pale, just a little.

"I need to see the other rooms first, before I can make such an avowal."

With a simper, he promises, "I'll move the world to make it so."

But first he moves me.

Gaston whisks me down a hallway to a room ornamented with artifacts from nearly every land east of the Mediterranean: hundred-year-old blossom-motif tapestries of Japanese silk; Grecian red-figure pots encased on pedestals; jolly Buddhas shaped from jade; Hindu figurines with glittering eyes and a sextet of arms; African tribal masks, tusked and toothed and intimidating.

"Did I not promise you would have the world?"

"You did," I say, with staggered breath. "It's like the Louvre."

"Better," he says, "because it's yours. As am I."

I'm not sure my legs could bear me under the weight of his stare. He's strong. I feel the bulk and bulge of his arms around me, and his ursine shoulders, as I keep from tipping. How he can hold me this long without growing tired, I don't know. But I wish he'd put me down.

"Shall I show you the library next?" he asks, setting off

in the supposed direction. It's entirely possible he'll carry me over every threshold of every room of every *wing* in this leviathan of a house, just to secure himself in knowing no ill luck will incur. Blessedly, upon reaching the aforementioned library, Gaston comes to his senses and sets me down.

This room I like best of all, lucent and open with blossomy crown molding above the bookshelves, which are tucked into niches like enchanted portals to imaginative lands. Plopping down on a plum-colored sofa, I take up a book resting on a table and flip arbitrarily through its pages.

"Have I satisfied you?" he says over my shoulder. He asks it seriously.

At the risk of sounding like an ingrate, I answer, "Almost. If Anna and Mamma were here to share my joy, then I think I really could call this home."

A sly smile. "That is easily remedied. I've already sent for them. For a short visit, mind you, for we are weary from our traveling."

I fly to my feet, nearly knocking Gaston's chin as he stoops over me. "Gaston, that's"—*kind, thoughtful, devoted*—a whole slew of adjectives I never thought could apply. But when he's like *this*—in full view of the sun without a shadow creeping in—they do, indeed, apply. He's realized my love for my family and sought to increase it. "That is the most wonderful thing you've done for me yet," I declare.

"I would do anything for you, Beatrice." He reaches for my hand. Strokes my wedding band. "As I hope you would do anything for me."

My rapture falls, sinking into my belly like curdled milk. Of course. All these gifts are just indicators of Gaston's conditions for our marriage. To receive, I must give. I shouldn't have expected anything less. I married him, after all, for his money.

Anna and I run to each other, squealing over the butler's announcement of visitors. "A Mrs. Tilney and a Miss Tilney to see you, sir."

"Thank you, Mr. Crawley." Gaston waves him away as Quincy yaps at our feet. I squat down to nuzzle him, and he licks my face. Gaston crinkles his nose at the bulldog, who growls at him.

"Stop that, Quincy," Mamma says, handing her capelet over to the butler. Though she seems improved, melancholia still films her eyes. She was an envy of the world once. Her straight teeth would sparkle through lips rouged with berries, and her costume, prim and meticulous, would deign display a wrinkle. Once her golden tresses curled carefully into ringlets, pinned into order, but now they hang limply, lifeless against her shoulders.

I kiss her cheek. "I've missed you, Mamma."

"Look at you," she says, cupping my face. "A woman."

I blush under her hand, and she runs her finger over the little divot in my lower lip. A dimple. A *woman's* dimple, she likes to say. Just like hers. A mark of maturity. Of secret experience. I remove her hand, only to kiss it to hide my dismay.

"Oh, Beatrice! You *have* to see my new piano." Anna claps her hands, buoyant on her toes. Her voice, her smile, her whole person is like that of the little girl she was when Papa was alive and Anna was his delight. This jubilant energy is something I've not seen in years. Indeed, she looks older, a maturing young woman who's no longer shy, but coy, almost coquettish. It makes me nervous. How could she have changed so quickly?

"New piano?" I say. "How could you have afforded that?"

She beams at Gaston. "Your new husband gave it to me. It's even more beautiful than my last—and its *sound*—oh, Beatrice, angels could not produce a more heavenly intonation."

"Blasphemy," I tease.

"But that's not all he's done for us. He's replenished the furniture, rehired Molly and Archie, *plus* two others to help with the chores, but best of all"—she sucks in a breath—"he has repurchased the orchard!"

At this, I look to him, a peculiar blend of esteem and dismay commingling in my breast. How much did it cost him to buy back my dreams, my childhood playground?

How much will it cost me?

"Let's move you to the salon," he says, with a smile I find a bit smug, "where you may be alone to chat and gossip to your hearts' content." He escorts us, and as we shuffle down the hall, skirts swishing, we pass the ballroom.

Anna looks about to swoon. "How grand it is," she says, halting our travel. "What spectacular balls you must have hosted, *monsieur*!"

"In truth, I've hosted none," he says.

"Oh, but you must! Beatrice, tell him. Wouldn't a midnight ball be the loveliest, most romantic—"

"Anna, your manners—"

"Hold peace, my dear. Your sister has wisdom in this. For nigh a decade the ballroom has lain unused. Why, look at these webs. Frightful! And this prolific carpeting of dust. My nose dogs with a sneeze at the sight of it." He actually sneezes, and Anna laughs, a tinkling fairy sound which delights him. "A ball sounds like a marvelous idea. Of course, as this is a domestic affair, the decision lies with the mistress of this manor and, therefore, the keeper of its keys."

There again with that smirk. He's teasing me, torturing me, and enjoying it thoroughly.

Anna bats her doe eyes. I roll mine. "*Please*, Beatrice?"

The last ball we attended, I was forced to dance three waltzes with Mr. Whitley, who, incidentally, has two left feet *despite* his being the town's cobbler. He went on and on about the shape of my slippers, which he had designed.

But as Anna pouts at me, her lower lip sticking out with an infinitesimal quiver, I can't help but yield. I suppose, now that I'm married, a ball wouldn't pose the same threat as it once did. And, as hostess, I wouldn't have to dance with anybody I didn't like. Or anybody at all.

I sigh heavily. "I'll choose a date."

Anna whops me in a clobbering hug.

Gaston claps his hands together. "Splendid. Now, if you'll excuse me, there is some business I must see to." He goes clandestine, leaning facetiously low to whisper to us. "While Beatrice and I were honeymooning, my vessel journeyed to the West Indies, cutting against wind and tide to return to us with a shipment of tobacco." The mere mention of the tropical clime induces a mousy squeal from Anna, as it might have me had I not already heard most of Gaston's gripping, albeit exaggerated, tales of his exploits.

After he has seen us comfortably to the salon, Anna remarks, "How fortunate you are, Beatrice, to have married such a noble man as him."

"How fortunate we all are," adds Mamma, settling onto the sofa. The butler, Mr. Crawley, has brought in the tea, and as hostess, I brew and serve it to my guests.

Taking a sip, Mamma pinches up, the tea too bitter for her. She stirs in sugar with a silver teaspoon. "Now, if we could find a match for Anna half as rich."

My hand slips, spilling tea on my dress. "Mamma, she's only fifteen." I take Anna's offered napkin. I don't like hearing her talk like this. If Papa were here, he'd be livid. I won't let her put Anna up on the auction block like she did with me.

"I'm only thinking of her future," she says sharply. "Unfortunately, that future has come more quickly than we anticipated. I want my daughters to be taken care of."

I taste a lie, coppery, like blood in the mouth. Her haste reveals something greater than finding safety for us, and I sense a guilt that must be shriven: the sooner her children have grown and left her, the sooner she can join her husband in that eternal sleep. Like Simon and Byron, she is abandoning us.

"*I* will care for Anna," I say, strangling the napkin in my lap. How can she think so selfishly when I've sacrificed my life for her?

Mamma feels my scorn like nettle, yet her voice is dead. "You can't save us all, Beatrice, no matter how strong your will. You are like your father in that way."

Tears bead in my eyes at Papa's mention. I blink them away.

Dusk dims into nightfall. The moon, a pale crescent, rises. Now that we're in the privacy of our own home, I fear Gaston will try again to bed me. It's a threshold I never want to cross, and one I will keep Anna from traversing at all costs. She will never know this fear. When she is of age, she will wed the man she loves, and she will be happy forever. She will have a love like our parents', the love I forfeited to protect the only heart I have. My family.

"Papa would have wanted me to try," I say reverently. "I won't give up on you, Mamma." I won't let you slip away.

She doesn't hear me. She's already slipped away, lost to her thoughts and her longing, absently stirring and stirring and stirring spoonfuls of sugar into her undrunk tea, gone cold with her neglect.

"We were lucky your eyes are blue," she says, her voice a ghost disembodied.

"What do you mean?" says Anna.

"It's been said the Monsieur has a fascination for blue eyes. Each of his former wives had various shades of the color. All but his first wife, that is."

An eddy of nausea whirls through me. Is that why he chose me? If my eyes had been brown like my siblings' or hazel like Papa's, would Gaston have passed over me for someone like Felicity Crane? Her eyes are blue. Why me? Why my blue eyes?

A shudder wracks my bones as a new, more disturbing question surfaces. How long have I been Gaston's obsession?

Before they depart, I take Anna and Mamma to the Hall of Artifacts. Anna *oohs* over a set of savannah animals, lions and zebras and wildebeest carved of ivory tusk, as Mamma trails her hand over a smooth moonstone pendant dated to the Roman conquests. Gaston says the power of the moonstone reunites lovers lost or estranged, restores passion, cures insomnia, and protects travelers from the dangers of nightfall. I don't believe it. A stone is just a stone, inert and ineffectual. Its alchemy can't affect the mortal world.

Quincy whines suddenly, ears pricked. I crouch to pet him, but he darts from the room. Chasing after him, I whisper-shout his name to call him back. I fear letting him wander, having noted Gaston's distaste for dogs.

Paws slapping the wood floors, Quincy's pudgy body careens down a gloomy wing of the house. When I catch up to him, he's stopped in front of a door, whimpering and scratching at its ground.

I don't remember Gaston showing me this room. A single candle burns on a table across the hall, above which a mirror hangs, reflections smirched with dust. The flame shudders, hit with a current of air.

"Quincy," I hiss, "come away from there." His complaining stops, head cocked inquisitively to one side. "What is it, Quince?"

But then I hear it.

Faint.

Effeminate.

*Whispers.*

The candle sputters and chokes, smothering the hall with darkness.

## CHAPTER 13
# ROSES

Snowflakes fall starlike, set against a canvas slicked black with pitch. The sounds of laughter and carving ice. Visible breaths. Anna grabs my hands, and we twirl in figures of eight. *Spin me*, I shout, taking to the air like a dove with wings spread in a suspended pirouette. I land, and the glittering heels of my boots split the ice, schisms chasing schisms, rending open the pond to claim my sister for its own.

In the dream, I'm brave. I dive in after her, sinking, reaching for her hand. But no matter how tightly I hold, my fingers keep slipping. My lungs burn, and I scream. I suck in water. My heart stalls its beating. My eyes dip shut. And I drift with the pond's placid current.

I feel a kiss on the back of my neck—light, quick—passing like a breeze. My eyes open, and I turn.

"You whimper in your sleep," Gaston says. "I worry

you are in pain."

Pain. Yes. In my lungs. I stopped breathing. Eyes watery and disoriented, I bat at pictures of ice and snow, fingers of the dream still caught in my hair.

Blink by blink, the pictures fade, but the emotions stay. I stare at Gaston lying next to me in bed, and the need to cry seizes my chest. "I think it's that I am caught in a dream," I say, "and I want to get out."

His forehead creases. "I know what will soothe a fretful mind."

He slides back the bed curtain and feels his way through the darkness. A match strikes and sizzles, giving life to a trio of candles. He returns to the bed with a long-necked bottle cast in silver. A rosewater decanter. "Lie down," he directs.

I hesitate, though ultimately submit, laying my back to the pillows.

"My first wife was Indian," he says, and I listen at full attention. "When the nights were cold and the wind alive, this would allay her heartsickness." Using the wand, Gaston wets the blue vein in my translucent wrist, drawing a line up to my elbow. "'*Nīlakantha,*' she'd chant, 'to Shiva, blue-throated one, dancer of *Tandava,* primordial. Subdue my heart, absolve my sins, and bless my husband.'" Twice more he repeats the mantra, manipulating the wand in smooth, stimulating strokes.

My body loosens, relaxing into the downy mattress. I breathe in a garden of tranquility, exhaling flowers in slow, soughing breaths. Gaston inhales with me, exhales with me. Then sows a succession of kisses along my arm, making my blood jump below the skin.

"My goddess," he mutters, all desire.

Coming awake, I jerk my arm away.

"Have I offended you?" There's a guttural edge to his voice.

"No, it's nothing. It's just—" As I struggle for a lie, clouds part, and the moon casts a ribbon athwart his face, giving his beard a bizarre, spectral aura. "Your beard," I say. "It tickles."

A laugh, like a lion's purr. Blushing, I run my finger along the seam in the sheets. Gaston brushes my lip with his thumb. My lower lip, over my woman's dimple.

"Are you happy?" he asks.

*So long as you are merry and glad, so shall I be. Nothing can make me sad if you're smiling.*

"Yes," I lie again. "Are you?"

He rolls to his back, silent, the room suddenly cold. No. Of course he's not happy. He's given me the world, but I haven't given him the only world he desires. *Me.*

I flop onto my stomach, pressing my face into a pillow. Did his other wives resist like I do, or did they give themselves freely? Did they honestly love him?

"Your other wives," I begin with caution, "what were they like?"

He answers without feeling, as if resenting the question. "My second wife, Clarimond, was English. She played the pianoforte almost as well as your sister. Angelique was French, like me. She bred Papillons, little lapdogs who barked too much. And Lenore..." He pauses, and I think I hear tenderness catch in his throat. "She sang me lullabies, her voice like silk."

"They sound lovely." They sound like women who lived through their passions. The fire, the *focus* they must have felt driving them forward—I wish I had it. Then maybe I wouldn't feel so forlorn in this new house, this new life. I have only my fear of losing what I've barely grasped hold of.

"They were."

"And they each had blue eyes?"

He looks at me. "What of it?"

"No reason," I rush. "Just curious." I hesitate asking, but I want to know. "How did they die?"

"Illness. The same that took your father."

"Even the first?" She was different from the rest of them. Her eyes weren't blue.

"She yet lives."

I cant my head off the pillow, surprised. "What do you mean? Where is she?" When he doesn't speak, I graze his arm, the first voluntary touch I've given him.

The bed shifts beneath me as he turns. "She left me for another."

Gaston's grief is a weight of icy water, morphing his face, deepening the lines around his eyes like a footprint in snow. I can't imagine the betrayal experienced when the person who professes to love you loves you no more, or the shame that accompanies a writ of annulment, forever divorcing him from her. Such tragedy is often treated like Brutus falling upon his sword: better to perish with honor than live with remorse.

Tears rim my eyes, unrelenting.

"Don't weep for me," Gaston says. "Weep for her. Weep for the happiness she forfeited."

He misunderstands. It *is* her I weep for. Whatever her reasons for marrying Gaston, it mustn't have been for love, because she reclaimed herself. She set herself free. Such infidelity should not be celebrated, and yet I *do* celebrate her. I revere her. I yearn for her courage.

But I can never be her. I put myself in this cage and gave Gaston the key. For my family's sake, he must never let me go.

"Promise me you will not betray me, Beatrice," he says, turning back to me. "Promise me you will not break my heart as she did. I could not suffer it a second time." His fingers twine into my hair, flowing down my back.

I stiffen—a reflex I must learn to fight against.

Gaston retreats, throwing back the covers and rising from the bed in a torrent of frustration.

*He can't let me go. I must make it right!*

"I promise," I say, goose down muffling the words. He halts, anticipating more, but I can't summon any more courage than that.

The bedchamber door bangs shut behind him.

*Meerut, India*
*10 March 1857*

*Dear Sister,*

*We were surprised to receive your announcement of marriage, especially when it was made known the town enigma would be the groom. Really, Beatrice, how could you have said yes to a man you barely know? He's rich, to be sure, but was it necessary? Your previous letters made out the situation to be benign and uninteresting, but to agree to a contract so final, so binding, there must be something more you haven't divulged. Is it Mamma? Is she dying? Or Anna? What's happening, Beatrice, and why won't you tell us?*

*As I write this, you're likely speaking your vows, or have even begun your honeymoon tour. Whatever your reasons for this decision, I hope Monsieur Dumas will be kind to you and that he's capable of making you happy. ~~And if he doesn't you can tell that frog I will personally stick my rapier up his~~— Scratch that last bit! Byron commandeered the pen from my hand. In all sincerity, sister, I hope the Frenchman will be good to you.*

*As for life here, Byron and I are making do with following commands, patrolling the mosque, and losing ourselves to the thrall of the bazaar on days we're allowed to go into town. The women here are beautiful, but their parents are protective and refuse the favors of soldiers. I can't say I blame them, what with the way Byron flirts. He'll incite a riot one day, I assure you.*

*Grievances, though checked low, do not go uncirculated by the cavalry. There are complaints among the sepoys concerning the new rifle-muskets at our use. When we are to load the cartridges, we must bite them with our teeth to unwrap the paper, which has been greased with beef tallow or swine fat, substances our Hindu and Muslim soldiers find offensive to their faiths. Our commanders remain indifferent to their protests and won't even listen to the objections made by their Indian superiors, whom, despite rank, they judge to be racially inferior. Hierarchy is not a foreign ideal. Even among the sepoys there is a caste, and soldiers are recruited exclusively from the classes of Brahmin and Rajput, and some very wealthy Muslims. Despite their positions, they're ignored, and what's worse, they're paid less.*

*At home, I never would have thought such differences could be met with such hatred. But hatred is all around me here. I feel it reach for me in the night, while in my tent I lie hot and awake, turning to the sound of the wind buffeting the canvas. Until I realize it's the dire noise of a flogging in the street, a poor washerman who drew water from a well from which he was forbidden. His touch polluted it, the soldiers said, excusing themselves from all blame.*

*My soul despairs, Beatrice. Mine is the soul of a Christian, and yet I, in my inadequacy, question what God can do to thwart the spread of darkness. Does not the task lie to me, the lowly cornet, to put out my arm in defense of the villager, be he an Indian or a Briton? And if I do, will I, too, be punished for polluting the system of men? I disparage these questions, because the answers are hard and are the words of a coward not fit to wear his rank—not of cornet, but of man.*

*Give me courage, dear sister. Courage that I might do something good while I'm here.*

*Your humble brother,*
*Simon Tilney*
*~~Cornet~~ Man, Bengal Light Cavalry*

# CHAPTER 14
# STAR-CROSSED

*Love looks not with the eyes, but with the mind;*
*And therefore is wing'd Cupid painted blind.*
*Nor hath Love's mind of any judgment taste;*
*Wings and no eyes figure unheedy haste;*
*And therefore is Love said to be a child,*
*Because in choice he is so oft beguil'd....*

Laughter sounds from the hall, disrupting my reading. Two voices. A booming bass—Gaston—but the other is soft, a cadenced baritone laughing airily at Gaston's wit. Setting my book aside, I follow the mirth into the Hall of Artifacts, where Gaston is showing off a 17$^{th}$ century kirpan he recovered in the Punjab. Though intrigued by Gaston's penchant for storytelling, the young man at his side stifles a yawn.

With no proper reason, my face blooms with heat. My

chest swells, a rolling motion, like my heart is tumbling downhill. Light freckles bedeck the man's face as if the sun has oft enjoyed embracing him, and his eyes—the richest brown I've ever seen—crinkle at the edges, deepening as he smiles.

"My dear!" says Gaston, returning the knife to its display. "Come, come. Meet Monsieur Swain. Henry, this is my wife."

Surprise flits over the man's face, passing quickly. "Madame," he says, taking my hand, which Gaston has given to him. He bows, releasing me before he's made vertical again. "How do you do?"

"Well," I answer, throat dry. "And you?"

"Very well, thank you."

"I've commissioned Monsieur Swain's services," Gaston explains, "the most gifted painter to have entered the halls of the Royal Academy."

Mr. Swain holds himself humbly, head tilted at a modest angle. He throws glances at me, though I resist meeting his eyes. I focus on Gaston as he marshals us into the library.

"This wall," Gaston says, swiping his hand over the paneled oak across from the great oriel windows, "is too bare for my taste. I wish Monsieur Swain to put a fresco there. What do you think of it? My love?"

*He's speaking to you.*

I've been distracted by Mr. Swain's russet hair, glossy with sunlight. Like tiger stripes. "Wonderful." I draw in a breath. "I mean—yes—an excellent idea." Shaking myself from my own idiocy, I blink until my head clears and my attention is fully on Gaston.

*What on earth is happening to me?*

"Good. What will it be, Swain?"

Roused from a thought—perchance on the cost of my shoes, which he's fixated on—Mr. Swain answers, "Perhaps Madame Dumas would care to choose the scene?" My nose wrinkles at the word *madame*, pretentious and gray and downright *old*.

Searching the room, my eyes land on the book of Shakespeare I'd previously been reading. "Perhaps a scene from the Bard?"

"Ah, *Hamlet*?"

"No," I muse. "Too morose, I think."

"*Julius Cesar*, then."

"Too gory."

"The Scottish play?"

"Too gothic."

Gaston belts a laugh. "She's a hard woman to please, is she not?"

Mr. Swain smiles, drifting for a moment into thought. "It would appear she never settles for less than what she wants."

A blush speeds down my neck, but if either man noticed, neither comment.

"The star-crossed lovers would be the better choice, don't you think, my love?" *My love.* The pet-name is like a slithering reminder in my ear as Gaston snakes an arm around my waist. Discomfort grows along my spine, the move too intimate for the presence of a guest.

"Perfect," I say, all lightness abated.

Mr. Swain clears his throat. "Capital. The lovers it is. I'll return tomorrow with my accoutrements."

"Nonsense," says Gaston. "I will purchase everything new. I want only the best."

"But sir, consider the expense. You've already insisted on paying double the commission price."

Gaston bats this away with his hand. "It's nothing to me. A young man of your talent requires the finest mediums. No less will do."

Mr. Swain looks to argue—a smidgen of pride showing through—but he quite sensibly thinks better of it. He bows, cutting me a final glance before allowing Crawley to see him out.

I'm drawn to the windows in a flurry of distracted thoughts. If I crane my neck, I can see the curve of the road at the front of the house, though the flap of a coat hem in the wind is all I catch of Mr. Swain's departure. It feels as though a match has been lit in my abdomen, its quiet flame emitting a simmering strand of smoke, filling my chest with heat. It's a foreign sensation, nothing I've ever experienced before. Except maybe once, when I found myself alone with a stranger in his darkened carriage. Yet that felt like a thrill fueled by fear, while this feels...like attraction.

That can't be right. No, it *isn't* right. I know nothing of such things.

A buzz of blue-gold flits past the corner of my eye—the wings of a scarab vanishing into thin air. I'm sure I've just imagined it, as surely as I've imagined any feelings for the artist—a man I've barely met. A man I am decidedly *not* married to.

I prod my temples with my fingers, fearing the pending emergence of a headache.

Gaston comes to my side, obstructing my view of the road, where still I watch, though the artist, Mr. Swain, has long since left. He speaks low, with deliberation. "Monsieur Swain is a handsome lad. What do you think of him?"

*Step carefully.* Gaston has shown himself to be the mercurial sort of gentleman. One wrong word will bruise his ego, and I can't allow that to happen. My worst fear is losing his grace and in consequence losing everything else.

"I suppose he's handsome," I say.

"No doubt he's the starring figure in many a young woman's dreams."

Gaston's ship, a three-masted barque christened *La Gitane*, drifts in the bay, constrained by the wind inflating its sails. A longing to be on it surges and descends. I think he's testing me. Probing for a tell of infidelity, an inconsistency in my words. I'll give him nothing of the kind.

"No girl is foolish enough to dream of a man before

she's certain he has first dreamt of her," I say. I read a similar line in a book somewhere. One of Miss Austen's, I think. The one with the girl named Catherine and her overactive imagination, much like mine.

Gaston smiles, and it reaches his eyes, if just. "How wise you are, my love. And how cunning."

I remain still as he kisses my temple, resisting the impulse to recoil. He's pleased with my tender efforts, and so am I. I breathe through my trepidation, reaching for whatever bit of courage that's in me. Everything I say and do must serve the interests of my security.

"Read to me," Gaston says, "while there's still light."

As he settles himself into an armchair, I pick up the book I'd left on the settee and begin reading from where I'd left off.

*As waggish boys in game themselves forswear,*
*So the boy Love is perjur'd everywhere;*
*For ere Demetrius look'd on Hermia's eyne,*
*He hail'd down oaths that he was only mine;*
*And when this hail some heat from Hermia felt,*
*So he dissolv'd, and show'rs of oaths did melt....*

My voice soothes him. Before an hour has passed, Gaston has fallen asleep. He snores softly, his abdomen swelling and receding, an ocean unto its own. A fiery sunset pours into the library, warm orange subduing the cold, eerie blue of his beard. In sleep, the gruff expressions of his face smooth away. He looks tame. Harmless. He looks like a man I should love.

I conjure up the memory of our first meeting, in his funeral coach. I know I felt a thrill in his dark presence then, but whether that was attraction or adrenaline, it's hard to parse out. What is love, exactly? How do you feel it? Know it? Summon it from its dormancy? In books it's like spellcraft, in poetry life or death. It seems impractical to think of it in such terms, to leave no room for nuance. To dive head first is foolish; if only Romeo had waited a moment longer before plunging in his knife, he'd have seen Juliet stir, awaken. And yet the urgency of his pain—to be without his love for even that singular moment—was too powerful to resist ending his own life. Surely love must be less impulsive, must wait a moment more, to be sure it's true.

Rising silently, I unfold a blanket and drape it over Gaston, leaving him to rest. The servants have been dismissed for the night, and in its desertion, the house seems to bend and sigh around me. I drift through the halls, my slippered feet soundless.

A suit of Mongolian armor projects the shadow of a man along the floor, his horse-tailed helmet a formidable apex of war and massacre. Once wondrous, all the artifacts have grown dark. The tribal masks wear scheming, sharp-toothed sneers, and the figurines appear warped, insidious.

I stop suddenly, my skin prickling, iced over with a

sound in the empty house. It starts soft, humming like an insect from down the corridor and then crescendoing into a mass of whispers.

Voices.

They're coming from the wing near the back of the house, where I chased Quincy. Such strangeness that night. When the candle went out, the susurrations ceased, and the air stood still, so still, not even my breath stirred it. Quincy bolted, and I ran after him towards the light that now flickers deceptively on the walls, shrinking and shrinking as the whispers gain fervor.

They're women.

Holding fast to a candle, I follow the voices as they marry into a single, unintelligible sound, guiding me to that obscure corridor with the incongruous table and mirror. And the lone chamber, sequestered from all the others, with dust seeping under its door.

No. Not dust.

*Sand.*

Tawny grains whip at my feet, pelting, stinging, biting, stirred up by pocket-sized whirlwinds. And from within the chamber, something cackles. Something feral, like wild dogs.

They hush at my presence, leaving only the sounds of my heart thumping in my ears and the splatter of dripping rafters. An *urge* yawns inside me. A puzzling, seductive urge to open the chamber door and release whatever creatures are trapped inside. In my curiosity, the same curiosity presumed to be inherited from Eve, I reach for the handle of the chamber door.

Hands grab me from behind, reeling me around.

"What are you doing here?" Gaston dominates the corridor, his shadow doubling his terrible size. "Did you think you would unlock the door? Did you think you would see inside of me?"

My mouth opens but nothing comes. I don't understand. *See inside him?* I feel as though I've been sleepwalking and am now waking up in a place that's not my bed. "I d-didn't know," I stutter. His brace on me is painful, enough to leave bruises.

"No, you didn't. And you never will, not until you've proven—" Gaston's eyes flash suddenly with something bestial. Something *hungry*. And I swear his beard sparks with blue flame.

Gaston pinions me to the wall, pressing himself against me. The kiss is erratic and sloppy and desperate for feeling hardly slaked. There's no room to struggle or scream, only to retch and pray that it ends soon, that it will be enough, *please, God, let it be enough to quench him.*

He jerks back as if stung, though I didn't move. My eyes are shut tight, my body a curled, quaking mass as I suppress my sobs.

"Beatrice." He makes my name a pitying noise, an anguished breath against my hair.

He lets me go, and I slide down the wall to the floor.

Staggering away from me, Gaston covers his face with

clawed hands. He berates himself, violent, scolding words in French that's too fast for me to follow. It sounds terrible and raw, and I gawk at him, at his back contorted in agony as if tormented by his own wretchedness. How awful—how *animal*—it looks, like some brutish creature has possession of him. Like he truly is a wolf transformed—no metaphor of his duplicitous nature, but an ancient, corporeal being with a will of its own. And before me is a battle for its exorcism.

The wolf writhes, ravenous, bent on Gaston's destruction.

And mine.

The fight is altogether baffling and fierce, ending abruptly. Gaston uncurls, his shadow shrinking to its normal size, yet he still seems too large—too heavy—to be held within the confines of this claustrophobic hallway.

"Forgive me, wife," he says. "I forgot myself." He won't look at me, though I stare at him without flinching. *Is it shame I see in his face? Remorse?* "It's late," he adds, smoothing his hair mussed by the paroxysm. "You should be in bed."

My laughter surprises us both, hysterical and crazed, bursting from my chest. How efficiently he's pushed aside the terror of the moment! He *forgot* himself? The excuse is absurd, and yet a contrarian part of me believes that it's true. Something *real* took hold of him.

Didn't it?

"I heard whispers," I say, as if explaining myself will rectify everything. "And there was sand blowing under the door." But when I check, the floor is as clean as if the maid had recently swept. "Where did it go?"

Gaston frowns into the mirror, combing his beard—neither aflame nor aglow—with his fingers. He prods the haggard, purpling flesh under his eyes. "Go to bed, Beatrice," he says evenly, finally meeting my eyes through my reflection. "Wonder no more at what you think you saw and heard. If it was ghosts, then let them rest in peace."

The dismissal is firm and bewildering, leaving me stunned. To bed, Beatrice, like the child you are.

I lie awake, alone. The clock measures the passing of hour after hour, but Gaston never comes to bed. I should feel relieved, but instead I flitter with doubt, agonizing over what could have possibly been real and what was merely the contrivance of my own imagination, drunk on the notions of this dark house.

# CHAPTER 15
# BRUSHSTROKES

Gaston insists I stay with Mr. Swain in the library, to supervise him and keep him company while he paints.

"Be sure he is comfortable. I will be out. I have some plans to see through." He makes to touch my waist but reconsiders. He's hardly met my eyes all morning, and when he does it's only for the briefest of seconds.

Sympathy is an interloper in my stomach, hunched alongside the terror I felt last night as he forced himself upon me. It nauseates me to consider what might have happened had Gaston not restrained himself.

Papa's senseless platitude to extend mercy only adds confusion to my misery. Gaston is only mortal, after all. A mortal who saved my family from destitution. Shouldn't I show mercy, if only to ensure that his generosity continues? He needs to believe that I'm warming to him, that his advances are not unwanted. It's another sacrifice.

Addressing Mr. Swain, he says, "Whatever you need, Beatrice will provide it."

Somewhat flushed, Mr. Swain bows, though it isn't so much of a bow as it is an inelegant thrust of his upper body. "Thank you, sir."

Gaston gives him an encouraging nod, much like a proud father would. The gesture fills me with a peculiar warmth, making *mercy* a little easier.

Mr. Swain isn't one to fritter away his time. As Gaston leaves, the artist straightway opens his oaken box of new supplies and pulls them out one by one, tabulating the brushes by length and width, coding the freshly mixed paints into their spectrum. I'm so engrossed by his meticulous behavior that until I hear an *ahem*, I don't notice he's been waiting for me to give him permission to begin his work.

He rubs his neck, a mite abashed. "I find if I organize myself before I start, the muse is more easily coaxed."

I ease into a chair, tucking my poufy taffeta skirts around my legs. "I wasn't aware an artist required a muse. A writer, surely. I hear they're hopeless without one. But I thought an artist's vision flowed through his hands more than his mind."

"The hands are vital instruments, to be sure. But the true producer of an artist's work is his imagination.

Otherwise, he wouldn't know where to cast the light from the sun, or the moon, so as to achieve the correct mood of the piece, or even what hue of dreamy blue to give Juliet's eyes."

"Are her eyes blue? Shakespeare was never specific. They could just as easily have been green or hazel or—you're laughing at me. Have I said something foolish?"

Mr. Swain presses his lips together. "No, madam. I'm laughing because you've proven my point. It's the details that make a piece of art what it is, but without a vision, I cannot divine the *right* details. It may not have mattered to Shakespeare what color eyes his characters possessed, but to the artist, it's that color that matters most."

I fall quiet, his oration rather passionate. To think that something's color could be what inspires an artist to achieve a masterpiece is a lovely idea. I wish I had the gift for portrayal as he does, or even the ability to draw music from an instrument like Anna. When they enter their secret worlds, the true world falls behind them. And there, in those private dreams belonging only to them, they hope and think and love, and they forget the mordant rules of society. They simply create, and the creating heals them.

"Well, then," I say with a breath. "What hue of blue will you paint?"

A droll smile plays on his lips. "Something bright, I think. Like sky." Eyes widening with some thought, Mr.

Swain goes red. "Forgive me," he says, abruptly busying himself with prepping the wall, blocking out a section in chalk.

My heart dances. "Forgive you for what?"

"For wasting time."

I haven't realized how closely I've been leaning in, to better hear him, see him, feel his movements pulsing the air. Our conversation over, I rise from my chair and go to the bookshelves, where the maid, Alice, is dusting the tomes.

"Shall I bring the tea now, mistress?" she asks.

"Yes, thank you," though I barely heard her. My heart attempts to play an erratic, three-beated waltz, and I can't comprehend its meaning. I wring my hands, wishing these bothersome feelings would depart from me. What magic is this—for magic, certain in its fiction but real in its ability to beguile, is what it must be?

A novel will distract me, for within its pages I, like an artist or musician, can make an escape from the world. Selecting a volume Gaston purchased in Paris because of its scandalous publicity, I return to the couches, slumping down to read about the eponymous Madame Bovary.

I read the first page, realize I didn't comprehend a word of it and read it again, only to pause halfway through. Mr. Swain is a curious fellow. I peer over the top of the book, watching him lay down a small square of grayish plaster, spreading it paper-thin with a palette knife. He aligns his cheek to the wall to look parallel over the plaster's surface. Satisfied with its evenness, he begins applying a glistening white paint with slow, inveterate brushstrokes. Up and down. Up and down.

"Why white?" I ask, *Madame Bovary* forgotten. "Why not a dark background, like the Romantics do?"

His mouth quirks up in amusement. "It all goes back to the colors. The white, wet ground is like a foundation, illuminating the colors that will be painted on top of it, making them brighter and jewel-like." His coat removed, Mr. Swain's sleeves are rolled up to the elbows, a canvas smock glommed with paint stains protecting his clothes. With each turn of his wrist, his muscles flex, rippling his lean, tanned arm.

Unexpectedly warm, I flap the cover of the book to fan myself.

Up and down. Up and down.

My throat is parched. Where's Alice with that tea?

"Did someone teach you to paint, Mr. Swain, or are you what they call a prodigy?"

"A prodigy," he deadpans. My eyebrows inch up, and he gives a saucy smile.

Up...and down. Up...and down.

"Now it's my turn to ask a question of you," he says.

"Go on."

"How long have you been Madame Dumas?"

Stalling my answer, I pretend to adjust the flowy

sleeves of my blouse. "Three weeks." Though it feels much longer than that. And longer still is left.

Alice finally arrives with a pot of Grey's Tea, as well as a plate of beef sandwiches and shell-shaped madeleine cakes. I invite Mr. Swain over, and he reposes on the sofa, waiting for Alice to leave before saying, "Then why do you look as though you've not yet entered that dream of marital bliss?"

I flush with heat and more than a little annoyance. The nerve of him—prying into my life as if it were an opera! "Mr. Swain, I'm not one of those silly girls who titters over frivolous romances hardly lasting a minute. If I were to answer your question—which I *won't*, because it's private and utterly facetious—I'd tell you there is much more to marriage than embracing."

He chokes on his tea. "No, of course. I didn't mean—excuse me. I meant only, why don't you look happy?"

Thoroughly irked, I argue, "What makes you think I'm not?"

He laughs, an exasperated sound. "Please, madam, it's not my intention to offend you. You're right, I *am* facetious and, quite frankly, I can be an incorrigible prat. But please, I beg you, don't mistake my impertinence for insincerity." He puts on another of his sundry smiles. I turn away from it.

I suppose it's not his fault, though that irritates me more. Mr. Swain is only curious, like every other invitee

Gaston so gleefully entertains. He attracts people's curiosity like flies to honey, delighted when they find themselves trapped in their own impertinent chin-wagging. Another hapless guest in our mysterious home, Mr. Swain is only showing himself to be inquisitive, if not indelicate.

I huff, loosening the last dregs of fury. "If I appear unhappy, it's likely due to my lack of sleep. The house cracks and chirrs, and I'm not yet used to it."

"I see." Chewing on a sandwich, he considers me, then drops his voice. "What made you do it?"

"What made me...?" What made me marry Gaston, he means. A man twice my age. No doubt the moment his boot slapped the platform of Town Station, Mr. Swain was barraged with rumors about his new employer, the enigmatic Frenchman who's married more women than most men would bother with, and a majority of them barely matured. What must the rumors say about *me*, the youngest wife of them all, who married Gaston within months of his fourth wife's passing?

Fly or no fly, I'd be loath to let Mr. Swain believe anything untrue about me.

"My father died. I had to do what was best for my family. What are you staring at?"

Several singular eternities pass between us until I feel like I'll burst from the discomfort. But then he says, "My heart breaks for you."

The *tenderness* of those words. They melt into me, a liniment for heartache, validation for choices made and sacrifices endured. It's like Mr. Swain has heard me calling through the bars of my self-made cage, and he has answered me.

"I should return to the fresco. Before the plaster dries."

Voiceless, I nod. He goes back to his work, and I open my book to read and reread the first page. Confined to its track, the sun journeys across the afternoon, appearing to stop when Gaston returns to us.

"How is our artist getting along?" More jovial than this morning, he fondly slaps Mr. Swain's back, inquiring, "Might I steal my wife from you, *jeune homme*? You must have learned by now she is captivating company, and I wish to take a turn."

"Of course, sir. Your wife is all yours." Mr. Swain returns his brush to the wall, and I want to stop his arm, reverse the clock to a few hours ago and replay those words, *my heart breaks for you*, over and over again.

"I have a surprise for you, my love. But first, you must change into your riding habit. Wear the blue one."

GROOMED AND SADDLED, Hastings waits alongside a dappled gray in the crescent-shaped driveway at the front of the house. The evening is cloudless and temperate, perfect for riding. In accordance with Gaston's request, I wear my navy riding habit with a veiled top hat. He helps me mount my horse, and we gallop along the chalky cliffs through hills blooming wildly with yellow samphire and pyramidal orchids. My veil flaps behind me, picked up by an April zephyr. I breathe in, scenting malt from the barley fields.

A feeling of pure contentment inhabits me. Out here, under the sky with open air expanding my chest, there's a sensation of freedom, of independence. I could ride anywhere—to the stalwart castle erect on the cliff, or Kearsney Bottom where my old home resides. Or I could run west, never stopping, never turning, until I reached England's other shore. There, I'd dig my feet into the sand and call it Haven, where I'd grow gray and soft and sink into the earth, my soul preserved. My body safe and untouched.

Instead, I follow Gaston. When we reach the paper and flour mills along the river, he holds up a hand for me to stop. "We'll walk from here," he says.

Our stable master, Leopold, has been waiting to take our horses, a leather purse jangling from his waist. I slide from Hasting's saddle before Gaston can offer me his arm, but quickly apologize when he curls his fists at his sides. One of Mamma's silly maxims breaches my mind—to let gentlemen be gentlemen, even when it's inconvenient.

Gaston takes a blindfold from his pocket. "To ensure

the surprise is not spoiled before I have a chance to reveal it."

I wear the blindfold willingly, though there's hardly a use for it. I recognize every bump and dip in the path, and the brambles grasping at my skirts with their thorny claws. I hear the chitters of buntings, the knocking of a thrush. I know exactly where we are.

Verdurous and wick and beginning to bud, Eden greets me with a burst of color. The scene is a decadent romance: glittering streamers strung from the branches, tinkling chimes and glass baubles spinning sunlight in soft gyrations. Gaston ducks under them to sit on the giant root of a Greensleeve, where at its base a picnic of champagne, a baguette, a rind of Camembert cheese, and sweet clementines and pomegranates is spread on a Persian rug.

"Is this what you've been at all day?" I kneel next to him, tracing my finger along the rug's complicated floral patterns, dyed carmine and indigo. Prisms of color rollick on his face as he serves me an apple tart.

"Your favorite, I'm told."

"Who told you?" I say, taking a bite. It's still warm, all oozy and sweet with cinnamon.

Foxy-eyed, he taps the side of his nose. "It's a husband's duty to know everything about his wife. Her every thought. Her every dream. Her every desire."

"And you snuck into my dreams, discovering my want for pastries?"

He laughs. "No. I had only to listen to your sleep-speech."

"Oh, no—I don't talk in my sleep, do I?"

"Only when you're dreaming. Tell me, my love, what is it you see in that netherworld?"

Dark things. Things of nightmares. I've seen this orchard burning. My father's pale lips and his handkerchief spotted with blood. My brothers in their yellow cavalry uniforms, black targets on their chests. I've seen Anna drowning, and Mamma decomposing like a flower in autumn. But most frequently of all, I've dreamed of Gaston, his hand outstretched. Beckoning.

"Apple tarts," I say.

Gaston harumphs thoughtfully. Selecting a pomegranate, he scores and breaks it, scooping out the arils with his fingers. He offers them to me, ruby juice like blood staining his sleeve. The Grecian myth of Persephone comes to my mind: stolen away by the god of the underworld, Persephone is tricked into consuming the seeds of the jeweled death-fruit, thereby tying her to Hades for six months of the year. The story chilled my bones when I was younger. Now it signifies my life. I am Persephone, eating, without question, the seeds offered to me.

Their juice is sweet and tart and utterly addicting. I take more.

"Have you decided on a date for the ball?" Gaston

asks, purling champagne into two flutes. Too guarded to drink, I set mine aside.

This spontaneous outing is motivated by more than the intent to charm me. I think Gaston is placating me into forgiving him for his igneous attack, and although I feel like I should, his spell is having the opposite effect on me. I wish he'd just say it. *I'm sorry.* I need to hear the words. I need to know he'll never do it again.

"I thought the twenty-ninth of this month would do," I say.

"Is that a Wednesday? I've heard it said dances held in the middle of the week are unfashionable. The first of May would do better. How many guests?"

"A small number, I think. Intimate parties are more pleasant than grand ones."

He waggles his finger at me. "Nonsense. I think that is the modesty in you, *mon amour.* Always trying to hide your beauty from the world. No, this ball should be a sweeping affair."

I bite my cheek, irritation pooling at the base of my skull. If he's going to contradict all my decisions, why should I even bother planning this ridiculous event? I seem to recall Gaston saying once that I knew my own mind, and that he shouldn't like to dispute it. What happened to that gentler, more supportive man? Had he even existed?

"We must invite the Cranes and the Fields," he continues, speaking more to himself than to me. "The families are like figureheads to the town; we'd do well with their presence. Haven't they daughters?"

"Felicity and Georgiana," I mumble.

"Yes, yes, they'll do. The Bells, of course, will be invited, as well as the Culpeppers. How about that Irishman—Whitley or whatnot? He's a sensible fellow."

Phantom pains surface at the memory of Mr. Whitley treading on my toes, and I wince. "Not him," I rush. "What I mean is, he's not fond of dancing, and I'm sure he'd decline the invitation."

"I see. And Monsieur Swain? Do you think *he* will accept?"

I go back to tracing patterns in the rug. I should like very much for Mr. Swain to come. But I dared not consider it, thinking Gaston would disapprove. Yet again the suspicion returns that he's testing me. Despite his flattery and his fawning over me, Gaston doesn't trust me to be faithful to him.

"I'm sure Mr. Swain has more pressing obligations than attending a dance," I say.

Gaston reclines against the tree, his legs outstretched and crossed at the ankles. He swivels his glass in his hand, contemplative, watching the champagne bubble and swill. He quaffs it down in a single gulp.

"I don't believe Henry to be the contrary sort," he says. "I'll ask him myself. He would not presume to decline me."

I push down my hurt. Gaston's correct; Mr. Swain

seems different than me. He's submissive, attentive, devoted to his art. He doesn't withhold what is due, nor shirk any of his duties. He does what's necessary to please those whom he serves. As should I—because I don't know how I can expect to keep Anna and Mamma sheltered when I consistently resist the wants of our benefactor. Notwithstanding his sleights, and his impetuous temper, Gaston must have *something* in return.

Swallowing my hesitation, I touch his knee. "You are kind to consider him," I say quietly. "I must strive for your goodness. Husband." It's the first time I've called him that, surprising us both.

Gaston palms my hand, his fingers warm and wanting. "And I must strive for your humility and the sincerity with which you call me *husband*."

My lips go dry, expecting him to kiss them. But he doesn't. If any affection is to be shown, he's waiting for *me* to show it. He's waiting for me to prove myself.

Even as I consider it, a line from *Jane Eyre* comes into my mind—where the chastened Mr. Rochester asks to prove his pardon by a reconciling kiss. Jane's response, in jest, is that she'd rather be excused. She consistently vexed him, yet he adored her.

It was the intellect of these two characters that drew them together—the stubborn, autonomous Jane befriending the irascible, sarcastic Mr. Rochester. Their love grew out of conversation, out of testing one another's mettle. Tricked into a loveless marriage, Rochester longed for a gentle wife to love him. And Jane—she wanted to be treated as an equal. She did not fear the possibility of marrying a haunted man, nor the reality that she must leave him to protect her dignity. She was young, an ingénue attracted to a man more experienced in matters of the heart. Ultimately, she knew she must grow independently from him before they could ever flourish together.

I think I can learn from Jane. If I can befriend Gaston first, maybe in time I will love him.

"I've not seen your smile in several days," he says, our fingers twined together like on our opera night. "I have missed it."

I let my smile grow. "Would you like to know another secret about me?"

"Desperately."

"I love a good ghost story. If it's set on the moors in a crumbling castle, the master a brooding romantic, that's even better."

Gaston throws his head back in a laugh. "Then allow me to regale you with a tale of the occult. You see, there was a time when I wintered with a German *Freiherr* and his vampiric daughter..."

His tale is luscious and dark and surely hyperbolized, yet my body thrums under the mellifluent tones of his voice. It's twilight by the time he's finished, when the crepuscular hedgehogs and foxes emerge from their burrows to hunt for their dinners. I'm disappointed when it's time to return home, for I miss watching the moon rise over the orchard, and I was hoping to hear about another of Gaston's adventures.

He takes my hands to assist me up, wisps of tinsel brushing our shoulders as he leans me against the apple tree. I sweep his knuckles with my thumbs, boldly studying the handsome cut of his beard and his roguish pompadour.

"I have sorrowful news, my love. The Company has summoned me for a voyage. I shall return before the ball, but it's likely I will be away for the month."

Worry comes suddenly, sharply. Though I loved the moment of return, when I'd throw my arms around Papa's shoulders and kiss his cheek, watching him walk up the gangway to one of his merchant ships always filled me with a certain dread. I feared his ship would get swallowed by a storm or that some giant sea-beast would rake its tentacles across the hull, dragging my father into the ocean's irreclaimable depths. What if Gaston's own vessel should sink, leaving me widowed and once again destitute? Then I will have to start all over again, praying that miracles are not as rare as they seem.

Although, a month alone might be just what I need to ease myself into the rest of this life with him. A whole month of privacy, of solace, of sprawling across the bed and hoarding all the covers. I can turn down the lights without the tension of Gaston's expectations. I can finally let my guard down.

As he expects, I look disheartened, casting my eyes to the ground. "That is sorrowful news. When do you leave?"

"In the morning." His fingers graze my chin, and I abide it. Like it, even. His touch is soft, insistent. The way he leans—*into me*—he wants more, and I pull in my lips, deliberating.

I kiss him.

# CHAPTER 16
# PROVIDENCE

Through the bedchamber window, I watch *La Gitane* sail from the harbor, shrinking into a white lily petal until the pink dawn engulfs her. Arms in praise, I twirl to the bed, laughing when I skid on the rug and land face-down onto my pillows. I curl up like a cat, nestling my cheek into the sumptuous Asian silk.

Alone. Alone, alone, *alone*. I am completely alone.

A knock at the door.

Well, as alone as the wife of an aristocrat can be.

The door opens quietly as Alice takes two small steps into the room. "Pardon me, mistress. Mr. Swain has arrived for the day's work. Shall I help you dress?"

I consider the dresses Gaston purchased for me in Paris, all stuffed into the armoire, but ultimately go to my trunk in the closet. "I think I'd like to dress casually today," I say, airing out the frock with a whip of air. A plain yet pretty olive dress with lavender stitch-work on the bodice. A dress I can actually move in.

Alice helps me with my wardrobe, and then I go meet Mr. Swain in the library. He's already begun mixing fresh paints, first grinding the colored pigments with a glass muller and then incorporating the powder into a viscous, oily matter.

"A curious procedure," I comment, coming up behind him.

He jumps. "Mrs. Dumas, I didn't hear you there. Ah, you're shoeless. That's why."

"I know it's improper," I say, blushing a bit. "I thought my dress would be long enough that you wouldn't notice."

"Only a man as thick and ignorant as a slug would fail to notice a change in such an enchanting woman."

"What a particularly malapert thing for you to say," I tease. "Honestly, Mr. Swain. Too bold."

He gives a mock bow. "My apologies. You must dock my pay for such effrontery."

I move closer to examine the narrow swatch of completed fresco. If he continues to work at this molasses pace, he'll be fortunate to finish by next Christmas. Curiously, the idea is a comfort to me.

"I've heard it said most artists are starved for food, so I could hardly dock your pay without aggrieving my conscience."

"Food? Not at all. Our clients pay us in dinner parties."

I giggle, and Mr. Swain spreads his hands in emphasis. "Now, acknowledgement, adoration—*these* are what we're truly starved for."

"Unfathomable. A man like you, un-adored? Somehow, I can't believe it."

"Careful, madam. Now it is *you* who is the malapert."

At once, a warning tolls, echoes of a promise made. Here I've been, shamelessly flirting with this artist when I know Gaston doesn't trust me.

"Excuse me," I say, wending away from Mr. Swain and his paints and this niggling feeling—this misplaced attraction. Just his presence in the room distracts all my thoughts, which are anything but rational. I need to distance myself from him, before something regrettable happens.

I rub the spaces behind my ears, another headache imminent.

My solitary time is mostly spent reading, often in the gardens, bounteous with the season's perennials: fuchsias, ferns, and verbenas edging the great lawn; cleome and snowcaps lending soft color to the rockery. A damask rosebush winds up and over a trellis-arch, where an ebullient fountain with a statue of Janus, the double-faced roman god, sluices water from his two mouths. I sit on a bench, my eyes heavy with sun and concentration. When

I begin to nod off, my brain gives me a little kick, snapping up my head. But I'm tuckered, and the day is unusually warm. I float onto the green and lay myself down under a dogwood tree, furred in white blossoms. I doze, for days, it seems.

The buzz of an insect wakes me, and I open my eyes to see Mr. Swain seated a few paces away, sketching in a book bound with moleskin.

He is sketching *me*.

"And the sleeping maiden awakens from her hundred years' slumber," he says.

"How long have you been there?" I tuck in my feet, dirty and unpardonably bare.

"Long enough." He snaps the sketchbook shut, heading for the house.

I chase after him. "Aren't you going to show it to me?"

"Show what to you?"

"The drawing, of course. The one you just did of me."

"You're mistaken, Mrs. Dumas. I was sketching the dogwood." His smile is far too frolicsome to be telling the truth.

In the library, Mr. Swain plunks himself down on the couch by the windows. I think to sit next to him—rethink it—then think it again. Finally, I sit, leaving a good gap between us.

"If you won't show me, I'll just have to take it." He makes no motion to stop me as I snatch the book from his hands. Pausing at each, I flip through pages of moorlands, seascapes, and self-portraits, admiring the softness of line, the fastidious detail. He drew each strand of hair, every eyelash, even the freckles on his own nose. I compare them to their originals, smiling to find they're spot on.

I gasp, arriving at the sketch of me napping under the tree. My hair curls into the grass, cambering over my arms spread above my head. Dogwood blossoms fall into the folds of my dress, the slim curve of my breast. The bluish beetle that must have awoken me glimmers next to my hand.

"You've made me look young," I say.

"Have I?" Mr. Swain scrutinizes his work, the sketch-book in my lap. "I must practice more. I thought I was drawing a woman." I goose his arm—a spontaneous gesture that leaves me blushing.

"Are you never serious? It's perfect. When I was little, I'd fall asleep just like this in the orchard. Papa said if I slept too long, the trees would take me, swallow me up in their roots like gaping mouths until I became one of them. It was hardly a surprise to him that my summers were spent napping outdoors."

"*Gaping mouths?* What an odd child you were, exciting over such frightful imagery."

We chortle.

"I was ten. Nothing frightened me."

"That still holds true, I'm sure."

Our knees touch, a spark running up my thigh. We

shouldn't be sitting like this. *Together.* But I can't bring myself to move away. I like the way it feels, being close to him. I crave friendship, someone to laugh with, to return the joy that's been absent from my life since Papa got sick. Growing up, I had few friends besides Ami Rose. My ideas were too big, too scandalous, for the other girls my age, and no mother would let her boy be corrupted by me. I spent my summers napping in the orchard because I was alone in my daydreams, left to only imagine what it was like to have a friend who accepted me, who encouraged my dreaming. While I've learned in my life to love solitude, being alone in this mammoth house has begun to weigh on me.

Mr. Swain works diligently through the week, completing the upper portion of the fresco's background, a midnight sky with bright stars and a luminous, full moon. As I study it one day, he comments, "A schoolmate of mine, John Millais, painted a scene from Shakespeare's *Hamlet*."

"I've seen it," I say. "In a gallery at the Royal Academy. You attended there?"

"Aye. And John, too. We were prodigies together." He winks. "He was sixteen. I was eleven. It's providence I attended at all."

"Well, go on," I prod, standing a little too close to him. Our elbows bump, bringing a delightsome tingle to my skin. "Tell me the tale."

He laughs, the sound breathless. "All right, then. Once

upon a time, in the slums of East London, there lived an orphan."

"Oh."

"Sometimes stories begin sadly, and this one is no exception. This orphan was a gawky chap, puny and too paltry to be taken in by any civilized English family. But what they didn't know is that he had a gift." He smiles, and I smile, too. "I'd practice on pavements and stone walkways, with pieces of charcoal from the burned-out fires that kept me warm at night. Sketching was the only way I'd keep sane, especially when I was pressganged."

"Pressganged?"

"Into a street gang of urchins and pickpockets. I was what polite society considered 'a common criminal.'" His face reads strained, repentant, and I desire suddenly to reach for his hand, but don't. He shakes his head. "High Society is ignorant of the security of its privilege, while its castoffs are neglected and left to suffer. Even children."

I look at the hardness in his eyes, the grief and disappointment there, and my throat goes tight. "But surely there was hope for the lad? After all, he's now a young man, and an accomplished artist at that. He found a way out."

"The way found him." His smile returns, showing teeth and crinkled eyes. "One day, a teacher found that delinquent little boy and took him to the Academy. He said I'd been awarded a place there and that my tuition had been paid in full."

"In full! But who was the benefactor?"

"I don't know, but I intend to find out. His compassion gave me a place in this world. A purpose. I'll find him and repay every cent."

"Have you any idea who he might be, where he might live?"

"Only rumor. I once overheard the headmaster speaking about one of the school's major patrons. He could be a different man entirely, but it was said he lived here, in Dover."

"So that's why you came here."

"That, and to draw beautiful girls while they sleep." I flush, looking away. Mr. Swain burns. "I'm sorry. That wasn't meant to sound so..."

"It's all right." My wedding band fluctuates hot and cold against my skin. Feeling faint, I sit in a wingback chair, gripping the armrest for support. "I understood your meaning. But it's late, Mr. Swain. Aren't you expected to return to your lodgings for supper? At the Lord Warden, wasn't it?"

He scrubs his hands on his trousers, his face grim. I look away again, embarrassed for him, and for myself.

"You're right." He begins to gather up his materials, throwing a brush into his painter's box. A nervous heat emanates from him, making me quake with its meaning. "Forgive me," he says, twisting his smock in his hands, "but I must ask you this. When I'm not with clients, I spend my time on personal works, many of which require models. I should like it if..." He swallows. Swallows again. "I would like for you to be one of those models."

Model like those provocative women in the French fashion magazines? I couldn't. It wouldn't be proper. "I'm not sure what to say, Mr. Swain."

"Consider it, at least. Tomorrow is Sunday, my day off. I'll be in Elmswood at sunrise. Come if you wish. I won't like you any less if you don't."

That last phrase loops through my mind, agitated like a pinwheel in a storm. *Like-you-any-less. Like-you-any-less.* He likes me.

He *likes* me.

Gnawing on my lower lip, I offer an uncertain nod.

# CHAPTER 17
# REQUIRED: ONE MODEL, FEMALE

My dreams are sweet. Blurred pictures, like watercolors. Mr. Swain is in them, painting flowers on my palms, my fingers the petals. Then the pictures warp into the image of an eagle, brass and sharp, and there's a cracking sound—smudges of black and red and blue. A blue beard. A devastating inferno of—

Passion.

"Gaston." I wake with a gasp, my arm reaching across the bed, until I remember.

I'm alone.

He's right; I do talk in my sleep. What is it he's heard me say?

Wick with sweat, I cross the room to the window seat. I hug my knees to me, listening to the inbound train whistling in the distance. If I sit very still, I can feel its rumblings as it charges through the tunnel under Shakespeare Cliff, right beneath my feet. For a moment, I wish the train were going out, and that I were on it.

The lighthouse on Admiralty Pier sweeps its beam across the water, and when the light comes around again, a ship appears. I pretend it's Gaston's ship, come home after a voyage that has lasted years. I prod the tender parts of my emotions, these feelings of melancholy and loneliness. There's an impression of loss, like a piece of me has been removed.

I *miss* him.

Admitting it eases the tightness in my chest, so that when I breathe, I smell the rosewater from the decanter on my dressing table. And next to that, bergamot, from a bottle of beard oil. Gaston is rather vain about his facial hair, but I like it. When I kissed him in the orchard, his beard against my cheek felt like silk, a marked difference from our wedding night, when it repulsed me.

Briefly, I wish to be able to return to that night, to talk frankly about my fears. I wish that I could have negotiated my marriage on my own terms, insisting that Gaston wait until I grew a little older before taking me to the altar. I could have prepared myself for him then, rather than try to learn how to swim while in the midst of deep water. If I knew for certain the core of who I am would never change, then perhaps in time I could have—could still—give myself fully to him.

I'm not sure dwelling on my regrets helps me any, but it feels good, at the very least, to voice them.

The Sabbath breaks, a pale, pale light vying with the spin of the lighthouse. Like the sun, Mr. Swain's entreaty that I model for him brightens with the morning sky. I have an idea—a way, perchance, to prove to Gaston that I have a stalwart heart.

I'll give him a homecoming gift.

The thought stirs my heart up into a flutter, and I smile to myself, resting my chin on my knees. I sit at the window an hour more, watching the lighthouse guide that ship safely into port. The anchor drops and little figures of men pull up the sails, while behind them the sun rises, its light all the better for clarity, for sight.

"Please, ma'am, allow me to send for Alice to accompany you," Crawley enjoins, overwrought with anxiety as I climb into Hastings's saddle. I've lied to him, telling him I'm going to take a basket to Ami Rose, though the basket is really for Mr. Swain, should he want to break from his work for lunch.

"I'll be perfectly safe, Mr. Crawley," I assure him. "But to ease your concerns, I'll make it a point to return by dinner."

"That would set me at ease, ma'am," says the uptight man, worried, no doubt, that if he lost me his head would end up in the crate of a guillotine. Gaston is French, after all. Passionate and, now I've learned, capable of violence.

I give Hastings a signal, and we take off at a clip. I pull the pins from my hair to let it fly, relishing its lightness. The sky hangs low, smeared gray with a shower to the south. Mr. Swain will have to work quickly before it reaches us.

He waits for me at the edge of the wood, a satchel slung across his vestless chest. Dressed in breeches the humblest shade of brown, a loose shirt, and braces, Mr. Swain looks emphatically like an underpaid, barely-fed artist. And I must admit, he has never been pleasanter to look at.

"You came," he says, his relief apparent. "I feared I'd have to write an advertisement in *The Express*. 'Required: One model, female. Will offer payment in the form of shoddy humor and cheeky remarks.'"

"I do expect reimbursement for my time," I reply, winking. He takes my waist as I dismount, and although he releases me the moment my feet touch ground, I feel the aftertouch of his fingertips for minutes afterwards.

Returning my wink, he says, "If this portrait impresses the critics, I'll split the proceeds sixty-forty."

"How generous of you, Mr. Swain, but will forty percent be enough for you?"

"Will sixty be enough for *you*?" he retorts, laughing.

I suppress my grin, all business. "Before we start, Mr. Swain, I have one stipulation."

His eyebrows rise. "Go on."

"You must gift the painting to Monsieur Dumas. No—I won't negotiate." He closes his mouth, my word final.

"Very well, I concede." His smile quirks to the side, worrying me for a moment. "I was right, it seems. You do not settle for less than exactly what you want." Thunder clashes in the distance. Glancing at the sky, he adds, "We must hurry."

He takes Hastings' bridle and hustles us further into the wood, over the carpet of bluebells. As he hunts for a suitable backdrop—squaring his thumb and forefingers and squinting, one-eyed, through them—I press a hand to my stomach to quell the apprehension there. Am I making a mistake being alone with him? The artist flirts with abandon, though he projects an air of wholesomeness. He wouldn't think to jeopardize my virtue. Would he?

My nerves remain unsettled as Mr. Swain turns back to me. "If you would," he says, gesturing to the base of a beech tree, its roots spread across the ground like earth-veins. After three heartbeats, I recline against it.

His pulse works rapidly underneath his skin, pumping blood into his ruddy cheeks. "May I?"

I nod, and he positions my right arm akimbo behind my head, carefully draping my left arm over an open book in my lap. He goes so far as to arrange my hair, drawing a curtain of tangles over my shoulder and making no attempt to unravel it, even smiling at its chaos.

"Your shoes," he says next.

I hesitate, unsure.

*He's already seen your bare feet.*

Surely, it's for the romantic effect of the portrait.

I allow him to undo the row of buttons on my scalloped boots but stop him when he means to remove my stockings. It feels too much like being undressed.

He lifts his hands. "I won't hurt you." Gently, "I would never hurt you."

At once, my mind quiets. The world slows its spin and even time forestalls. Sincerer words have never been spoken to me, and I believe him. With all my being, I believe him.

Inch by inch, Mr. Swain rolls my stockings down, carefully rounding my heels, and tosses them by my boots.

"Now," he says, bending my left knee, arranging the folds of my dress. "Don't move, and think of the dreamiest thing you can."

It's been half an hour, and my arm has fallen asleep, though I'm afraid to even twitch. Mr. Swain's temples sheen with light perspiration as he bends over his sketchbook. Every so often his mouth pulls into the smallest of smiles until finally, I have to ask him what he thinks is so amusing. Are my feet muddy? Is my hair too much like a bird's nest? I can't stand it any longer.

"What's so funny?"

His smile widens. "Keep still. And look straight ahead, into the distance."

In a broody manner, I do as he says. He curbs a laugh.

"What is it?" I say, laughing too, though I've no idea at what. The book slips from my lap and with that the pose falls apart. Doubling over, I snort into my knees, and it's wonderful, laughing until my sides stitch. I haven't laughed like this since Papa.

"Now that you've ruined my scene," he says, wiping the jollity from his eyes, "I suppose now would be a good time for a break."

"I brought food."

I toddle to my feet as Mr. Swain moves first, a root snaring his foot. He pitches forward, his body plunking into mine. We stay there—*hooked*—lured in by each other's bewildered stares. His eyes are so bright I can see my own reflection in them: tussled hair and lips parted in breathless abandon, as if waiting for his own. I glance at his mouth, and he looks at mine. Carefully, he pries my hands away from his suspenders.

An impossible thought thrusts into my side, nearly cleaving me in half. *Doesn't he want me?*

Of course not, Beatrice. You're married.

I break past him, covering my humiliation. Is this how

Gaston feels each time I reject him? Umbrage, embarrassment, bitterness—not towards Mr. Swain, but towards myself. This was a mistake. Being alone with him here looks like I'm in the midst of tryst, no matter how innocent my intentions.

"I don't know why it is," the artist says, speaking with a caution I resent. "But I always find myself apologizing to you about something." Resolved to un-feel everything, I snatch up the basket from Hastings's saddle. "There—you see? I've upset you again."

"You haven't!"

"Then what is it, Mrs. Dumas?" He steps forward, and I step back, a dismal look coming into his eyes. "What plagues you?"

What *plagues* me? I laugh at the archaic word. A bitter laugh. A forced, humorless breath. This certainly is a plague, isn't it? Worse than what Papa had, for this is a passive disease, taking its time, defiling its host bit by bit.

Shivering, I whisper, "That name." That name is what plagues, unrelenting in its pursuit of me. My name has *changed.*

What else will?

Thunder breaks. A raindrop splashes down the artist's face, and he curses, our squabble forgotten as he moves to save his work from the rain. "Let me see you home."

"No," I say quickly. No one can know Mr. Swain and I were alone together.

I bury my face in Hastings's mane, trying not to cry.

The artist doesn't argue but picks up my boots, saying, "Don't forget your shoes."

*Meerut, India*
*2 April 1857*

*Dear Beatrice,*

*Terrible news has reached us from the cantonment at Barrackpore, near Calcutta, where I'm acquainted with the soldiers transferred there after their indefensible beating of that washerman. Upon the parade ground, a disgruntled sepoy—reported to be under the influence of bhang, an intoxicant—shot at his commanding officer. The officer was unharmed, but his horse was wounded and a skirmish ensued. When it became clear the man wouldn't succeed in his coup, he turned the musket on himself but missed. They're calling it a rebellion. A botched rebellion but insurgent, nonetheless. It's presumed this soldier will be court-martialed and then hanged.*

*I'm afraid of this growing violence. The sepoys, my friends, are restless. And not just them, but the villagers, too. The people pace and growl like tigers restricted to a cage, emboldened with each swipe at the hand between the bars. I fear it won't be long before more blood is spilled, and in greater quantities.*

*Forgive my dark mind. I'll move on to a more lighthearted*

*topic. Byron claims he has fallen in love…with the Rani of Jhansi. We'd just exited the canteen, stepping into the congested marketplace, when suddenly the crowds parted as if Moses had thrown down his serpent-staff. And there she was, traveling south in her palanquin. Except she wasn't in the palanquin. No, this queen rose above us on the back of a great, gray elephant bridled with tassels and precious jewels.*

*The effect was quite stunning, and Byron nearly swooned. He thinks she smiled at him; however, as I was beside him, I know the upturn of her lip was really a curl of revulsion. Byron will have to be content with the modest nature of Lilly Coons. Actually, she's quite fair. If he doesn't want her, I think I'll try to court her. She should have no objections—my face is as handsome as his, being that it's identical, and my dancing is far better. (Byron has just read what I've written and cudgeled me for it. I laugh at him.)*

*Of course, whether he or I are granted the opportunity to court any young woman is dependent upon whether we should ever be sent home. ~~I fear~~ I hope we will, when our service is complete.*

*Pray for me, sister, and for Byron. We may need a miracle yet.*

*Your devoted brother,*
*Simon*
*Cornet, Bengal Light Cavalry*

*Postscript—*

*Tell our mother and sister that I love them. I didn't say it enough when at home.*

## CHAPTER 18
# WINGÈD THINGS

I set Simon's letter aside on the breakfast table, nibbling my lip. The conflicts in India are growing more turbulent, and with them my fear that my brothers might not leave the country unharmed. If they ever choose to leave, that is. They may never want to come back to me.

Venturing from the dining room, I evade the library—and Mr. Swain—as I go. I've barely spoken to him since our non-tryst one week ago. I've taken instead to reading in Gaston's study, where I'm continually reminded of him.

A portrait of him as a sportive, clean-cut young man hangs above his desk. Eyes sparkling with some naughty joke, he swings a cherrywood walking stick over his shoulder. His beard was merely scruff then, raven black without a streak of grayish-blue. He must have been no more than Mr. Swain's age of twenty-two when this was painted.

I sigh into a chair, dangling my legs over the armrest. My thoughts always seem to circle back to the artist, no matter how hard I try to avoid him. He follows me everywhere, like Quincy used to.

The butler slogs into the room with a message for me. "Mr. Swain requests to see you, ma'am. He says there's a problem with the fresco."

I frown at him. "Are you well, Crawley?"

The man is sweating, pulling at his collar as if struggling to breathe. His face is gray, almost ghostly.

"Yes, ma'am," he says, but I don't believe him. His eyes shift around the room in skittish movements. He jumps suddenly, pointing at the floor. "There! Do you see it?"

I stand, looking about. "See what?"

"There, by your foot!"

I jump, lifting my skirts. "There's nothing!"

Crawley covers his ears. "There—there they are again—you must hear them!"

"Hear what, Mr. Crawley?"

"The whispers!"

My stomach drops. "What do they say?"

Removing his hands, Mr. Crawley stares at me with a blankness I've only seen in a corpse. "'Look inside,'" he says.

All at once the butler straightens, perfectly composed

as if nothing unordinary has occurred. "Mr. Swain requests to see you, ma'am. He says there's a problem with the fresco."

He seems unaware that he's repeated himself.

I gawk at him, not knowing what to say or think. What just happened? Did he hear the same whispers I did, tricks played by this gloomy house, its empty halls toying with our imaginations?

"Thank you, Mr. Crawley."

He bows to me, nothing amiss.

In the library, the artist yawns. I cough discreetly. "You asked for me?"

"I did. You look pale—are you all right?"

"Yes. Though I just had a rather strange encounter with Mr. Crawley. The man is hearing things. He *is* getting on in years, perhaps that's all it is."

Mr. Swain nods, though I can tell he's not listening. He wrings his already untidy necktie, and as if to match him, wingèd things fly circles in my belly.

"I have something to show you." I glance at the fresco. Except for a blank patch in the middle where the star figures will go, I see nothing disastrously wrong with it. "Not that," he says. "Not yet." Like an illusionist, he reveals a canvas from behind a white sheet, snatching the breath from my lungs.

“It’s me.”

It’s the portrait I posed for in the wood, under the beech tree, its lowest branches shading me like green umbrellas. My boots spill onto the ground at my side, my dress a vibrant white, my wedding band highlighted by the sun funneled through the canopy. Mr. Swain saw everything: the bend of the bluebells, the quirky curve of my foot, even the wistful gleam in my eyes as my mouth, full-lipped with its womanly dimple, wilts with an expression I can only describe as *ennui.*

“I couldn’t rest until I finished it.” Mr. Swain takes a breath. “Do you like it?”

I’ve never liked anything more in my entire life. He’s captured the likeness not just of my person but my *soul,* split between reality and a world of dreams, the world I want but know I can’t have. Maidenhood versus matrimony.

How is it possible he knows what I haven’t revealed to him?

I’m afraid if I speak my emotions will tumble out in some blubbering mess. So I nod, and Mr. Swain releases his breath.

“I’m sure Dumas will like it, too.” The sentence takes me aback, until I remember the request I made. The painting must be a gift for Gaston. This image of me as a vestal maiden, romantic in white, will belong to him.

“Yes,” I whisper. “Yes, I think he will.”

“Now, to the fresco.” Mr. Swain crosses over to it.

"Juliet is ready to take the stage, but her part needs an actress."

He's asking me, again, to model for him.

It didn't feel right, sneaking behind the servants' backs so word wouldn't get back that I'd spent an afternoon, unsupervised, with the artist. Not only do I need Gaston's trust, but I find myself *craving* it.

As if knowing I'll refuse him, Mr. Swain adds, "Please," and the way his voice falls into reverence swells my chest with the easiest of swoons. "Please. Please, I cannot finish without you." He brightens strangely, eyes sparking like flint as if he meant not, *I cannot finish without you*, but *without you, I am unfinished.*

Like swallowing the sun, emotion burns down my throat into the furthest parts of me, where I'm in a welter. Such double meanings are the concoctions of my own mind—no more substantial or real than the whisperings of ghosts. And yet those are the meanings I cling to.

Heaven, help me.

I think I want to be so much *more* to Mr. Swain than his model.

*Professionalism*, I remind myself.

Even Michelangelo had his models. Granted, they were male with womanly anatomy painted onto the appropriate places later, yet professionalism remained the impetus of the Sistine chapel. And with Crawley or Alice incessantly bustling in and out like chaperones, behaviors bordering on indecorous are kept in check. It's odd, though, that I haven't seen either servant today.

My modeling as Juliet has spanned a little more than two weeks. To any outsider, Mr. Swain would appear to be working tediously slow, taking breaks every hour or so. His pace is intentional; he wants to lengthen his days with me, and I'm glad for it. I've determined to be his friend until he's finished, cherishing our banter as he paints. He's lovely and pure, and I'm sure that had we met as children (him without a mother to disapprove) I would have dragged him everywhere.

In my modeling, Mr. Swain has me stand with my hand abaft, as if Romeo were grasping it from behind, imploring Juliet to turn back and embrace him. It's an exhausting pose, so I'm grateful when he sets down his brush and says, "Tea?"

"I'll ring for Alice." I go to the little bell by the door.

A balmy sea gale furls in through the open window, billowing the curtains and nudging a barque along the waters of the bay. Clouds scud across the sun, swaddling the ship in momentary darkness. The slightest quiver runs through me. How quickly the brightest light can be extinguished. But no, the sun hasn't dimmed entirely. Still, it burns, even when concealed. Oh, to be like it.

My mouth waters, thirsty for something more vivifying than tea. When Alice comes along, I'll ask her to bring us lemonade.

"Juliet is looking well," I note, my back to the breeze and the bay and that little ship, skirting the chalky reef.

"She practically blooms with color," says Mr. Swain, his smile growing a little wider.

The sun has heated up my neck, my face, which I hide behind a fan. *Professionalism.* The air cools my blush, and the constant fanning prevents me from looking too long at him. That, more than anything, is what bridles me.

We sit, silence gliding over our heads like seagulls scouting for a perch.

"Would you like to try your hand at it?" he says.

"Painting? Oh, no. I'd ruin it."

"You won't." And then with vigor, "Any mistake can be fixed."

I pause, an audacious thought coming to me. "An interesting notion, Mr. Swain. I wonder if it applies to life, as well as to art."

He frowns, and my fanning stops.

"I dearly hope so." Such hazy words, dressed in doubt. I'm confused by what he means, then a theory dawns: *he's made a decision.*

It feels immoral, but I want to know what that decision is. I want to know *all* of Mr. Swain's intentions, all his secrets. And, secretly, I hope they have to do with me.

"Will you show me? How to paint, I mean."

At the fresco, he places a paintbrush in my hand, and,

standing behind me, shows me how to move it in slow, deliberate strokes. Up, and down. Up, and down.

Heart racing.

We're cheek to cheek, almost touching. Mr. Swain has so many freckles. Grains of sand, each of them. I want to bottle them up to wear on a chain around my neck.

Up, and down. Up, and down.

It's intoxicating—the heat of his hand over mine.

"Mr. Swain—"

"Call me Henry."

"Henry."

Who knew there was such intimacy in a name? I say it again, and his lips curve into the sweetest of smiles, tipping fractionally towards me.

The lyrics of a ballad swim into my head as his gaze drinks me in:

*Drink to me only with thine eyes,*
*And I will pledge with mine;*
*Or leave a kiss but in the cup*
*And I'll not ask for wine.*

His breath blows on my mouth, and I have the wickedest thought of him kissing me. I want him to. More than life, I want Henry to kiss me.

*What am I doing?*

This must stop.

I break from his arms, the sudden absence of his body

next to mine sending a chill through me. He feels it, too. The absence. The chill. The beginning of a splintering between us. How easy it is to slip, to find yourself too close.

"Would you like some lemonade?"

"I would. Thank you."

I fetch the drink myself. I need the air and the distance running brings. How could I have let him get so close to me? I was practically in his arms. His solid, strapping arms.

My goal forgotten, I let my feet carry me where they will as I get lost in a discordance of thoughts.

Euphoria burns in my veins like a vexatious fever, a myriad lines of poetry springing to my mind. Over a cauldron in some sodden cave somewhere, three witches prick their thumbs—*fair is foul and foul is fair*—and with their blood, I'm spellbound.

Cursed.

*Foolish, silly girl! How can you be so flippant with your heart?*

Suddenly my mind goes quiet, as I look to where my feet have brought me. The empty wing in the back of the house, where a single chamber door stands locked.

Dusky light streams in through the shuttered window at the end of the hall, eerily silent. No imaginary whispers. No doggish laughter or siren calls. Nothing here but the door.

I wonder what's behind it.

My wondering grows, a tingling sensation running along my arm as I reach, unthinking, for the doorhandle. I jiggle it, discovering that it's locked.

*But why?*

The knob twists under my hand, and I leap back, the door swinging out, pushing me to the wall. I nab glimpses of shapes swaying inside the lightless room, as Gaston slinks from it like a shadow.

His eyes are bloodshot, his beard wispy and in need of a trim. He shuts the door, locking it with speed.

*Ah, so there's a key.*

He drops it into his waistcoat.

"Beatrice," he says, face drained of blood. "What are you doing here?"

"I was just wandering," I rush, "and my wandering led me here." And wincing at the memory of him crushing me against this very wall, I whisper, "Please don't be cross with me."

His nostrils flare as he exhales. He leans his cane, a simple carving, against the wall. And then he embraces me with fondness and care, and it startles me—how opposite this embrace is from his last. The wolf absent, there is only the solidity of Gaston's mortal body.

"No, I'm not cross with you."

Relief rushes through me, and I relax into his arms, savoring this feeling of security. He reads it as passion, holding me tighter, and I rest my head against his chest.

"I didn't expect you home so early." An odd smell

exudes from his clothes, something feculent and reeking, burning my nose. It must be a spice of some kind, picked up from his travels. "When did you arrive?"

"Not but a few hours ago."

Panic slams into my chest. Hours! Could he have seen me with Henry—our closeness?

"Why didn't you seek me out the moment you arrived?" If Gaston discovered us, why hasn't he turned on me, unleashed his wolf to punish me? What has he been doing all this time?

His eyes flit to the chamber door then back to mine. "Did you miss me, my love?"

He acts as if he's seen nothing. As if his trust in me was justified. The guilt is sharp, knowing it wasn't. I almost broke the only promise he's ever made me swear to, never to betray him like his first wife did. If I tell him I missed him, then maybe he won't suspect I've done anything wrong.

"Desperately," I say, and he leans me against the wall, wanting proof. *Desperate* describes me perfectly. I married him because I was desperate for his fortune, for the salvation it would give my family. I'm desperate now to keep it.

The kiss is longer than our last—beseeching and slow, and I almost get lost in the sensation of tingling lips.

"Did you dream of me?" he asks.

I did more than dream of him. I *called out* for him.

The part of me that's cunning instructs me to tell him everything. That the night brought frustration and sleeplessness. That I'd become too used to the weight of him next to me in the bed and would jolt awake at every creak in the walls or scraping of the wind against the house. And then in the morning I'd wake, wretched, only to soothe myself—not with thoughts of him—but of Henry. No, I can't tell him everything. It's impossible to do so without hurting him.

Smiling weakly, I swallow the tightness in my throat. "I'll never tell."

Gaston chuckles, tracking a finger down my throat, leaving a trail of gooseflesh.

"What treasures have you brought?" I ask, before he can think to kiss me there. The spot seems too...*carnal*... and I'm not sure I could bear it.

He grins. "Come with me."

With haste, we thread through the house to the entrance hall. Henry has been searching for me; seeing Gaston, he tucks into a hurried bow. "Welcome home, sir." His voice cracks, the same panicked thoughts on his face. *Were we seen?*

"*Henri, mon cher camarade!* How is my painting?"

"Good, sir. Excellent!"

"Excellent," Gaston parrots as he tugs me up the staircase. I glance back at Henry, staring up at me with such loss in his eyes that I feel a second splintering snap between us. But this is how it must be. I must follow Gaston, forever looking back to what could have been if only my story were different.

Reaching our bedchamber, Gaston tells me to close my eyes. I squeeze them tight to crush the threatening tears.

He whispers in my ear, his breath warm, raising the hair on my neck. "Open."

A headless mannequin stands at the center of the room, wearing a striking gown of Indian make. Soft satin and sheer mull, embroidered with emerald lotus blossoms and wingspread beetle motifs, and a shawl to match.

"It's beautiful." A tear escapes, but I wipe it quickly away. It's more than beautiful; it's a piece of the world brought home to me, like Papa would do. The love I felt for him was immense, knowing that as he traveled—as the world distracted him with all its colors and wonders—he'd always spared a thought for me. Just as Gaston has done.

"As are you. Wear it for me." Not a question or request but a command. *Wear it for me.* I slip the shawl around my shoulders, bringing the silk embroidery to my nose, my lips. It feels like cream, smells like saffron. I sigh around the fabric as it covers me, captivated.

*Spellbound.*

"And this." Gaston fastens around my neck a weave of gold and diamonds, dangling pearls and raw, uncut emeralds. A wish granted, the choker covers most of my neck, protecting me from unwanted touch.

"I want only to please you," he says.

"You have." It's the truth. Anna and Mamma are safe and looked after, and so am I. "I have something for you, too. Close your eyes, please." He shoots up an eyebrow, smirking as I quote him. "I don't want my surprise spoiled before I have a chance to reveal it."

I go to the closet, retrieving my portrait. I had it framed, gilt roses and fleur-de-lis motifs twisting prettily around my image. Holding it aloft, I allow Gaston to look.

"*Mon Dieu,*" he says, his breath robbed from him. I hide my face behind the canvas, pleasantly demurred by his response, but he'll have none of that. He sets my portrait aside, so he can plunge his hands into my hair.

"Let me see your face, my wife." He turns me toward the windows, the last rays of sunset bouncing off the crystal-cut glass. He pores over my face like an ancient text, as if he were trying to read me. He seeks paradise, *aches* for it to calm the punishing storms of his eyes, opposites of mine. "How is it you've bewitched me so?"

"I'm certain I've done nothing like what you imply," I whisper, discomfited by his stare and his breath on my face. I feel my body clamming up, inching furtively away from this intimacy, though I fight for calm. I can handle a kiss or two.

Minutes later, he pulls away from my panting mouth. "Thank you for the gift. I will cherish it, and will thank Henry for painting you so perfectly."

I blink, my face burning as I look down, away,

anywhere but at Gaston. That's when I notice my open bodice, my loosened stays. Did I do this myself or—?

Gaston sheds his overcoat for a dinner jacket, grinning to himself as he adjusts his cuffs. "I'll ask the lad to join us tonight," he says. But I don't reply, securing my corset with double knots.

The duck's encrusted eyes goggle up at me from its dish, trussed with herbs and citrus fruits. I imagine it blinks. What a terrible fate to be paddling in your pond one day under a brilliant sun, when a shadow meets your wake and snatches you up by the neck. Thinking about the bird's plight stirs up my stomach, which gurgles.

The dining room is uncannily hot, the atmosphere strained, dizzy. Any moment I'll topple out of my chair. Gaston presides at the head of the table with me on his left, Henry opposite me at Gaston's right. Shuffling glances, Henry and I keep our attentions on our bowls of Potage Crécy, a creamy carrot soup that is one of Gaston's favorites. I stir it with my spoon, barely tasting it.

"Tell me, Henry," Gaston says, puncturing the silence. "Did they train you well at *l'académie*?"

Henry looks up from his soup, his spoon dribbling onto the white tablecloth. "I was fortunate to have distinguished instructors," he says.

Gaston bobs his head approvingly. “Your parents must be proud of your accomplishments.”

“I hope they would be, if...” He falters, and my heart pangs for him. “If they were still living.”

Reverence falls over the table. Thick. Mournful.

“No doubt they’d think highly of their son.” These aren’t simple words of condolence, I think, spoken out of custom or unfelt sympathy. I hear sincerity in them. Gaston feels for Henry, and that alone reminds me of his compassion, something I’ve forgotten.

“If you don’t think it rude,” he continues, with deference, “might I ask how you managed to pay for this education?”

“Not at all, sir. I was blessed with a benefactor. He sent me to school and ensured I was well treated.”

“He must be a generous man, and wealthy.”

“Indeed, sir.”

“Who is he?”

Eyes down, Henry skims his spoon atop the soup, drawing patterns in the cream. “I don’t know. He’s chosen to remain anonymous. No doubt to belie his association with a former kinchin coe.” My brow ruffles, unfamiliar with the term, but Gaston appears to know it.

“Do not be ashamed of your past, Monsieur Swain,” he says. “The gods toiled with your life, but you took it back.” The words are dogged, inspiring. They straighten my backbone so that I sit up a little taller in my chair. Despite his affluence, Gaston knows much of life’s toil and strife. He's lost four wives. How wretched it must have been to bury each of them, to experience that remorseless, vitriolic pain not once nor twice but *three* times. But do their deaths equal the affliction of betrayal brought by his first wife, when he was told he was *unwanted*? Is this what I do to him, each time I thwart him?

The room reverts into an ambiance of clinking plates, gamey odors, and slow-burning candles. I've eaten little and spoken even less, neither of which goes unnoticed.

"Does Madame Dumas not look angelic this evening?" Gaston says.

A flux of blood to my cheeks. I fight the urge to look at Henry.

"I've never seen a lovelier woman."

I reach for my goblet of sherry but end up tipping the saltcellar, scattering the grains across the table. *Bad luck.*

Gaston cringes, though he manages to check his temper. "Are you seeking a wife, Monsieur Swain?"

A furtive glance. *Oh, Lord, I'm going to be sick.*

"I'm afraid that as an artist barely born, I'm too poor to suitably sustain one."

Gaston smiles wryly. "A wife is indeed an ephemeral creature. So easily lost to the caprices of life. When you find her, Henry, I would caution you to never let her venture far from you." He reaches for my hand, entwining our fingers, and I'm sure I'll vomit. If he knows anything, he's teasing us. Teasing and taunting and *toiling,* and I can't stand it anymore. My guilt is a parasite squirming behind my breastbone, and it's killing me.

I bolt to standing, rattling the plate settings. "Pardon me," I say.

Both men rise and reach for me, but I've already escaped, darting for the gardens where I collapse under the dogwood tree and regurgitate duck.

## CHAPTER 19
# BURNING, BURNING

Midnight churns black and silver. Thunder rattles the windows as lightning strikes the convulsive waves hurling against the cliffs. Papa worshiped nights like this. He'd gawp through windows, streaming with water as if the house had transfigured into a sinking ship. "Listen," he'd say when the winds had pacified. The world was an overwhelming calm, heavy on the lungs. "This is what peace is. You feel it only after a storm."

Tonight's storm wracks my body with tremors. With each tumultuous clash of the sea, I cower under the bedcovers, the bed empty on its other side. I feel Gaston's absence as fear, as abandonment as the world is rent to dissolution. For the first time since marrying him, I don't want to be alone.

The scream of the wind catapults me to my feet. I flee

the bedchamber down spiraled stairs, through passageways dark and sullen and creaking with shadows. Nervy, I ease open the door to his study, hoping to find him there.

"Gaston?"

No response from the darkness.

A piquant aroma stings my nose. I follow the scent trail to the wall, where a tapestry hangs. Curiosity evicting my distress, I brush the tapestry aside, skimming my hand along the cleft between two panels.

A breeze.

Curious. There must be a chamber behind this wall, a den for seclusion and secretive affairs.

There's a tic in my veins—a thrill—and suddenly I'm transported into the gothic novels I devour by the fireside. If I could just find the latch that opens the door...

*Click.*

The panel swings inward on a room aglow with firelight. Gaston rises in surprise, a mahogany pipe at his lips. My eyes water with the peppery haze, and I can't tell if he's annoyed with me for discovering his sanctuary, or if that harsh line between his brows is a shadow cast by flame. It doesn't matter. A concussive burst of thunder rips the air, and I whimper, that line melting into concern.

"Are you frightened, my love?" The question makes me feel puerile and small. I'm acting like a child.

Stuttering makes my fear even more obvious. "I-I just wondered where you were."

He sets his pipe on the table next to the armchair,

where today's cane, a brass eagle's head, is propped. "Stay with me, then."

I ease onto the floor by the fireplace, like I would at home with my siblings. I miss them. I miss their laughter, their teasing. I miss Byron's smug humor and Simon's eye-rolling. I miss Anna's cluelessness when she's being made fun of, and her blushing when she realizes it. It's hard to believe I ever thought of leaving them to go adventuring. At the time I wanted distance, but now that I have it, I long for time's reversal.

Gaston drapes a blanket around my shoulders, pulling me from thought. I whiff the spicy odor from his smoking jacket, sneezing once, twice, and he removes it before slumping next to me on the floor. His knees crack with age, catching up to him, and a flicker of sympathy runs through me, though I don't say anything. We just sit like this, in fire-crackling quietude, for a while.

I watch the flames, lithe little bodies twisting in a sinuous dance.

Dinner couldn't have been more horrible. What made it worse was Gaston and Henry both running after me to watch the glory taking place in the dirt. Panic-stricken, Gaston rushed me to our bedchamber and laid me down. "I'll call for a physician," he said, but I stopped him, catching his hand.

I saw the fear in his eyes, the same that seized Mamma when she saw Papa cough up blood for the first time. No doubt Gaston thought I'd contracted the disease of his previous wives. How helpless he looked, genuflect at my bedside. If he knew the true reason for my sickness, I doubt he'd have been sympathetic.

"Are you feeling better?" he asks now. I respond affirmatively, though a squeamishness still lingers.

He fiddles with a ring on his right hand, stroking the gold emblazoned with firelight. It's an envelope ring, a funereal possession containing hair clippings from a loved one who's passed.

"Which wife is it for?" I ask, my voice barely above a whisper.

Reluctance.

But then, "Parvati. My first wife."

The fire sparks, enlivened by the name. Reflections of the flames burn fervidly in Gaston's eyes. *He still loves her.* I don't know how I couldn't see it before. Though he's told me she lives, she's dead to him, and yet he's kept a lock of her hair to remember her. Despite her betrayal, he still loves her.

I've never heard of anything more tragic or heartbreaking. Or romantic. It softens me. It softens me like butter.

The house groans with the storm. And I think I'm only imagining the phantasmal tread of footsteps when Gaston utters sardonically, "Did you forget, *mon amour*? Our home is tenanted by ghosts." There's a low rumble in his throat—a laugh—but I'm not convinced. His demeanor sags grim, almost depressed, as if he truly is haunted. As if he hears the whispers, too. Are they the voices of those who've died in this house, or are they the sounds of those who've never been born?

"There are no children here. Surely, with four wives before me, you would have conceived many." I blanch at the word *conceive*, but that mystery has been niggling my mind since the time I arrived. I've never felt brash enough to ask about it, until now.

Gaston's mouth curves almost painfully, extending the lines around his eyes. "I am...incapable. That's not to say I can't show you my desire. I simply cannot produce a child. Four wives, each more nubile than the last, has taught me that."

A tenuous ray of sympathy filters into the space between my lungs, staying there awhile. I can see he wanted children. Though his patience with that shop boy in Paris was thin, at best. But if the boy had been his own blood and bone, would he have been merciful, patient? Would he still have needed a wife to warm his bed?

"Is that why you've kept your distance from me?" he asks. "You feared that children would come too soon?"

My heart flitters in my chest. If I say yes, he might try to ease me into compliance. If I say no, he'll demand to know what reason I have for not loving him. Love *is* my reason—but so is fear. Fear that I'll somehow be different. *Someone of his shaping.* If I give myself to him, will I still be *me*? The truth ought to be told, if not for his sake, then for mine.

I take a breath, holding it till it hurts and I have to release it. "Gaston. I'm grateful for everything you've done for me, for my family, but—"

"But you are not grateful enough to express it. Beatrice..." The fire dies down as if by unspoken command, bringing a golden glow to Gaston's beard. He pushes my hair from my shoulder, baring my neck and the emerald choker I didn't remove when I changed into my nightgown. I'd hardly noticed it was there, like it was a part of me, brand new and, somehow, *right*. A change, but good.

"I've been patient with you. Given you time to get used to me." His voice *croons*, and my head tips back as I'm masterfully lured in, a maiden ensorcelled. I wait for the tug of my body to resist, but it doesn't, and I think, *This is what Jane must have felt, when Rochester kissed her for the very first time.* "How much longer need I wait?" Gaston's fingers slip under the choker, lifting it dexterously away like it was the lid on a tureen and my flesh was the fare, and I can't move, can't think. I can only feel Gaston's fingers as they cup my neck, his husky whisper seeking my ear. "You are my *wife*."

Meditative kisses follow a vein up my throat to my jaw to my mouth, and he coaxes me open with his tongue. Something slips between my vertebrae like a spell, and my eyes grow heavy, fluttering with stolen breath. This isn't an emotion I've ever experienced before, overwhelming and—and *hungry.* The same lightning spark I felt with Henry I'm feeling now, ten times as much. With each kiss, every touch, the spark grows wider in my middle. My deepest middle.

Something like a moan escapes my mouth, some feral thing, and I lose all sense but the sensation of this inferno consuming my insides. *Am I not obligated?* thrums a sly, convincing voice inside of me. Did I not vow I'd be his, to have, to hold, forever?

Burning, burning. So much burning.

I start to shake, the emotion too much, too hot, too *fast.* I'm not ready for this. I tear Gaston's hands from my back and writhe away from him, wiping my mouth, scrubbing at those perfidious gems on the choker. How easily they could be plied and manipulated, providing no immunity at all. *Stupid girl, they're just gems. Just tricks. And you let them charm you.*

His joints click and pop, abhorrent. "Why must you be so cold? Don't you love me?"

I almost laugh. Of course he'd ask it when the answer is so apparent. But he doesn't care about the truth. He just wants the illusion.

My response comes as a murmur. "I'm just a girl."

He leans back as if surprised, like he'd forgotten. And for the briefest of moments, he looks as if he's realized his mistake. I'm too young for him.

Gaston's chest rises with a breath that looks too shallow. "Then I will have to find a woman."

Incensed footsteps beat the floor. A heavy scrape and a door slam and I flinch inward, miserable.

The room sighs.

When I've finished crying, it occurs to me how deathly silent it is.

The storm has passed.

## CHAPTER 20
# RUMORS

I insisted on choosing the design and fabric of my ballgown: a full-skirted, crème-colored silk moiré with vines of gold and silver beading delicately stitched onto the hem. Fallen shoulders and a flattering low bodice draw the eyes to my collarbones and bare neck.

I inspect myself in the mirror as Alice smooths my hair into place, pinning sprigs of baby's breath. She finishes right as Gaston comes to fetch me for the ball, a chill creeping through the doorway. Alice avoids him as much as she can, I've noticed.

I grow warm when I see him, hearkening to last night. I can't stop dwelling on it—the warmth of his mouth, his tongue. How, for a moment, I enjoyed it. It strains credulity, but I felt pleasure. Yet my passion gave way so quickly to panic, it almost didn't seem fair.

Gaston admires me from afar, his gaze flitting along my bare parts as if my choice in dress was subconsciously guided with him in mind. Before I even knew my fear of exposed flesh, I was offering it up as alms for his desire. If keeping in Gaston's good graces means embracing my vulnerability, then so be it. I don't want the rest of my life with him to be miserable, so I must work through the hard parts as best as I can. And, if possible, on *my* terms.

Gaston's gift of emeralds and pearls resumes its place on my neck, a reminder that, at the heart of it all, he wants me to be happy.

I hold onto his arm as we descend the stairs to greet our guests, entering a ballroom that's been transformed into an inharmonious mixture of fairy whimsy and Indian infusion. Our two worlds clashing for the whole town to behold.

Strings of roses and sweet-smelling violets garnish the walls, the room's marble pillars incandescently lit with sconces. Around the perimeter, snake charmers enchant our guests, mystified and scandalized, as jugglers juggle knives and women in *lehenga* skirts dance the fiery, barefoot *Kathak*. Casting glares, little mirrors ornamenting the women's costumes blind the men from ogling too long at their bare midriffs. As part of the dance, they wave their hennaed hands, as if to entice, or even to tempt.

The effect is mesmerizing, and as we draw nearer, I find myself wanting to join them. Their beauty, their grace—it's like asphyxiation. Like the ecstasy one feels when the air is too thin to breathe, yet breathe one must.

Gaston locks onto one dancer in particular, her dark eyes smoldering as she spires her arms above her head. By his look, I think he wants to breathe her in, too.

The tips of my ears starting to burn, I constrain him to walk. "When we sent invitations for a ball," I say to him, "a ball is what our guests expected. Not some spectacle."

"I don't care what others think," he replies testily. "There is more than one way to live in this world. Just because a man's ideas are different doesn't mean they're wrong."

"Nor a woman's."

I didn't expect him to hear the quip. He stops our revolution of the ballroom and looks at me, not with contempt, but fascination for what I've just said. It's not the same way he looked at the dancer.

I feel jealousy so clearly that I can name it without doubt. Good gracious, I'm *jealous*—not of the dancer, but of the woman this ball is in homage to. It's all for his first wife, Parvati.

*That I'll somehow be different. Someone of his shaping.*

I'm not her. No matter how much of myself I give to him, I will never *be* her. With this new truth my jealousy fades into something near hurt. Near *grief*. Because if I'm to be Gaston's wife, I want to be different from all the others.

"Nor a woman's," he says.

A surprised, shallow gasp escapes my lungs. He's rarely conceded to me, and it gives me *hope*.

Bowing low, Gaston kisses the back of my white-gloved hand. "Go. Enjoy the night."

He moves into the crowd, guests parting for him easily. He holds every one of their stares as if he knows what they all whisper about him—that he's magnetic, salacious, powerful. He'll steal their daughters if they're not careful. And then one by one he'll bury them.

He's beautiful, a dangerous prize, and no one can take their eyes off him.

Including me.

I bite my lip painfully, pushing every thought of him away as he disappears into this dream he's created for himself.

Henry stands across the room, speaking with the creditor Silas Mitchell. They laugh, shaking hands as if having made a business transaction. I move to join them when a turbaned man shoves past a gentleman in his way, pointing a sharp-nailed finger at me.

"You, girl!"

The man's bedraggled beard hangs past his shoulders, framed by an open vest. I try not to stare at his chest, naked but for the curly black hair plunging to his loins. A capuchin balances on his shoulder as he waves away some silly girls hoping to get their palms read.

He's a soothsayer. A mystic. A man of illusion.

I try to step back but find I can't, my feet affixed to the floor.

"Look into my eyes," he says.

The soothsayer's eyes eddy black and gold, and I feel myself falling into a whirlpool of stars, weightless, lethargic. The monkey screeches, its head bobbing madly with its lips folded back into a gummy smile. "I see it too, Aakaash," says the soothsayer to his pet. "He hopes you will be the one."

"The one?"

"The one with the key."

*The key.*

Everything's drowsy and dark, and I can't—I can't wake up. "The key to what," I hear myself say in a stranger's voice. Afar off. A soulless echo in an empty space.

The soothsayer hisses low, drawing out the final word and biting down hard. "His heart."

But my addled brain can scarcely comprehend his words. It's like I've inhaled one of Gaston's spicy cigars.

"Find the key."

"The key," I echo.

Puckered, floating lips blow air into my face as the heel of a brown hand bumps against my forehead. The din of a hundred voices explodes in my ears, and I press my hands to my eyes, keening with flashes of light.

A turbaned man grins queerly at me as a collared monkey bounces on his shoulder, teeth bared. The man wears a vest but no shirt, exposing his hairy chest. I avert my eyes.

"Would you like to know your future?" he asks, waiting for me to put my palm in his.

He's a soothsayer. A mystic. A man of illusion.

I blink, feeling as if I've missed a minute of my life. "No, thank you. Please help yourself to the food and drink." I move away from him, a puzzled hostess. I had something I needed to do. Baffled, I pause. Not a moment ago, I saw Henry and Mr. Mitchell shaking hands, but now Henry has disappeared and Mr. Mitchell has been snatched up by Felicity Crane.

The two are engaged to be married. Their fathers must have negotiated the union, senior partners adamant on keeping their company within the Noble Bloodlines. Felicity has Mr. Mitchell clinched to her side in a vise-grip. I've never felt sorrier for him, though Felicity looks truly happy. Mr. Mitchell tries to look pleasant, but under that pasted smile I can tell he'd rather be home with a decanter of brandy. While he must have a companion of sorts—a hound, perhaps, bred for the foxhunt—I can't see matrimony being agreeable to him.

They don't see me approach. I hide myself behind a column to eavesdrop, taking no shame in it.

Felicity's cousin snickers at her side. "Did you see how stiff he looked next to her?" Georgiana's whispers are unsuccessful. "Must be a lovers' quarrel."

"Well, *I* heard ever since their betrothal she can't satisfy him."

"What do you mean, 'ever since'?"

"You mean you don't know? Why do you think they married so quickly after his previous wife *just happened* to turn up dead?" Georgiana opens up her mouth to *umm*, and Felicity huffs. "She was his *mistress*."

Georgiana gasps.

"It gets better." Felicity goes so low that I strain to hear her over the string quartet. "A late servant of Monsieur Dumas's told his wife—who works for Daddy—that he'd seen his master carrying a *body* into one of his chambers! And what's stranger is the very next night, after the day's work had finished, the servant never returned home."

"Was he murdered?" Legitimate confusion pulls Georgiana's face into a pinch.

Mr. Mitchell, who has been growing increasingly irritable with each word, finally breaks. "Honestly, Felicity, I've never heard a more ludicrous story. This is England, for goodness' sake! It's not right to slander a man, especially in his own home. And as for that servant, I knew him. He was a spineless drunkard who left his wife and children to drink himself to death in some tavern in Folkestone. It's despicable the way you prattle on about people as if they're characters in a novel."

Felicity jabs a finger into his chest. "And the wedding? Do you think I'm making that up, as well?"

Anxious for the conversation—and this night—to be over, Mr. Mitchell takes an underhanded peek at his pocket-watch. “I admit, the timing was unorthodox.”

“See?”

“But you’ve no right to besmirch the Dumas’, especially Beatrice. You didn’t know her circumstances.”

“And you did?”

He refuses to answer, glancing at his watch again.

Felicity lifts her nose, her rant ended. Georgiana suggests they go try the ices being served in the refreshments room, and the girls totter off, their crinolines swaying about their waists like floor sweeps, poor Mr. Mitchell dragged behind them like a spoil of war.

Guilt for having been so rude to him during our last encounter eats its way through me. He did nothing wrong, but I treated him like a swindler. Yet he still defends me against Felicity’s venomous defamations.

I’m about to follow Mr. Mitchell to thank him, when a thin, gristly voice invades my ear.

“Is it true?” it mocks, and as recognition comes, I feel all goodness tapped from me. “Were you Dumas’s secret paramour?”

Mr. Haskell weasels a hand down my glove, his voice hard, dangerous. He clinches my forearm tight enough to bruise. “So that’s why you resisted me.”

He pulls me behind the curtained pillars, keeping me pinned, unable to see his face with its chasmal pockmarks and scars. The face of a reprobate. A villain.

"How are you here?" I struggle against him, my chest heaving with rage and panic. He smells drunk. "Coward—you ruined us. How dare you show your face again?"

"Ruined? You don't look ruined to me." He sniffs my hair, rubbing his cutting, stubbled cheek against my own. "You smell like roses."

My stomach burns with revulsion.

*Gaston. Where's Gaston?*

No one can see us here.

I struggle harder.

Haskell's slavered teeth graze my neck, and my body tightens. I kick backward, catching his shin.

His fingernails stab into me. "Do you know why I stole from your father?" he hisses. "Because I was *nothing* to him. We founded the business as partners, but he treated me like a bloody desk clerk. He said I was better suited for the books than the politics." He laughs—a wet, bloated sound. "He was right."

My voice is savage. "What did you do with the money?"

"Does it matter? I won."

"Then why come back here? They'll catch you."

"Who are *they*, you delicious thing? The constable? Dumas? What evidence did you show them, hm?"

Haskell turns me around, gripping me above the elbows. He looks the same as when I saw him last, except for one thing. His look is more determined—more crazed

—a vein throbbing at his temple. I don't think he'll run away this time.

"Your father signed away everything to me. The business. The money. Even you. You had no right to marry without my permission."

My lip curls. "You left us to starve."

"Did I? I seem to recall a matter overseas that duty required me to attend. The common sense of any magistrate will recognize your elopement to that braggart Frenchman as an act of rebellion against me, your guardian."

"He's no braggart. Gaston rescued us from the consequences of your filth."

"Well, then. He'll have to come to your rescue yet again." He lets go of my arms, propping his hands against the pillar, caging me in. His breath is rank, and I fight against the reflex to gag as he opines. "The servant who reportedly drunk himself to death in Folkestone, I knew him, too. As we exchanged pints, he told me the most interesting things about your *husband*." He spits the word, flecks of saliva spritzing my cheek. "He's not what you think he is."

*He's a wolf.*

"Whatever he is, he can't be worse than you."

"I'm not a murderer."

My heart sinks into my stomach.

*Be vigilant, Beatrice.*

I grit my teeth. "You're a liar."

"You heard it yourself from the Crane girl. Your husband murdered his servant because he witnessed another's death and had to be silenced."

"Those are just rumors—falsehoods."

"Every rumor begins in truth."

I can't breathe, my chest squeezing tight. I fold my arms over my stomach, fighting for control over my body by forcing in breaths. I won't believe anything Haskell says. I won't be bested by him.

"I have a new proposition for you," he says, looking me over. The lion prowls, paces. He has me in his den.

*Breathe. Just breathe.*

"Find me evidence of the Frenchman's dark deeds, so that I might take advantage of his financial standing. Or else I go to the judge with a suit of annulment, stating you married without your guardian's consent."

"My mother gave her consent."

"Your mother is not a man. You're underage until your twenty-first birthday, Miss Tilney. Which means your marriage is invalid without my approval."

I falter, my anxiety slipping out, and a numbness slipping in, spreading from my hands to my head where my mind is a blank. I don't know what to do.

"Help me blackmail him, and I'll not interfere with your marriage."

The room's gone cold and dim, and my hands feel punctured with needles. I find myself nodding like a puppet, a lever on my neck pulling up and pushing down. Powerless.

Haskell's tone changes, engrossed by something else. "My, my," he purrs. "Your sister is maturing nicely."

I wake up.

I reel forward to tell him to stay the bloody hell away from her, but he's already slinked off into a set of couples dancing a minuet, his throaty laugh hanging above the crowd.

I push through the mass of party guests, standing on my toes to search over their heads. I can't find my sister, and my lungs start closing again. Someone calls my name, but I ignore it. I have to find her, protect her—our pearl! Where is she?

"Beatrice!" My mother yanks me back onto my feet.

"Where's Anna?" I shout at her. People stare; Mamma shushes me.

"She's dancing with Mr. Swain."

I scan the faces of the dancers, hating myself. It was *me* Haskell wanted, not my sister, and I should have just let him have me.

I spot Anna—there—dancing with Henry, as Mamma said. She's safe.

*She's safe.*

I sigh painfully, my chest on fire. I should have let him have me from the beginning. His sights would have turned eventually, but I could have done something

—*anything*—to keep them trained on me, to keep Anna safe from him.

"Beatrice, what is the matter?" Mamma grips my hands. I stare at hers—ungloved, veiny, and frail—near lifeless. Reminders of her eventual surrender from this life.

I pull from her grasp to rub my arms, grateful for the long gloves covering Haskell's purpling fingerprints. "I just wanted to show Anna my gown," I say, my voice a rasp.

The lie is weak, and Mamma sees through its transparency. Her lips thin, though she keeps silent. She won't argue with me in so open a place, with so many prominent people to overhear. She takes a breath, and it propels her into a cough.

"Mamma? Mamma, are you all right?" I brace her shoulders. She removes her handkerchief from her mouth.

Clean. White. Snow white.

"I'm fine, dear. Just a cold I'm trying to shift."

I close my eyes, pleading for a cool heart. I bring the flat of my hand to my chest and focus, tapping out the rhythm of the music. Anna's bouncy laughter floats above the notes of the string quartet. I open my eyes to see her but see Henry first. He turns her around the tessellated floor with lightness and ease, confidence and carefulness. He's a wonderful dancer, no doubt the favorite among the women whose balls he's attended. He must have attended many. His finesse of motion is beautiful to watch, taking me out of my head and into the moment, where I feel real. I wish I were dancing with him instead of Anna. I want to feel his arms around me again and hear him say how his heart breaks for me—a foolish girl caught in a trap of her own making.

Mamma tidies the single ringlet draped over my shoulder. "I wish you could have had more," she says.

"I have plenty, Mamma," I say, not looking at her. I'm on the verge of tears. "Gaston is wealthy and generous and—" Her hand, laid gently on my shoulder, silences me.

"That's not what I meant, Beatrice." Her eyes glimmer. Not mere misery or sorrow but *true* sadness. The kind where one feels hopelessly lost and thinks they can never be recovered. In her benign, apologetic tone, she says, "Your father hoped you'd be lucky enough to find him, your knight of valor. He hoped you would be happy."

One moment is all it takes. Just a few simple words to realize how poorly I've misread her. Since Papa's death, she's been a ghost, begrudgingly clinging to mortality, and I've resented her for it. Because I need her. I need her to see my pain and feel it and ease it. I need her to see the sacrifices I'm making for her, for Anna.

She *does* see them.

I tip my head to the ceiling to keep my tears from dripping. "Mamma," I say, and she hugs me to her. I hide my face in the crook of her neck, wanting to go back to before my regret, to before I said *yes* to Gaston. Mr.

Haskell has returned, and I don't know how to stop him from ruining our lives.

Mamma's comfort is brief, but enough. She nudges me upright. "As a lady, you could not look more beautiful," she says, but with her disciplinary look. "However, as a hostess, I'm unimpressed. I see far too many wallflowers without partners, and too few couples for this set. What's to be done about it?"

"Perhaps hire a new hostess," I reply, expressionless. I'm tired. I want to escape from this world and the men who control it.

She frowns but doesn't scold me. As the quartet draws out its final notes, the dancers applaud. The men begin their searches for their next partners while the women check off their dance cards. Henry escorts Anna back to us. Her face a burgeoning rose, she curtsies and thanks him. Henry kisses the back of her white kid glove, his lips not quite connecting with her hand. I flex my fingers, at once aware of how tightly I've been clenching them.

"Did you see us?" Anna says, her feet still trying to dance. "Mr. Swain is a lovely dancer."

On cue with the compliment, he flushes modestly. "A dancer is only as lovely as his partner," he says, and Anna blushes, too.

"I did see. Lovely." There's not quite enough feeling in the word.

"Anna," says Mamma, flattening her hand to her forehead. "Let us leave the room. It's warm, and I'm feeling faint."

"Yes, Mamma." Anna's voice reeks of disappointment. She was hoping Henry would ask her to dance another. I'm glad he will not.

I grasp Mamma's arm. "Keep her close to you," I whisper. "Promise me you'll not let her leave your side." Urgency darkens my voice, frightening her.

"Yes, all right," she says. I kiss her and Anna, watching carefully as they quit the ballroom, alert for Mr. Haskell's thin, slippery shadow.

"Are you well this evening?" Henry says. He frowns, perceptive of my ghostly face, of the sweat beaded along my hairline. I just want this night to end.

It's only for Henry's sake that I smother my emotions. I tug on the ends of my gloves, smoothing them over my elbows to hide what's happened to me. "Yes, I'm quite well."

A tremolo of trumpets signals the assembly to take up its positions on the floor for the next set, which will be a waltz. In that bashful way of his, Henry offers his hand. "I've already asked your husband."

Society dictates I'm not allowed to dance with my husband in public because it's too intimate, but not that I can't dance at all, if only my partner asks his permission.

"We have his blessing," Henry adds, trying to pull my attention to him.

*It's a husband's duty to know everything about his wife...*

*her every desire.* Gaston knows my desires, and he's tempting me with them. But I'll prove that I'm loyal, that I can dance with Henry and return to Gaston, my heart unattached. I will try to make him happy.

My knees are weak, my gut wobbly. "I'm afraid I'm not very good."

"You don't have to be." Henry steps to me and positions my hands. The dance begins, and we move fluidly through the expanse of couples, rotating around each other like cogs in a clock. Acutely aware of his hand on my waist, nudging me into the direction of a turn or a step, I don't have to think or anticipate, just trust his lead. It's effortless. Like our rhythms, our bodies, are one. He's the best dancer, the best friend, I've ever known.

He looks dashing in a gold vest and white gloves, paired with black pants and a dress coat. He wears a satin cravat and polished, low-heeled leather boots, his hair combed back in a dapper, almost dandyish style.

"How did a starving artist afford such an expensive suit?" I ask, not letting myself stare too long.

He grins at the pert question. "If you must know, your husband paid for it. Naturally, I refused, but he's not a man who likes to be rebutted."

"No. He isn't." The waltz's energy wanes, just a little.

"You look radiant."

"Nonsense. Sublime, perhaps, but never radiant."

In mock propitiation, Henry lays a hand over his

heart. "I stand corrected, madam. It's an honor to be in the presence of divinity."

I crinkle my nose. "I wish you'd stop calling me 'madam.' It's so..."

"Geriatric?" he suggests.

"*Yes.*" I laugh, taking my first easy breath all night.

A serious look alights Henry's face. "If I may, I'd like to say something to you."

But my reply never comes, my heart stilling altogether as I watch Gaston exit the ballroom with that hennaed dancer pinned to his side. His hand feels its way across her back as he leans into her whisper, his mouth rising, curving, pulling...into a grin.

## CHAPTER 21
# SECRETS THAT STING

I wish I hadn't seen, didn't know. Gaston is a hypocrite. He makes me swear my faithfulness while recanting his own. And he thinks I won't find out, that I won't even care.

*Of course I care.* What is marriage but a covenant of trust and confidence? How can I entrust my family —*myself*—to him if he lies to me? What else is he lying about?

My throat sears with pain, the floor blurring under my feet as I run through the corridors. My dress weighs me down, and I want to strip from it, shred it into ribbons in my outrage. Henry chases after me as I run ever faster, finally yielding to the floor as my knees give out.

"What's happened, Beatrice?"

We have left the ballroom far behind us. I jolt, seeing where we've come. Mirror, table, window. A lone door, locked. Why is it my running always brings me here, to the very place I'm forbidden from being? A place that, now, I fear is where Gaston keeps his secrets.

*Could it be true? Is he a murderer?*

"Please, answer me." Henry urges me to look at him. "Let me know you."

My conscience, that fanatical part of me enslaved to edicts and etiquette, reminds me that I cannot share what is personal with a man I'm not promised to.

But my feelings overwhelm me.

"He's upset with me," I say.

"Because you can't satisfy him?" *So. Henry has heard Felicity's baneful gossip.*

"Because I won't try." Stricken with discomfort, I yank the hairpins pinching my scalp. Henry helps me loose the curls, staring at the one between his fingers.

"You mean...you haven't consummated your marriage." Is that relief I hear in his voice? Not surprise or shame or criticism, as expected, but *relief*. The secret I tell may sting me, but it is nectar to Henry. "Beatrice." My name—he breathes it—and he takes that lock of hair in his hand and twines it around his fingers, the action pulling me closer.

Close faces. Close lips. Round and ample and enticing.

Henry is going to kiss me.

There are drums in my ears, tribal and heavy. Devilish whispers goad me on, and as I lean, as I part my lips to receive Henry's kiss, something savage cackles.

It scares me back into reality.

"No, Henry." I stop his mouth with my hand, a quaver knocking my bones. "We can't."

He sits back on his heels. "Beatrice, I—" Flush against his mouth, his desires tremble. "When I'm with you, I say things I'd never say, *do* things I'd never do. I think...I think I'm falling in love with you." His look changes, resolute. He takes my hand and doesn't let go. "I know you feel the same."

My cheeks flare with transparency, my heart tearing at its restraints. My feelings for Henry pulse and burn like swallowed suns, but I can't express them. I made a vow, and whether Gaston breaks his or not, I won't do the same. I won't hurt him like he's hurt me.

"It matters, Henry. I won't betray him. I will be *loyal* until—"

"Until death do you part," he finishes, his forehead pleating with resolve.

I shut my eyes, unable to bear Henry's earnestness, or the censure of my own.

## CHAPTER 22
# SHE LOVED HIM

Gaston's teeth rip into the buttered bread, crumbs sticking in his beard as the distasteful noises of mastication inflate the dining room. He chomps down on two more bites before swallowing. I've never seen him gorge himself like this, and I can't say I find it alluring.

Tension is a string between us, pulled taut. I don't know what to say to him, aside from, "Good morning."

"Morning." He hardly glances. Crawley has brought in the post, and Gaston sits absorbed, a rather troubled expression on his face as he reads. Some article about discontented sepoys and his beloved East India Company. His appetite slows. "Did you sleep well?"

"I had disturbing dreams." He was in them. Him and that dancer.

"That's unfortunate." He sips his coffee, cream sticking to his mustache.

My head drones with impatience. I want him to look at me, to talk to me. I want the truth from him. "You didn't come to bed last night."

"I had some letters to write. Business."

"Business." I bristle at the flagrant lie. *Business*, indeed. How many wives have heard the same excuse? How many of those wives were Gaston's? Did he play this game with them as he does with me?

"I've heard a rumor, Gaston. Concerning you and a former servant."

He folds up his paper and sets it aside. "And?"

"The servant saw you carrying a body into that chamber of yours, the one you're always sneaking into. He saw you, then the next day he disappeared. Rumor has it you're a murderer."

There's a beat of stunned silence, and then he bursts into open-mouthed laughter. "Murderer!" He doubles over onto the table as my face heats with irritation. The tip of his beard dips into his soft-boiled egg, smearing orange yoke onto his waistcoat. "Would you believe me," he says happily, wiping the laughter from his eyes, "if the 'body' the servant saw me carrying was actually a *rug* slung over my shoulder?"

I swallow the discomfort in my throat. "Then how did he disappear?"

He waves his hand dismissively. "The man was an opium addict who often hallucinated. He threatened me with his gossip, so I fired him." His humor subsiding, Gaston dabs at his beard with a napkin. "When I heard he had died, I felt sorry for his wife and sent her a sum of money to send her eldest to school. The lad had a penchant for naturalism and the physical sciences, as I recall."

*An opium addict.*

I've never felt more embarrassed in all my life. I remember Papa warning my brother Byron to shun the black pill, as he'd called it, because he'd seen his own father consumed by the drug. Toward the end of his short life, my grandfather hallucinated all manner of demons. It's certainly not a stretch to believe Gaston's former servant did the same.

Yet what of Gaston's infidelity, his hands on the dancer? *That* I saw with my own eyes.

I hide my trembling hands in my lap. "I saw you last night, leaving the ballroom with a woman on your arm. You seemed...interested in her." There's no more amusement in Gaston's eyes, but I press on, twisting the edge of the tablecloth in my fist. "Did you kiss her? Do...*more*... with her?"

His meal forgotten, Gaston leans back in his seat. "It hurts you to think I did." His brows pull together, pensive or troubled, I can't tell which.

I nod, feeling the humiliation of my inexperience, my innocence, as I fail to equate the kisses I've shared with him to the pleasure he took in that dancer. "I regret it, you know." My mouth is dry, the words hard to say. "Not being...willing...to give you what you want. But that doesn't mean I'm not grateful to you."

Of its own accord, my hand reaches across the table to take his own, the one with his envelope ring. Absently, I stroke it, a mixture of fondness and sorrow easing me into the next part. "Whether you believe it or not, you matter to me. I'm alive because of you. I'm alive and content, and I want *you* to be content, too, which is why..." I take a shallow breath. "I want to try harder for you. For the both of us."

His chair creaks, the noise sharp. Gaston looks stricken, milk-white under his bluish beard. "I've no words, except those to dispel this other rumor. That woman you saw me with—she is my former sister-in-law. Not only would it have been immoral to bed her, but considered incestuous under English law. I did no such thing."

I'm dumbfounded. "Parvati's sister?"

"Her name is Indira. She arranged the entertainment for the ball, as a favor to me."

"So, you didn't kiss her."

"On the cheek only, when I escorted her to her carriage."

I hold back a sob, confused and mortified and something else I don't understand. I've just accused Gaston of terrible things—of being a murderer, an adulterer. By listening to rumor, I've built the image of a villain around him, a beast that takes what it wants and tears out women's hearts. I imagined him tearing out *my* heart.

I almost tore out his, in my nearness to Henry.

I drop my head in my hands. "I'm a wicked, horrid girl."

Gaston reaches across the table, pulling my hands from my face. "No, *mon amour*. You are young—it's true—but you're no girl. You have a strong mind and a will to act for yourself. This spirit, trying as it may be to my passions, is what I admire most in you." He holds my attention like he held my hand at the opera, the moment ours and ours alone. My tears flow, and he wipes them away with his thumbs. "Beatrice, you are the first of my wives to have ever voiced your desires to me, and I thank you for it. Your veracity moves me in ways I've scarcely felt."

He looks at me like he adores me, and the mood shifts between us. I marvel at my own honesty, at its power to bring out his understanding, even amplifying his passion for me as he waits, with bated breath, for me to kiss him.

I do.

I give Gaston a kiss deeper than I've yet known or experienced. I allow it to linger and play, to explore the texture of his mouth, his beard. I feel my heart hasten in time with his own and the thrill it excites in my depthless spaces. This is when my fear begins, when I start to tighten and resist the beckoning warmth because it feels foreign and shameful. But for just a moment I push through my hesitancy to invite a pleasure that *I* control. I control when it starts, when it ends. It ends when I feel his fingers start to unknot my bodice from my skirt. I'm not being untruthful when I say I want to try harder for him, but with pleasure this powerful, I also want to take my time.

I pull Gaston's hands away but kiss him again to show it's not a rejection, just a redirect. A boyish smirk comes into his eyes, and he wiggles his eyebrows, breaking into laughter.

I press my lips together, fighting a smile that's part bashfulness, part exhilaration. I kissed him without prompt or concern—I just acted. Because it felt natural and...I wanted it. I wanted the indulgence of his mouth against mine, this heady rush that comes afterwards. I wanted it for *me*, not just for him.

During the kiss, I'd made my way into his lap. I stand now, brushing my hands down my skirt, his eyes following my every movement with rapt attention. I've rendered him speechless, gripping a napkin in his hand like it's all he can do to keep from ravishing me right here on the table. Appreciating this Herculean effort, I retake his hands, running my thumbs along the wedding band on his left, the envelope ring on his right. His present, his past. If I'm ever to be the wife he desires, I need to know more about him, though I won't ask him to relive what hurts him.

"I'd like to visit Ami Rose today, if you'd allow it."

Gaston frowns at this, but I hold my chin upturned, uncompromising. He's explained away the rumor of his alleged murderousness easily enough, but I need to know for sure—because his life depends on it. The obsessive determination in Mr. Haskell's eyes was a warning: I've underestimated him and the depths he'll sink to get what he wants. Wealth, power, dominance. Haskell wants to possess me because he hates me, the daughter of his enemy past, the wife of his enemy present. I'm simply a pawn, but I'll do whatever it takes to outmaneuver him.

After a moment of dissatisfied silence, where Gaston weighs whether to fight or offer me freedom, he nods his assent. "But return to me before dark."

Hooded with ivy, Ami Rose's graystone cottage roosts on the edge of Kearsney Wood, where the orchard lies, a scroll of smoke puffing from the chimney. Tawny shutters peek through cords of wisteria, flower boxes overflowing beneath the windows. She putters in her garden, which is populous with foxgloves, coralbells, and blue bearded iris. A collie barks, hearing hooves clop across the bridge, over the rill trickling through the yard.

"How like a queen you look!" Ami exclaims, kissing

my forehead the instant my feet touch ground. "Ooh, look at my hands—filthy." She runs them down her dress, smirched with mud at the knees. But even caked in dirt, Ami Rose is what Gaston would call a Breathless Beauty. I understand why he was once infatuated with her. "How was the ball?"

"Tedious," I say, with an eye-roll. As I pet her frolicsome dog, Millie, my manner dampens. "I wish you could have been there."

"So do I, dear. Gaston holds a grudge like a Roman Emperor. *Eternally*."

"I wanted to invite you, Ami. Please know that."

"I *do*. Truly, there's no offense."

Mist rises from the road, encroaching on the flowers. "Dreary weather," she says, shuddering. "It was like this the last night I saw Benjamin, before he disappeared." She wanders far into the memory, getting lost, tangled in the brambles of distorted re-imaginings. But she finds her way again along the bread trail of the present. She shivers. "Let's get inside."

Ami's modest parlor doubles as her kitchen, with a stove in the far corner and a glowing hearth next to that. Herbs, hung to dry on the rafters, permeate the room with savory smells, mingling with the sweet redolence of daisies furbishing her table.

"So," she says, pumping water into the kettle and dropping it onto the woodstove. "How is the Old Wolf?"

"He's...tolerable, actually." I unpack the basket, avoiding her skeptical look.

The dimming hearth diverts her attention; exhausted logs spark and split under the weight of the new and crumble to ashes. "I knew his first wife, you know," she says.

I still, a pot of jam suspended in my hand. "What was she like?" I'd meant to broach the subject slowly, forgetting how adept Ami Rose is at reading everyone's intentions. She knows I came for a story.

She beams. "She was the most beautiful thing I'd ever seen. Exotic and delicate like a lotus blossom. When she looked at you, it was like she saw—not only to your soul, but *past* it—into your true being. That part hidden even to you, known only to the universe. *Karma*, I believe she called it. She was enchanting." The kettle cries out, and she transfers the hot water into a teapot with a chipped spout. "It's a shame her family didn't approve."

"What do you mean?" I settle into an armchair with my tea and a plate of muffins with jam. Ami Rose does the same, seating herself in a rocker. The mist from outside finds cracks in the doorframe, sneaking its way in to settle at our feet.

"She was engaged to a wealthy Brahmin when Gaston met her. His family had money, but not like the Brahmin. Gaston was able to win her with his charm, and they eloped. Her family disowned her."

"All of them? Gaston said she had a sister, Indira. They must have been close."

"I don't know anything about that. My knowledge of her family tree is limited."

I nibble my muffin, thinking. "She loved him?" I finally ask. With all these rumors being dispelled one by one, I wonder if I'm wrong about Parvati, too. All this time, I've imagined her as a woman pressured into a contract. I thought she'd reclaimed herself, but perhaps she was pressed by her family to leave Gaston for the Brahmin. Her loyalties were split, and she had to choose.

"Yes, she loved him. You could see it in the way she clutched his arm when he escorted her, or how she hid herself in his shadow at social gatherings. People treated her like some artifact for Gaston's private exhibits, but she was a woman with spirit and influence. He loved her. Zealously."

Wistful, Ami breathes in the steam from her tea. "Gaston was so different then. Indelibly jolly, and wonderful company at parties. He whistled—can you imagine it?" I try to. "And then one day he was called away to an excavation in the East somewhere, and when he came back, it was like he hadn't come back at all. What I mean to say is, he'd changed. He wasn't the gentleman we all knew. He'd grown cold, even to Parvati."

Despite the size of the fire and closeness of the room, I shudder. My mind travels back to the Louvre and its exhibit of Egyptian Antiquities, where Gaston told me the first of many magical, outlandish tales. Could that have been the expedition that changed him, that left him cold? He'd said the tomb had been cursed, which I took to be a metaphor for something real and dangerous, like raiders or pestilence. Gaston relives his stories even as he tells them, but I wonder if he embellishes the good while wrapping the bad up in riddles. Rumors abound in his life because he cultivates them, secretly reveling in the attention scandal brings. With one exception, I think.

"Parvati," I say, "did she leave him for the Brahmin?"

"I can't say for certain." Bundling a stole around her shoulders, Ami Rose rocks complacently in her chair. "But if she did, it was after Gaston's affections for her had faded."

The encroaching mist seems to have seeped into my brain; I'm having trouble thinking past it. If Gaston has changed, as Ami says, it isn't in his love for Parvati. To this day, he aches for his Indian flower. He has never stopped loving her.

"What about his other wives?"

*Did Gaston worship them as he did Parvati?*

Ami pauses her rocking, her sagacious, downturned eyes crimping at the corners. She understands my need to know the women who came before me. I need to know why he chose them. Why he chose *me*.

"I know only that one of them was an aristocrat," she says. "French, like him. And that the other two came from humble English families." This I knew as well. I have more questions, like which of those wives immediately preceded me and how long their marriages to Gaston lasted, but Ami Rose stops me with her hand. "That is all I know, nothing more. After declining his proposal, I moved to London to be a governess. Those women came after my time."

Disappointed, I pick at the crumbs of my muffin.

Ami's spent. She rests her eyes, continuing her gentle pitch to and fro. But I have one more question for her. I ask it carefully. "Ami Rose, have you ever been in love?"

"Once," she says, her smile falling. "But it was just a dream."

"A dream?"

"I taught school to her children."

A thick brume of silence falls over the parlor, and I imagine the daisies wilting imperceptibly in their vase. Interest, more than shock, holds my thoughts. That's why she's never married, why she rejected Gaston's own proposal. She wouldn't have loved him, or any man.

Ami's eyes creep open. If I once looked like porcelain to her, she now appraises me as if I were diamond. "You are in a precarious situation, Beatrice. You may believe you owe Gaston everything, but you don't. Your body, your heart, they are your own to give, and only ever for your happiness. One might call that selfish, but I call it brave."

I want be brave. Brave like Parvati, who loved despite opposition, reclaiming herself when her marriage went cold. Brave like my mother, who dove into love heart-first, fiercely and forever loyal. And brave like Ami Rose, who knows who she is and what she wants, living every day for herself.

Gaston's other wives must have been brave, too, to face a wolf and love him.

The question is, can I?

# CHAPTER 23
# WE REGRET

June sails toward us on a falcon's wings. Henry estimates he'll finish the fresco by then, and with each sunset comes our inevitable parting. Ever since our near-kiss the night of the ball, I've tried to keep my distance from him, though his persistence has yet to wane. Each day, I find a dogwood blossom tucked into the cushions where I sit—on the far side of the library, near the windows, with my back to him. My modeling as Juliet is finished, but Henry insists his fondness for me is not. I've asked him not to push it, and he has obliged, if reluctantly.

Mr. Crawley announces the arrival of a guest, Mr. Mitchell, come with his briefcase. My stomach lurches at the sight of him—afraid he's here on Mr. Haskell's behest. But my fears assuage when he shakes Henry's hand.

"He's here to see me," Henry says, slapping the solicitor's shoulder like they're best mates. Together, they look like my brothers. Spirited. Steadfast. Loyal to a fault. I can only imagine what mischief they'll get up to.

"You know each other?" I ask.

"Only just."

"We met at your lovely party," Silas adds. "I've offered Henry my services in the search for this mysterious benefactor of his."

I raise an eyebrow at Henry as he grins, unaware that he has a splotch of paint on his nose. Silas makes a swiping motion to alert him, and I stifle my laugh. Henry takes out his handkerchief to wipe the spot away.

"I came to Dover for employment as much as to find my benefactor," he says. "But the job is almost over, and I'm running out of time."

"Actually, it's the job that might lead us to him." We follow Silas as he heads to the writing desk near the bookcases. He clicks open his briefcase and shuffles through a stack of papers until he finds the one he needs, showing it to us.

"It's a financial contract," I say, studying the document.

"That's correct. This is a copy of the contract Henry's benefactor used to secure his place at the Academy. But there's something odd about it, a stipulation that's unusual for an anonymous educational endowment." Silas underlines a sentence with his finger as Henry and I both lean in to look. "This line appears to be a caveat of the gift. It states the money is to be released to the Academy only on the grounds that, upon graduation, Henry must accept employment under the benefactor, who is always to remain anonymous."

Henry pushes his hand through his hair, mussing it. "But that means any one of my previous employers could be him. That's well over a dozen since I've graduated."

Silas frowns. "There's more. Should you decline to take the job offered by your benefactor, the Academy will strip you of your degree at his word."

"Could they do that?" I ask, astonished.

"They could, and they'd hardly lose a wink of sleep over it. This endowment is a substantial sum of money. The Academy would have been hard-pressed to go without it." Silas looks at Henry, tension in both men's faces. "This whole agreement, it's like playing Russian roulette. Almost as if your benefactor required some leverage over you."

I grab Henry's sleeve, not wanting my theory to be true. "Gaston? You said you'd heard rumor that your benefactor was here, in Dover."

"He's not the only one to have offered me employment in this town." Henry looks ill, like he'll vomit. I direct him to sit down. "Mr. Crane commissioned me last week to paint a series of political advertisements. He's heard of the East India Company's demise, and he means to exploit it. But that doesn't explain why he would fund an orphan's education for ten years."

Silas rubs his chin, thinking. "My uncle is a known philanthrope but also a cutthroat. He'll just as easily demolish an orphanage as finance it. He's a collector of talents, of assets he can control. He could most certainly be our man."

We're silent, each of us trapped in his, and her, mind of horrors. How cruel this world is to allow the exploitation of people, of children, proffering opportunity only to warp it for their use in some wealthy man's deleterious schemes. Henry's crushed, his whole life a turn in someone's game.

The desire to take his hand—to comfort him—weighs on me. I fold my arms instead, pushing aside these feelings of adulation for a boy whose only fault was falling in love with me.

Henry and Silas leave together, taking the next steps of their plan with them. Henry won't stop searching until he's facing the man responsible for saving his life, whether for good or for ill.

Gaston finds me as they leave. He's been rending his beard, parts of it twisted and knotted up. Yesterday, a courier delivered news that the East India Company had been disbanded in India and reabsorbed under the purview of the English crown. Gaston said not to worry; he'd been offered the role of a Queen's agent. Essentially, he's under new management. If I'm not supposed to worry, then why does he look so upset?

"My love." He takes my shoulders, and the fixity of his grip fills me with dread.

"What is it?"

His eyes flick to the hall, where Alice is polishing the woodwork. "To the garden."

We sit on the bench next to the bubbling Janus fountain, a sea breeze rustling the flowers. The irises seem especially blue today, funnily reminding me of Gaston's beard.

He smothers my hands in his. "Beatrice." Already, my gut twists, and he's only spoken my name. In a rare moment, he struggles finding his words. "There has been a rebellion. Your brother... He is dead."

I blink at him.

"What?"

Gaston slips a piece of paper into my hands. A telegram.

DOVER, VIA CALAIS
20 MAY 1857

TO THE FAMILY:

WE REGRET TO INFORM YOU CORNET SIMON TILNEY OF THE BENGAL LIGHT CAVALRY WAS KILLED IN

ACTION 10 MAY IN THE SERVICE OF HER MAJESTY THE QUEEN VICTORIA—

I rip the paper in half, in half again, not bothering to read the rest of its contrived condolences. I choke for air, tears constricting my throat. He promised. Simon promised they'd be safe.

It hits me: "Byron—"

"He's missing."

I curl inward. Something ruptures inside me, dispelling an alluvion of sharp-edged sobs so great it feels like it's *me* who's died. Not my brother. *Please, no, not my brother.*

Gaston cradles me as I wail, a terrible sound. "Not Simon! Not my brother."

I bunch bergamot-scented fabric in my hands, arms tightening around me. The sun beats down as droplets splash into my hair, and I pull away to see my husband, crying for me. Gaston's storm-black eyes drip and run and shine with tears. I've never realized—never cared to know—how fatigued and worn those deep-set eyes make him look.

And his freckles. Though they're just blurs, I brush his cheekbones to test their realness. Gaston has a whole shore of the lightest freckles, brought out now by the sun. Mementoes from his days in the desert, digging in the tombs of pharaohs.

They're beautiful.

I desire so suddenly to lose myself in him that I pull him to his knees in the dirt, clutching his jacket to keep him close. I wish to feel anything besides this pain, this rawness at losing Papa and now my brother. But my passion overwhelms me, a converted tide of desperation for comfort—but then rage about my brother—and I'm shaking so much that I push Gaston away in frustration—in fractured, ineffable self-pity. I want and I don't want. I hate myself for both. I bury my face in my knees, unable to face Gaston's bewilderment, his anger as he leaves me there to cry. He kicks at the dirt, yelling French obscenities as he tramps into the house.

Folding myself among the irises, I watch the watery, haunting vision of a scarab land on my fist. Fluorescent blue and phantomlike, it appears to wink at me, vanishing the moment I realize it's not real.

Meerut, India

9 May 1857

*Beatrice—*

*Please excuse the brevity of this letter, but in light of what has just happened, I don't imagine I could write more. My hand shakes. My pen judders with rage and disgust. I must start from the beginning.*

*On the morning of 24 April, the garrison was on the parade ground. 90 of our sepoy brethren from the 3rd regiment were ordered by the lieutenant colonel to perform their drills using the tallow cartridges. All but 5 of them refused. Today, those 85 men awaited their court-martial. In front of their comrades, they were stripped of their ranks and their uniforms. Ferocious words shot like arrows from all sides—the condemned, berating their fellows for not defending them—and the guilty, ridiculing the shackled and the shamed. Those men will face ten years imprisonment for their beliefs.*

*I sorrow for them. I hate their enemies as my own. I realize I am that enemy—a Briton, who has invaded their country. And I despise myself for it. What is this good I have committed myself to achieve?*

*Tomorrow is Sunday, the day of rest.*

*I'll not rest. Somehow, I will prove myself a man of peace.*

*—Simon*

## CHAPTER 24
# TIME TO WAKE UP

Simon's final letter to us lies crumpled on the drawing room floor. Anna's weeping is soundless; she's cried a lifetime of tears and can't shed any more for ink-smeared words. Yet there's something more she cries for. Something she, in her reluctance, presses back with her palm.

Like a hand to a skittish horse, I speak calmly to her. "What is it, Anna?"

"Simon," she says.

"You're lying."

"I'm not." She hiccups. Frustration hums under my skin. She's as stubborn as me; that's how people tell we're sisters. But Papa had his tricks with us. Like a serpent charmer, he could always lure the truth from our mouths.

He'd begin by making us laugh.

"Do you remember when Byron lost his shoes in the

Dour," I start, "and he was mortified of telling Mamma for fear she'd punish him by making him ask Lilly Coons to dance at the Culpeppers' ball?"

The vestige of a smile. "He bribed Simon into giving him his."

"And a few days afterward they turned up at the sluicegate—"

"—dredged in mud," we say together, giggling.

"Lilly Coons was never happier than when Byron stepped on her feet," Anna says, her smile in full form. She holds it there, and I hold mine, and we let the moment ring with our cheer. But moments are fickle things, always moving, never kind enough to stop.

"Sisters shouldn't keep secrets," I say. "There's something you're not telling me, Anna, and I must know what it is. How else am I to keep you and Mamma safe?" *There* —she looked away—she turned away when I said—"It's Mamma, isn't it?"

I pull her hand from her mouth and she blurts, "I found blood on her pillow this morning."

Blood.

That red word spills across my vision, washing the rugs and the walls with death. I once was bucked from Hastings's saddle and landed back-down in a patch of hard dirt. I thought my lungs had ruptured and I'd never breathe again, but this feeling, this lack of breath, bucks me tenfold.

At the ball she was fine—*she was fine*—Mamma was fine.

"If she dies, I'll be all alone."

That stirs me, draws in air. "I'll never let that happen, Anna. Mamma won't die, but if she..." *If she does...* She won't. "You'll live here, with me. I'll keep you safe."

"For how long?" My sister's face is scarlet, her mood escalating to distress. "Indefinitely? Would I be your captive, shut up in a tower and never seen again?"

*What?*

I'd laugh at this—this nonsensical, adolescent melodrama—if she didn't speak so vehemently. "What are you talking about?"

"You!" she shouts. "You and your sheltering. Your smothering and—and *mothering*. If Mamma dies, you'll take her place and then I'll never get married."

Now I laugh, a full-bellied belt of incredulity. "That's what these tears are for? You want to get married? You're too young!"

"There! You see? *Mothering*. I'll be sixteen next week. The age of consent."

I shake my head, stunned and a little sick. "Oh, Anna. You don't even know what that means."

She stands, her skinny legs pushing back the settee a few inches. "I'm sorry you don't like your husband," she says hotly. "But I will like mine, and I won't be bitter about it. Unlike you, I *want* a man to love and protect me. I want a man like Mr. Swain."

I must have misheard her.

"Henry? He's the man of your affections?"

Anna's smitten; sentiment-dripping words about dancing with him, smiling at him—and him smiling at her—shrivel into the background of our conversation. And in the foreground, bristling skin. Fulminant jealousy popping, fizzing underneath. He danced with *me*, smiled at *me*. It was me he almost kissed. If I weren't married, he would have.

But I am married. Until death.

How can Henry waste his life pining after me when he could have Anna now?

She's blathering on about something, but I'm barely listening to her. "...We would rent the Rose Residence on St. James Street, and our children would attend the school there, and play together with yours—"

"*My* children?" I stand, gaining height on her. I pace to the window, seeing into the garden to the dogwood tree where Henry drew me sleeping. He dared not wake me from my dreams.

I wish he had.

"I don't intend on having any children." My voice has grizzled into its darkest pitch. "And you shouldn't either, not for a long while. You're too young for Mr. Swain. For *any* man."

Silence looms. And in that silence, Anna gathers up her dislike and her hurtful words, low and harsh. "I wish

Papa were here. He wouldn't hate Mr. Swain like you do. He'd want me to be happy."

I turn on her. "If Papa were here, I wouldn't have needed to surrender my life for an ungrateful sister, or for a mother who'd rather die than protect her daughters from the men of this world!"

I gasp, my hands pressed to my mouth. Too late to keep it in.

I didn't mean it.

*But I did.*

It's not her fault.

*But it feels like it.*

Resentment has been a canker in my mouth as I've watched Anna bloom into the young woman I've wanted to be, happily naïve to the expectations of marriage. She doesn't see how many doors might be shut, locked to her the moment she says I do. She doesn't see how trapped she'll be. Trapped like I am trapped.

She trembles. Her tears shake her like earth, and she flees, and I chase her, cursing myself for my venom and cruelty. I'm a callous sister. Her wails percuss off the walls, torturing me, and I know she'll never forgive me.

She runs from the house as Gaston enters it. We crash into each other.

"*Que s'est-il passé?*" he says. "What's happened?"

How can I explain to him that I've ruined everything? That I've realized the futility of the marriage that was meant to save Mamma, but now that she's dying will have been for nothing? I've suffered all of this for *nothing*!

"Speak to me. I'm your husband."

What meaning is there in the word? Anna believes a husband is a man who loves unconditionally. His marriage vows say he worships and endows. That's his duty—a duty I've resented. I've barely allowed Gaston to enter my life, to worship me as he did his first wife.

And here he stands, having waited months for my acceptance.

For my love.

I fall into him, pressing my face into the warmth of his neck, delving for the balm I sought when he told me Simon had died and Byron was missing. Even if it was desperate and fraught, he faded my pain. He made me feel like I was all that mattered.

I want to feel that again.

"She's dying. Mamma is—oh, Gaston."

His fingers comb through the curls rolling down my back. The motion soothes me, drawing me deeper into his heat. "*Paix, mon amour.* Peace."

I whuffle into his vest. "There must be something you can do."

With my head against him, I hear his heart accelerate. The silence crackles strangely, my skin needling with dreadful anticipation. There's something wrong, subversive, about the pause between his breath and his answer.

"No. But there is something you can do."

My whimpering quits, and I stare up at him, into his eyes so black the blackness consumes that speck of light Papa told me was a person's soul. I can't see it, and that stirs up my fear anew.

Gaston's beard pulses with the fluorescent, fiery blue of an Egyptian curse.

"It's apparent you will not love me without some inducement," he says, but it's not his voice. It's the guttural, ensnarling ultimatum of a wolf. "Because of this, I have no choice but to barter for your affections."

*Barter?*

I untwist from him, and he pursues my backward movements. I step, he steps—a chase, a trap. I'm pushed into the alcove of a window, his mass of muscle blocking the outlet.

"You have my word your mother will receive all the care she requires from the most esteemed physician. But in return, you must—"

"Don't say it." I feel every vein in my body pulsing to the point of pain. Irrationally, I never believed this moment would come. He's making me choose: my family's preservation, or my own.

With my every refusal Gaston has withdrawn himself, never subjecting me to his desires except for that night, when his own passions overpowered him. Was that his true nature—his actual self—as I see now before me? Or is this man in front of me enchanted, a wolf in human skin?

"This can't be real," I utter. "This can't be you."

"Show me your devotion." The wolf reaches for my face.

I despise him.

He fists his hand at my rebuff, bringing it coolly to his side. His voice is ice. "I expect your answer by sunset."

The wolf moves aside, and I spring out of his trap like a hare. I sprint to the stables. I unbolt Hastings's stall, mount him bareback, and spur him to run.

ELMSWOOD SHOUTS BLUE, bluebells everywhere, blanketing the floor. It's said the flowers ring out with a summons only the fey folk can hear, but if that's true, my keening drowns them out.

I slip from Hastings's back to the roots of the tree where I posed for an artist's dreams, and I batter my fists against its trunk. There's poison in my heart, spreading through me, spreading lies, and I veer numb at its persuasion. Whether man or beast, I can't hope to win if Gaston holds my every resource. No matter how far I run, I will always turn back to him.

"Beatrice?" The voice startles me, though I know it immediately. I pick up and struggle away from it. "Wait!" Henry grabs me but I beat against his chest. He wraps me in his arms, and I *melt* into him.

These affections I've had for Gaston are daggers to the

heart for all the pain they've caused me, even now, as they invoke my shame for the treachery I'm about to commit. Eternities seem to pass in Henry's arms. I become a girl no longer scared of her own desires. Because the tighter he holds, the more adamantly I know this is where I feel safest.

Time will not allow me forever. But it might give me this moment.

"Kiss me."

Perplexed, he lets go. I hold onto his shirt, saying it again. "Kiss me, Henry." My eyes rivet onto his. "*Take* me."

If I am to lose my innocence, it won't be to Gaston's demon—his wolf—his accursed doppelganger. It will be to the man whose love is guileless and giving, unselfish and pure. The man who's proved himself capable of governing his basest passions, respecting my power when no other man has. "It's you, Henry. I choose *you*."

His eyes—his lovely, adoring eyes—flit about in their sockets like moths desiring to land on a flame. But getting too close, singe their wings. Writ on his face there's conflict and want, and there's fear. Fear of consequence, scandal, sin. Fear of *me*.

He won't touch me.

He raises his hands, warding me off. "I can't."

"You don't want me."

"That's not true. I want you—now, tomorrow, everyday—but I will not take you. Beatrice." He swallows, and it sounds like he's swallowing sand. "It isn't right.

Again and again, you've reminded me of that. I'm finally listening to you."

Aching with their grip on him, my hands slacken and fall to my sides. The woods don't breathe. Shrews rustle in the cowslips and birds eavesdrop in the trees, but there are no other sounds. No wind to blow me away.

"My mother's dying." The words slit the air. "The only way Gaston will help is if I... He wants me to..." I seal my eyes, tears leaking through.

But Henry understands. His voice goes hard. "Don't do it."

"I've lost a father and a brother. I can't lose my mother, too."

"If he loved you, he wouldn't force you."

"He's not forcing me."

"He's *coercing* you!" Henry takes my shoulders but rethinks it, and I want to scream *touch me!* Touch me. If you don't touch me, I'll wither. If you don't hold me, I'll fade.

My coarse name is like a song in his mouth. "Beatrice, I know I have no right to ask you this, and I wish—I wish I could save you from this anguish. But please, wait for me. Wait for me, as I will wait for you."

He's right.

*This is anguish.*

My soul has wrested itself from my body, and I feel...nothing.

*This can't be real.*

I must be dreaming.

*Sit with me,* I say in this dream. I sit at the roots of the beech tree with Henry, and he tells me again to wait for him, to wait for him. I see his open sketchbook neglected in the mead of bluebells, but there aren't any pictures. Instead, there are words, elegant words in an elegant hand. They're Shakespeare's words. *Read them to me.* And the sonnet's serene cantillations play like an aria inside my head.

*Now see what good turns eyes for eyes have done:*
*Mine eyes have drawn thy shape, and thine for me*
*Are windows to my breast, where through the sun*
*Delights to peep, to gaze therein on thee;*
*Yet eyes this cunning want to grace their art:*
*They draw but what they see, know not the heart.*

CHAPTER 25

# At the Moonlight's Edge

I wear the same nightgown Gaston laid out for me on our wedding night. The slippery silk, ephemeral lace, glides over my skin like mist along a river. Spellbinding. Desolate.

I wait for him in the darkness of our bedchamber, my hair undone, my legs drawn under me at the window seat. The sun takes its final bow, making way for the moon as it rises to its mark above the sea.

I imagine Gaston's shadow stretching toward me in the shape of a wolf, black fur on blacker night, his impatience pawing at my insecurity even as my dread slips away. I've made my decision and will not shrink from it.

An azure glow evaporates off of him, but I dare not think it's the beast retreating. He waits at the moonlight's edge, the only barrier between us. "Well?" he says.

I rise, my movements lacking vitality or forethought.

I'm caught up in quicksand, my skin liquid hot as I cap the distance of the room. Gaston wears his night-robe of Indian silk, the cord loosened about his waist and baring everything down to his navel. My tongue dries at the sight of all his skin, flocked with hair like fur. Like fur because he's a wolf, and he'll devour me.

He promises a gentle devouring.

*Le petit mort* is what the French call it. *The little death.* That moment when pleasure is too much and too little all at once. That breath taken when there's barely any air at all, and your head is high, up in the treetops.

I recall the burning I felt in his den, by the firelight. I feel the phantoms of his touches and they *were* gentle. But they were also hungry. I was hungry, too.

A shiver dances down my back. My body *wants* this pleasure. But my mind, my emotions, know that bedding a man is far more complicated than feeling his hands, his heat. Ami Rose said the pleasure should be mine as well as his, and I should want it with enthusiasm. Yet how swiftly want can change when panic creeps in.

An electric quiver jumps from my thigh to my foot, and I take the final step, shattering the division between us. "Well," he says again, a welcoming purr.

I kiss him. Softly, sweetly. And then I step back into the moonlight, a single word vibrating on my tongue stronger than it's ever been before. "No."

Not now. Not like this. I learned something from Henry even as he shattered all my hopes: courage can mean denying yourself when the moment's not right, stepping back from your desires until they come into focus. I want Gaston as a man, not a wolf. I want to believe him—the amulet, the whispers, the impossible sands blowing underneath the chamber door. I want to believe in his curse, if only because it justifies his willfulness. Gaston entered a tomb of treasures as a good man but returned from it cold. Something real and vanquishable changed him, and I want to change him back.

Gaston pushes forward until the moon illumines every rill and valley of his abdomen, and my breath catches at the beauty, the allure, of him. "If that's your answer—"

"It is."

The curse works its way through him as a flame of blue, his eyes ablaze with lazuline. Fully transformed, the wolf works his tongue against his cheek, and I brace myself, ready to defend my body if he tries to force his way in. He will have to destroy me before I break.

The wolf clamps his jaws, straining against the champing of ferocious, wife-devouring teeth. Sparks leap from his beard, illusions vanishing as they hit the floor. His walking stick—the one with the beetle trapped in amber—jumps from his hand, and he stumbles forward. I catch his shoulders, helping him to his knees as he clutches at his heart. His breaths come in labored bursts, his head falling onto my shoulder, and I hold him there.

Until his chest begins to move evenly again. Until his curse fades into obsolescence.

The moment is incomprehensibly long. I barely breathe throughout the length of Gaston's convulsions, his tormented howls, his battle with his wolf. Pain registers in my palms, and I peel my fingers away to reveal bloody half-moons. Sitting up, Gaston looks at them, looks at me, with exhausted eyes.

He releases a sigh of exertion like a beast of burden lying down to die. His irises, a moment ago ghostly blue like his beard, now darken to their bottomless black pupils. "You disdain me," he says miserably. "All of them did."

His admission surprises me, my sorrow matching his. "That's not true. Parvati loved you." The others did, too, they must have. How could they not love him when he fights so valiantly against his darkest self?

He doesn't respond, numb to everything but this pain inside him. And even while his throbbing desire to claim my body visibly bewitches him, I reach out in one last, foolhardy concession for his mercy. "I don't know whether I'm talking to you or your curse," I tell him. "All I know is that I want to cure you of this wretchedness."

His breath is a warm puff against my face. "I'd hoped you would be different from my other wives. Indeed, you are. You are like a spark, impossible to crush. Once pressed, you spit flame. You spurn me with your every rejection and yet I—" His voice breaks. "And yet I am in awe of you."

Validation for living. For being. Gaston uncovers my deepest need for acceptance of who I am, a girl with conviction and veracity, who will sacrifice her autonomy to save her family, who will remain true to her heart despite every danger.

Finally, he hears me. He sees me.

He groans. I help him into bed, holding him as he sleeps, and I wonder at it. I am untenably tied to him like Jane to her Rochester—an indisputable truce betwixt my mind and heart. And I know that if this cord between us were to snap, I would actually take to bleeding inwardly.

## CHAPTER 26

# FIND THE KEY

The morning tide licks my toes, travels up my legs. Gaston slept soundly in my arms, but I couldn't, too disturbed by the tumultuous sea clashing against the cliff. I rose around dawn and went outside, though the air nipped at the tips of my ears, my nose.

I've lain here for hours. The sky is gray vastness, pressing down on me as I lie beneath it. The chalky white palisades of Shakespeare cliff bend upside-down to look at me. Not far from me, energetic sanderlings dig their pointed beaks into the wet sand. The braver ones wade into the foam, buffeting their wings to evade the undertow. The relentless forward and backward rush swallows one up, but the bird fights, tirelessly beating against the impulses of moon and tide, only to get caught up in the swills once more.

For the briefest moment, I wonder if Gaston was telling the truth when he said he'd be gentle.

A frigid wave hits the strand and the cold becomes too much to weather. Gritting against stiff joints, I rise. I shake the sand from my dress, my hair, and carry my shoes up the craggy slope to the house.

Dusky light filters through the stained glass in the foyer, muting the colors. The grandfather clock ticks out its diligent time; the Mongolian guards the entrance to that forbidden wing; and the Arabian scimitar smiles its curved, mortiferous smile. Light catches on its shorn point, like bleeding starlight.

The sight is daunting, but I choose to be dauntless. I rue that sword and its smirk. Stalking up to it, I say, "I'm not afraid of you."

Clouds layer the sun, darkening the hall and the scimitar. A peculiar mood, a foreboding, crawls up my skin. I step back, and with that step I come into cognizance: I'm talking to an inanimate object.

A tear squeezes its way to freedom, a sob cracking in my throat. Memories bloom of Gaston's hands on my skin, of every kiss I've freely given him.

"Henry." The name skates from my mouth, unbidden. I'm afraid to see him. Afraid of what he'll do with the gift of my abstinence. He'll worship me for it, throwing his life away as he waits for me to finally be his. As the years pass, his hope will wear his heart raw, as surely as it will wither mine.

He idles in the library by the windows, surveying the sea and the beach where I lay not ten minutes before. He's been watching me, with tormented expressions. They warp his brow, his copious freckles appearing mottled and indistinct. I ache to smooth them, to put them back into place and order.

"Hello," I say, the word a mere shred of air.

Henry's look sweeps over me, searching for the change, the hollowed-out space. "Look at me," he says, but I don't. I can't. "Tell me you didn't."

"I had to," I lie, because if I don't, he'll wait for me forever.

"But you don't love him."

"Does it matter?"

I hear Henry's heart stop beating. Hear the life culled from his lungs and his teeth grinding against each other. But I don't hear him leave.

No. I feel that.

Like a hundred times before, I wander the house, drifting through its halls like a ghost. A tranquil hush rests over Gaston's study, where I breathe in the fusty scents of mahogany and pipe tobacco, the urge to snoop persistent. A drawer was left ajar in his desk. I've learned that if he fears for his privacy he'll send away the servants. I'm alone in this house, Gaston having left for a visit to his bank.

Rumors of murder float through my head. Mr. Haskell's threat to undo me should I refuse to help him exploit Gaston. I'd sooner trust a wolf than a poacher, especially when I'm the prey. I'll prove Gaston is no murderer.

I open the drawer, finding nothing unusual or even interesting. Merely paper and quills and a flash of silver. Lifting away a collection of dusty letters, I reach for the silver plate. A daguerreotype, absent its case.

I recognize at once the image of Parvati. Her tan complexion and sultry, kohl-lined eyes with the glittering Bindi between them could belong to no other beauty than Gaston's first wife. And she is beautiful. Breathlessly so. She's the most beautiful woman I've ever seen.

My features can't compare. Though there are, perhaps, resemblances in the shapes of our eyes, upturned, or in the deep corners of our mouths. Otherwise, I'm nothing like her.

I drop the daguerreotype back into the drawer, the plate clattering against another metal. A key.

A flash of an image: a bedraggled beard and balancing capuchin.

*Look into my eyes.*

*Find the key...*

My actions are swift and automatic. I race with the key to the forbidden chamber, sparing no thought of what the consequence could be or what I'll find. Lost to my curiosity—my hunger to know—I jam the key into the lock. The tumblers move easily, and the door opens of its own accord.

I step into the chamber as if I were an archaeologist entering a tomb. As if I were Gaston, unearthing a curse. In the dampness of the room, whistling with an uncertain breeze, hazy forms take shape in my vision.

A dozen dusty canes collected over the decades.

And the crumpled roll of a discarded Persian rug, eaten through by moths.

## CHAPTER 27
# A PRIZE FOR THE AGES

There's something undeniably comforting about the affection of an animal. His whole backside wagging with enthusiasm, Quincy bounds into my lap as I kneel to spoil him with kisses. "Hello, old boy," I say, rubbing out his rolls of shoulder fat. "I've missed you." He licks my chin and nuzzles into the crook of my arm with a whine. "I see you've missed me, too."

My home feels just as familiar as it did when I left it. Using the servants' entrance, I slip in quietly through the kitchen and up the stairs, kissing Archie and Molly, my old servants, and introducing myself to the new ones, Edith and Thomas. Every room is clean and well-furnished, the pantry stocked, the larder full, not a comfort missing or out of place. The only disturbance comes from the upper floor, from Mamma's sickroom.

"She worsens, Mrs. Dumas," Dr. Field says by way of

greeting as I ascend the stairs into the hallway. Much like his brother-in-law, Mr. Crane, Dr. Field is a balding, stocky man who dresses a mite too extravagantly for his profession, his stethoscope hung next to a *checkered* cravat rather than the professional white. He carries a multi-bladed fleam and a shallow bowl for bloodletting.

My own blood surges. "Are you sure draining her is the solution?" The question is snappish and hard, disputing his skill.

"Venesection has been a practicable treatment for centuries," he argues, adjusting his rectangular spectacles. "Respected, even, by the Greeks. You'd do well to trust in its science."

"And you would do well to address my wife with more deference." I turn with a start. Gaston steps out of Mamma's bedroom, closing the door behind him. "You're too late, Beatrice." My heart stops. But then, "She has just fallen asleep."

Asleep, but not dead.

"I don't understand," I say. "Why are you here?"

"If I may answer her, Dumas." Dr. Field moves us away from the door, speaking low. "There is a place, a sanatorium in Bavaria where I've heard of some success treating maladies like your mother has. There, her diet will be improved. She'll have plenty of fresh air and will be encouraged to exercise." A glance at Gaston. "But it will be costly, which is why I did not prescribe it before."

"The cost is no concern," Gaston says.

The physician nods, and they shake hands, Dr. Field smiling uncomfortably as Gaston grips him too tightly. "I'll write to them immediately." He sees himself out.

Gaston and I stand awkwardly together in the hall. He makes to leave, but I pull him aside, into what used to be mine and Anna's bedroom. I shut the door behind us.

The original furnishings have been left untouched, including the two beds, woven rug, and lace curtains. I cringe at the dried violets in a vase by the window, given to me one birthday by the baker's son, with the scribbled misspellings of a love note. The note I tossed, but the flowers looked too lovely to throw away. Now, they just look faded.

I avoid Gaston's look. "You rescinded your threat."

"The man who made it was pitiless and desperate."

"But not cursed."

It's all been a fantasy. The psychosis of my own traumatic fear, playing with my mind. I saw inside Gaston's chamber, and there was nothing except dust and canes and a moth-eaten rug. I unrolled that rug, finding no bones but the exoskeletons of insects and one glutted arachnid. I've deceived myself, letting my imagination overpower my reason for far too long.

Gaston drops onto the nearest bed—what once was *my* bed—and wrings his jade-tipped cane in his hands. It looks painful, like he's burning his skin with the friction. I take the cane from him and prop it against the windowsill by the violets. He then fiddles with his envelope ring, twisting it around his index finger.

I sigh, sinking next to him. “She was everything to you,” I say, feeling the reverence of the phrase. “She was your first love, and none of the wives that came after her could fill your emptiness. Including me. I can’t give you what you need.”

“And what is it you think I need?” he says gloomily. “Love? I despise the word and all it has caused me to suffer. Love is fickle and short-lived. Love is a curse.” He leans over his knees, clutching his skull with hooked fingers. “A curse that will not end. No, Beatrice. You cannot give me what I need because the curse will not allow it. You are not the one.”

*He hopes you will be the one.*

*The one with the key.*

*The key to his heart.*

A nauseating knot forms in my stomach. If love is a curse, then there’s no cure for it but tolerance, to keep imbibing its poison until you no longer feel its effects. *Spreading through me, spreading lies.* Yet I’ve never felt more numb than when I’ve *resisted* its persuasion.

I won’t believe it. Love isn’t a curse. It’s a cure.

Needing something to do with my hands, I pluck one of the violets from its brittle bouquet and tuck it into the flower hole of Gaston’s jacket. He catches my hand before I pull away, pressing it to his heart.

"You said I'm like a spark," I whisper, more to myself than to him. *Lord, those eyes.* "All flame but no heat." Veiled and unfathomable. "But a flame can still give light."

His stare is eternity.

"Do you want to know why I chose you?" he asks.

A cool blush creeps over my cheeks. I nod.

"You've heard the rumor that I fancy blue eyes?" I nod again, glancing away. "That rumor is true. Each wife before you had blue eyes, each of different hues. But to understand why I chose them, why I chose you, I must tell you another story."

WITH THE PASSING of summer into winter, dry Etesian winds receded to the damper air, the oppressive heat, and the rise of the river Nile. His heart weighed down with sand and rue, the archaeologist loaded his toolkit into the paddle steamer, pointed north to Cairo. To leave the valley of kings was a bane, but the amulet that lay inside his breast pocket, next to his heart, urged him homeward.

It was a prize for the ages.

And it was his.

Warily, he guarded it from the prying eyes of the Fellahin laborers and his colleagues aboard the steamer, stealing himself into the darkest cabin belowdecks to look upon it. Surely, if those ingrates saw the stone's power, they'd want it for themselves. But the falcon's effigy was meant only for him. A gift from Horus. God of the sky.

The archaeologist would protect it through any means necessary.

From Cairo to Alexandria, he journeyed by barge along the Mahmoudieh canal, to port, where the Mediterranean Sea took him west into England and to home.

*Home.*

Home to his wife.

It was a long voyage, and with every knot and league, his anticipation grew like the land before him. How impatient he was to see her face again, to kiss her in the dark.

Indeed, their reunion rivaled even that of the god Shiva and his consort reincarnate, Sati. The archaeologist kissed his wife with tenderness, between her eyebrows on her Bindi mark of fertile red.

"You will not leave me so long the next time," she admonished him.

"Perhaps there will not be a next time," he said bitterly, and her golden hands went to smooth the rugged hairs of his beard.

"Blue," she said, and it was like a question.

She gasped.

"*Halāhala*!" she cried. "You have swallowed poison!"

He flew to the mirror, peering into it. "The amulet," he whispered, in French so his wife wouldn't understand.

The amulet's sorcery must have been great to manifest physically. But that didn't disturb him. No, it *empowered* him. He would wear his secret with pride, and like Samson, never think to shear off the source of his strength.

With a delusory smile, he turned back to his wife. "It's but the gray of age," he said. "Let it worry you no further."

An obedient wife, she heeded his word. Until a heaviness she couldn't shun grew over their house. She discerned a change in her husband, who'd become rougher in his ways and his love, like an animal had possession of him. She knew an evil spirit dwelt inside his heart, working its iniquity and chaos, and that her husband's soul was in danger of Yama's judgment. And so, on his behalf, she began to pray.

"*Nīlakantha*," she chanted, bathing The Destroyer's icon in a basin of cow's milk. "To Shiva, blue-throated one, dancer of *Tandava* primordial. Subdue my heart, absolve my sins, and bless my husband."

Despite all her prayers, his sickness festered. He took to abandoning their bed in the depths of the night, hiding himself away in a chamber in the forsaken wing of the house. She'd seen this behavior before, in the opium dens where she'd had to hunt for her youngest sister, Indira, and bring her home.

This, Parvati suspected, was not an addiction to any substance of man, but of the gods.

She confronted him one night, having followed him

down to the chamber and the shadows. "Why have you left me all alone?" she demanded. But in his paranoia, his distrust of her intents, her husband shut the door, locking her out of his heart.

She fell into a waste of malaise, the sickness of despair. Where one feels hopelessly lost and believes they can never be recovered.

Until Benjamin.

He was a daguerreotypist. And although she believed it was vanity, she sat for his portraits, his presence replenishing her joy. She listened, fascinated, to his explanations of how he came to capture her image on the silver-faced copper plate.

*First, I must polish the plate with alcohol and rottenstone, the white powder there. Then I buff it with rouge—yes, like your cheeks, your rose-colored cheeks. And then I place it inside the sensitizing box, which is inlaid with iodine crystals. Now for the bromide. And to make it susceptible to the light, I'll slide it into the camera and remove the lens....*

Parvati fancied the reedy tones of Benjamin's voice, hypnotic and soft like a bansuri flute. He reminded her of India, her long-lost home. She wished for his friendship, for his permanence, and soon her wishing acceded to graver things. She wished for a child, which her own husband could not provide. Her wish consumed her, compelling her to vice, and she slipped into the mistake of love.

While in his chamber, the archaeologist suffered. The

amulet burned in his hands as he held it, but he couldn't let go. It had fixed itself to him as an appendage, a parasite, sapping him of his goodness. He understood its vile effects when, in his lowest and most wretched state, he remembered his wife and his love for her.

"Parvati," he lamented, prostrate on the floor. The chamber echoed with twisted laughter. The amulet flared, lashing him with its evil light, and he felt lust and shame and desire and revulsion—all of these at once. But above all, he felt powerful. Impervious. Like he could have anything he wanted, if only he gave in.

It was a wrestle to rival Jesus in the desert, or Siddhartha on the river. Straining against the demon infecting his mind, the archaeologist escaped the chamber that had become his prison. He threw open the window at the end of the claustrophobic hall, his arm hardening to stone even as he raised it to launch the vile talisman into the sea.

He had to win.

*He would not lose his only love.*

A hellish wail broke through his lips. He ruptured his invisible chains, lobbing the amulet into the ocean where it dashed upon the cliff rocks, pieces snapping cobalt fire as they sank beneath the foam.

The demon's release flooded his lungs with air, and the archaeologist sucked it in, his eyes wet, his arms open to the wind. He hadn't realized how long he'd been drowning. And now he was free. He was saved.

And he could return to his wife, having been so long apart from her.

With her name on his lips, the archaeologist—a man reborn—quested through the house in search of her. He heard her laughter scattered over corridors. *The library.* He ran. *The bookshelves.* He wove between them, through their maze of texts and history. But then his legs gave out. As he grasped a shelf to stabilize him, the image before him knifed his heart.

Parvati and the daguerreotypist, Benjamin, *trysted.*

Entwined.

His wife's eyes, once a warm, hazelnut brown, lustered a phosphorescent blue as if magicked. The curse had claimed her, and it would work its evil in her heart as brutally as it had done to every living soul it encountered before.

*Who is this woman?* the archaeologist thought.

Not his wife, faithful and pure, who'd loved him enough to suffer the scorn of her family, to abandon her homeland, to be with him. His *true* wife would never have betrayed him. But she had.

She did.

Well, then. She would be his wife no more.

GASTON BELIEVES. He truly believes the amulet he found was cursed, and that it devastated his life with its chaos.

If he hadn't discovered the antechamber in Pharaoh Seti's tomb, then he'd have returned home to Parvati, and perhaps in some miracle conceived the child they'd yearned for. He could have been happy, if he hadn't pined after such perilous adventure.

"What happened next?" The question cracks, fear irresistible. I choose my words carefully. "When you put her away, divorced yourself, what happened?"

"I recognized the amulet for what it was. A curse, whispering to me, blackening my heart. It had returned. I awoke to a tremendous storm blasting the cliff, and there it was—restored to its whole under my pillow, ablaze with vengeance. It would not be rid of so easily."

Damp with sweat, he loosens his cravat. I help him remove it and open his shirt collar to cool him, feeling my ears heat as his flesh peeks through.

He meets my eyes. "But every shaman will tell you that a curse, no matter how thick or binding, can be broken. I needed only to discover how. So, I went home to Lourmarin, to see my Romani grandmother. People called her a *gitane*—a gypsy—but she was so much more than the sum of her culture. Though I didn't know it until I'd grown.

"When I was a boy, I'd mock her, tease her cages full of birds and upset the careful patterns of her garden. Young fool that I was, I didn't see her gifts for the preter-natural. Long before I boarded the ferry, she saw my return. She told me the hope I clung to was not a fool's hope, but that I could be rescued—*reborn*—in a woman's blue eyes. I needed only search for the hue that matched my curse, and she who held the color in her eyes would be my savior."

Gaston's hand goes to his breast pocket, deliberation pulling at the corners of his mouth. After several seconds of debate, he reaches in, and withdraws a stone.

An amulet.

Called lapis lazuli, the Persian sky stone is a vivid sky-blue with rivulets of pyrite. This has been carved into the image of a falcon. Horus's symbol. God of the sky.

Unlike the amulet in the story, this one doesn't glow, doesn't beat with a blue-white light, and neither whispers nor sings. It's just a stone. Inert. Ineffectual. The color of my eyes.

A miasma of confusion eddies through my head, and I fight to clear it, taking breath after ineffectual breath. It was just a story—a work of fiction told by a husband to titillate his young wife. But even as my hand yearns to stretch out, to feel the sublime relic, I begin again to question everything.

There's drumming in my ears. Puckish laughter, like wild dogs.

"Your eyes are the purest blue I've ever seen." And like on the day Gaston first said those words, the day he asked me to marry him, my body crests hot and cold and hot again.

I don't want to believe in ghosts. In specters, or gods,

or even curses. But I want to believe in Fate. In the power it has to unlock doors, revealing truth.

And the truth is, I was always meant to become Gaston's fifth wife.

## CHAPTER 28
# A MILLION TIMES YES

I knead my hands until they suffer. The truth is a shawl around my shoulders, stitched with apprehension, hemmed in hope. *His* hope. Gaston's hope.

He thinks I'm his rescuer. That I'm the one who'll love him the way he thinks his other wives couldn't.

I can.

I want to. For me, as well as for him.

I kiss him, gasping as his mouth travels instantly to my throat. I push his jacket from his shoulders to unbutton his shirt, where his skin burns beneath my touch. My spark. My light.

"You're certain?" His lips pause above the square of flesh along my shoulder.

The pause is too long, too much.

"Yes," I say.

A million times, yes.

~

He was gentle, like he promised he'd be, and I felt it. That exquisite, rapturous little death.

The sun has wandered close to the horizon. Gaston cinches up my corset, and I retie his cravat. He grins down at me. I blush up at him.

The door opens, and we fly apart, my sister frozen at the threshold.

"We came to see Mamma," I say, glancing guiltily as Gaston shrugs into his jacket. My hair has come loose of its pins; I do my best to smooth it down.

Anna hugs herself, looking mortified, and something else. Her sleeves are wrinkled, a trail of silvery mucus on her bodice. She's been crying—violently. I ask her what's wrong, and her eyes flit to Gaston, too embarrassed to say anything with him in the room.

Ever perceptive, he takes this as his cue to leave. He plants a kiss on my cheek, and I try not to grin, my satisfaction overwhelming.

Anna climbs into her bed fully clothed, boots and all. She pulls the covers over her head.

Her anger with me has yet to subside. I sit on the edge of her bed, not knowing quite what to say or how to say it. An apology doesn't seem good enough.

"I have a gift for you," I say, unhooking a dainty

emerald bracelet from my wrist. "I'm sorry I missed your birthday. I didn't think you wanted to see me, and I didn't want to ruin your day." When she doesn't respond, I hang the bracelet on her bedpost and try again, monitoring my voice so I don't sound like the patronizing mother she resents. "Sisters shouldn't hurt each other like I hurt you. I was wrong to say those awful things. I promised you happiness and I meant it; I still want that for you. I was just...jealous." It stings, admitting it aloud.

"Jealous?" comes Anna's voice, a muffled lump under the blankets.

"Of you. Of your feelings for Henry. You see, I—" My confession scrabbles up my throat, wanting freedom, though the truth is confused and contradictory, considering what I've just done with Gaston. "I care for him deeply."

Slowly, *slowly,* Anna peels back her covers. "You love him?"

"In a way. It shouldn't have been possible, Anna—I hid my heart. I told myself I couldn't love, and I locked it away. But Henry found it. He found it too late."

A tear drips off my jaw, Anna expressionless. I thought she'd cry or rage or curse me, and it scares me that she doesn't. My sister looks as though she barely feels anything at all, like her emotions have all been extracted from her.

My heart squeezes. "What's this?" A splotch of purple on her wrist.

She hides it. "Nothing."

But I grab her hand and push up her sleeve. Bruises. Ghastly bruises on her forearms in the shapes of fingers.

*In the shapes of fingers.*

"Who made these?" I demand. She yanks away, covering the wicked marks. I touch her shoulder, and she winces. There are bruises there, too.

I feel sick, knowing horribly who did this. "Anna, what did he *do*?"

The relinquishing paralysis of her limbs and surrender of her words are unmistakable. "I missed Papa," she says. "I just wanted to feel close to him."

She went to pray to him. In Papa's forgotten office on Snargate Street, Anna knelt in the dust, and she asked him to heal the pain I'd caused her. Mr. Haskell found her there. He let her cry to him, and while she wept at the feet of our father's ruin, Haskell locked the office door.

## CHAPTER 29
# PARADOXICAL GODDESS

I took Anna to stay with Ami Rose while Mamma convalesces in Bavaria. Ami put her in charge of harvesting the vegetables in the garden, and while Anna delights in the green, she can't stand the dirt, especially the way it cakes into the creases of her hands. She scrubs until they're chafed—exposing her delicate underskin—and then cries, saying she'll never be clean again. Ami Rose holds her for hours, just listening. She'll heal, but it will take time, and our most patient love.

The night is humid, filling the house with a suffocating mugginess. I roam the halls in a bone-deep fatigue, avoiding the library. Henry has isolated himself there and won't talk to anyone until the fresco is finished. I haven't the heart to face him again, though his avoidance still hurts.

Gaston's voice resonates from his room of artifacts. In a familiar scene, he shows off his $17^{th}$ century kirpan to a man turned away from me. But I don't need to see his face to recognize the man I hate most in this world. Mr. Haskell receives Gaston's attention with pretentious camaraderie, practically bloated with self-satisfaction.

I rush him like a bull, striking him.

"Beatrice!" Gaston hauls me away, but not before I rake my nails down Haskell's cheek, drawing slim lines of blood. I feel the rip of his skin under my fingernails and *oh*, how I crave another slash, screaming for revenge.

"Calm yourself!" Gaston plants my feet on the floor, wheeling me to face him. His fingers pinch and tweak, and I revile against them, wrestling free for another go at Haskell hissing in pain. It's not enough. His punishment must be so much more than a few quick lashes. I want him to suffer for what he's done.

Gaston clinches me to him, restraining my arms. "*Calmes-toi.*"

"He assaulted my sister," I say, spit flying onto Gaston's shirt with bedeviled speed. "He hurt her because I refused him!" Gaston's arms loosen, but he doesn't let go. I tell him everything—about Haskell's heinous proposals, his threats, how he put his revolting lips on me at the ball. "He threatened *you*, Gaston. He said he'd file an annulment with the magistrate—on the grounds that I'm underage and lacked his permission to marry—if I didn't help him blackmail you. He thinks you're a murderer, but I know he's wrong."

Gaston's neck flushes, flaming into his beard. He releases me, turning to Haskell and affixing his glare.

"She's lying," the wretch says, but his attempts are feeble as Gaston stalks up to him. A full foot in advantage, Gaston wraps his hand around Haskell's neck.

"Your injury," he says, pressing thumb to windpipe. "It's freshly mended, is it not?" A craggy scab forks into Haskell's hairline. Anna said she'd kicked him, her bootheel bludgeoning his face. I wish the wound were deeper, wider, uglier.

"Yes, but—" Gaston squeezes.

"And which of my family gave it to you?"

In his fear, Haskell's bulging eyes flick to mine.

Gaston reads it as his answer.

Mr. Haskell's face turns violet, Gaston giving no indication that he'll stop. I don't want him to. I want him to keep going until the villain's throat is crushed, so he'll never touch Anna or me or any girl ever again.

Haskell tries to push out some semblance of words. "Benj—"

Under his mustache, Gaston's lips press into a line.

He's gone pale as moonlight.

He shoves Haskell back, releasing his hold.

"You'd take the side of this cur over me?" I say, incredulous. How quickly he changed his mind about defending me. "He's taken everything from me!"

"There's nothing more he can do."

Gaston's nonchalance sets my teeth on edge. I grip his lapels, shouting, "He could take me away from you!"

"He won't."

"How can you know that?"

Gaston's casualness, his cavalier ideas of the world, terrify me. He's flesh and bone like me, like Haskell. To believe he's impervious is a delusion.

His hands go to my waist, moving lower as his expression transmutes suddenly into a shade of want. He is *remembering* me, in the grossest of moments. I don't know what calls the memory to him—my passion, my flush—but it weakens me, denuded by his look.

He has no idea what danger he's in.

Mr. Haskell nurses his face, watching us with prurient, amused interest. Like Gaston, he's not as afraid as he should be.

Terror rises up my throat. He's found something. Haskell has found his blackmail without even needing my help. He said something, while Gaston was choking him. It sounded like a name.

Benj.

*Benjamin?*

I've known only one Benjamin in my life. Ami Rose's brother.

The revelation emerges so slowly it's barely coherent. The daguerreotypist in Gaston's story and Ami's brother are one in the same. Gaston said Parvati ran away with him, and Ami's family never heard from Benjamin again. But what significance this has, I'm not sure.

"If you are quite finished with your connubial row," Haskell says, "I have some threats to make." He straightens his collar, and with showy insouciance runs his hand along the naked statue of Kali, paradoxical goddess of death and fertility. From her skirt of severed limbs to her arms of open benevolence, she can't be contained. She is feared and loved and bestows both of these equally. Haskell's touch defiles her image, filling me with fire.

"You can't hurt us," I say—a weak warning, and we both know it.

"*Au contraire*," he mocks, turning to Gaston. "I met someone rather intriguing the night of your ball. She had an interesting theory concerning the disappearance of your first wife. Her sister, I believe. What was her name?"

"Indira," I realize.

"Mm. Endearing." He chuckles. "She thinks you killed her sister, and I'm inclined to agree."

"Where is your proof?" Gaston says.

"Beatrice?"

I lift my chin. *He has no proof! Only rumor.* "There is none. I won't help you destroy us."

Haskell's smile falls. "Then it seems I have a complaint to file with the magistrate."

Instinct rears up in me. I don't know if it's the African masks or the effigies of ancient, vengeful goddesses, but they fuel me. I snatch the kirpan from its stand and brandish it before me like a Trojan. Haskell roars with glee—until I feel a force push me forward, stumbling with the knife into his chest.

## CHAPTER 30
# DO NOT OPEN THE DOOR

It's sickening, the amount of blood slopping out of him. The kirpan, which has a blade that curves upward, sticks out of Mr. Haskell's shoulder as he screams.

Gaston told me the Punjabi word *kirpan* roughly translates to "mercy." In the religion of the Sikhs, the weapon is a symbol, only to be used in self-defense, and only when the rift between good and evil threatens to rupture a person's soul. To use it for revenge, like I've just done, insults the faith of an entire people.

"You'll pay for this!" Haskell wrenches the knife from his arm, and it clatters to the marble.

I could have killed him—but wait, was it Fate that pushed me forward, or Gaston?

I drop to the floor, sick, commotion blurring around me. Haskell lunges at me with his good arm, but Gaston flings him back. Haskell's head hits the wall with a crack, artifacts tumbling down as he slumps into unconsciousness, blood trickling down his face.

Unnervingly calm, Gaston kneels before me. "Beatrice, don't worry. I will solve this. Oh, my Beatrice." He smooths my hair, the lines along his brow folding into impressions of recognition. Yet he looks at me as if seeing someone else.

"Can this be?" he says—disbelieving or enraptured, I don't know which. His eyes are a matte black, deflecting all light. Wherever his mind is, it's not here with me. "Have you returned to me?"

The room spins. "Who do you mean?"

"You, of course." He meshes his fingers in my hair. "Parvati."

Her name sticks in my quivering heart, a fishhook. "Is that who you see when you look at me?"

He realizes his mistake too late. "Don't be foolish," he says darkly. Picking up the kirpan, he wipes away Haskell's blood and reverently returns it to its display. "Go to bed, Beatrice. I will take care of him."

Haskell's chest undulates a shallow, thready rhythm. He's alive, but won't be if the bleeding doesn't stop.

"He needs a surgeon," I say.

"He deserves the gallows. He betrayed your father and stole from his business. He's a criminal."

"I never told you that." Gaston heaves Mr. Haskell's limp body over his shoulder like a moth-eaten rug. I try to stand, but dizziness pulls me back to the floor. "The embezzlement—how long have you known?"

"Your father told me, before his death."

"You...you spoke to my father?"

Anxious to leave, he readjusts Haskell's weight. "He asked me for a loan to cover Horace's indiscretions. I declined to give it. Though, I could not have foreseen your father's next step, practically signing you over to the lesser business partner. I should have made my threats clearer, but the rat came back."

I squeeze my head between my hands, comprehension a struggle. "Are you saying you could have saved us? You could have saved us, but instead you let us suffer? You let my *father* suffer so you could make me your wife after his death—because you *knew* he would never give his consent to you. Isn't that true?"

The wrath of a goddess channels through me as I presume the answer Gaston never gives.

"Isn't that true!"

All this time I've been powerless, my life mere puppetry. Gaston has been lurking in the background of my life far longer than I'd ever thought. He colluded, not just with Mamma, but Papa, too. No—Papa would never have given me over to a man cloaked in shadows. The logic is deluded, but he must have thought that by turning guardianship over to Mr. Haskell, he was saving me from someone far more deceitful. Haskell was the lesser of two evils.

I've been too consumed by grief to see that control was always Gaston's. It wasn't happenstance that he buried his wife the same day we buried Papa. It wasn't *fate* that his carriage found me on the road, or that Mr. Haskell ran before taking me as his prize. Gaston threatened to expose his misdeeds, foolishly believing himself untouchable.

I didn't notice Gaston leave, taking Haskell's bleeding figure with him. That was hours ago. Night has fallen over the Hall of Artifacts, where I haven't moved, tangled in a net of terrible truth. Another object for his collection, I lie immobile between Kali and the kirpan, surrounded by blood and shadows and the growing whispers of women's ghosts.

He moves like a somnambulist enslaved to a dream. Having returned from his disposal of Mr. Haskell—alive or dead or somewhere in-between—Gaston seeks solace. I follow him without candlelight, down to his secret chamber where a blue light glows beneath the door. I watch him enter, the door opening itself to him without his touch. When I try the door myself seconds later, it's locked.

The sensual music of a bansuri flute plays in melody with the wind fluted through the windowpanes, and the arrhythmic pounding of my knock as I beg him to let me in. I've given Gaston everything—my body, my life—but he hides behind this door, basking in his secrets.

He tricked me, lured me in with his fortune and snapped the trap shut. I was easily fooled, a panicked, self-sabotaging creature. But the worst of it is, the pain caused by his deceits is naught compared to my excruciating desire for my captor's liberation. The ties between us are a mess of ever-tightening knots that I can't seem to cut. I loathe him, but I want to *know* him.

*Did you think you would see inside of me?*

I startle backward, bumping into the table and tipping over the candle. The flame dies, but the chamber's blue light glows ever brighter.

The voice was corporeal, not in my head. I didn't imagine it.

"Who are you?" I whisper to the corridor. *What* are you?

The corridor whispers back.

*Look inside,* it says.

My vision blurs as something moves in me, a gliding out, a tearing away from my body. And once within, I'm without.

I float above myself.

Entrapped in the cobwebbed mirror, my reflection gapes at me, aglow with the azure light from Gaston's chamber. She is me and she is not. Her curves are voluptuous, her hot eyes dazzling with some secret experience, some knowing. A Bindi mark of fertile red appears between my eyebrows, and heat rushes through me, shifting, thriving, an oasis in the desert. I feel the most exquisite ache reaching through me as the Bindi melts, slipping thick and crimson down my nose.

Blood.

The drumming blaze in my eyes dies out. And there, in their middles, a new reflection.

Gaston.

His sullen face appears next to mine in the mirror, the chamber shut behind him. That prickling, rank odor I've smelled on him before fills my nose. Not a spice, perhaps, but a drug.

"What do you do in there?" It's just a room filled with rubbish and dust, yet he's drawn to it like rivers to the sea. "Gaston? Do you hear me?"

He just stares, his eyes bloodshot. He pushes my hair back from my neck, kissing me until I've forgotten what I asked. There's no more fire in me. No more rage or vengeance, only defeat. My heart is broken. This is what Papa feared, what he tried to warn me about when he told me to protect my heart.

Gaston murmurs Parvati's name, and I close my eyes. There's nothing in him but desire, but it's not me he wants. He believes I'm Parvati reincarnated. Does he visit her there, in his chamber where he stores his secrets, his memories of her? I wish he'd let me see.

"How do you expect me to love what I don't know?" I hadn't meant to ask the question aloud, but it wakes him.

He sees it's me—Beatrice—his fifth wife not his first. It confuses him.

"Please, Beatrice." I hear the travail, the misery, in his voice. "Leave it be."

"I won't. I want to trust you, but I can't do that if you keep me out."

His shoulders fall. He leans his head against the chamber door, sighing as if he can feel vibrations in the wood. The chamber has gone dark. "Behind this door is a part of me that must never be known. If it were, your sorrow would be too great." His eyes—his storms to my skies—search mine as the sun slowly rises. "I don't wish to hurt you."

"Then let me know you." I give to him my softest, most unsparing touch. Under his skin, his blood quivers.

"Please," he begs. He tilts his forehead to mine. "For your own sake, do not ask to see inside."

"I must. It's the only way I'll ever trust you."

His head lifts. Gaston wades into my paradise, exploring me as I hunt for signs of doubt, suspicion. But in the shadowed grooves of his eyes, his mouth, I find anticipation.

He waits for my invitation, my parted lips. His hand is rough with years and calloused from thrusting shovel upon shovel into sandy earth, and yet his touch on my cheek, steering my face toward his, is the softest I've ever felt from him. It surprises, settles, *soothes*, and I ache with its tenderness, its void of lust or heat.

Cool metal slips into my hand.

A key.

"Take my heart, but do not break it. Do not open the door."

I close my eyes, hardly believing.

"Don't break it," he pleads. "Don't open it." He kisses me again, long and deep and sweet, and it breaks me apart when it ends.

I clench the key, imprinting its shape into my palm.

It's different from the one I used before.

## CHAPTER 31
# MY LOVER'S KEY

I watch Gaston's dinghy roll upon the waves out to *La Gitane*, white sails billowing down her masts. The wind fills them up, thrusting the ship toward the sunrise where she shrinks to the size of a pearl and vanishes.

Ocean breezes bat at the curtains as honeybees sip nectar from the vine-flowers. Love is like a sunrise, I muse. Gradual. Refulgent. So easily clouded.

"A letter for you, ma'am." Crawley sets the post next to my plate of savory crêpes, stepping carefully back into his position by the door.

I wear Gaston's key around my neck, slung on a gold chain with the ruby he bought for me in Paris, its weight growing heavier the longer it's in my possession.

I slip my finger under the letter's seal to tear it open,

Henry's crisp, elegant handwriting shining up from the ivory paper.

*My Sweetest Bee,*

*Please, forgive me. Like a child, I've been avoiding you when I know you don't deserve it. The choices you make are yours alone, and I will never dispute that again. I made a promise to not interfere and I intend to keep it—but there is a conflict of heart I must acknowledge.*

*You wish for me a life apart, to find love with another. But here I tell you such an act would be impossible. My heart only has room for you, and until my love for you seeks to remove itself, I will forever remain in love with you. I can give no room, no affection, to another. And for that, regrettably, I am not sorry.*

*The purpose of this letter is not solely to profess to you what you already know to be true, which truth I hope you'll never doubt. After a laborious search of bank records, Silas has uncovered a pseudonym with an attached address, which he thinks belongs to the financial advisor of my patron saint. If we can find this man and convince him to give up my benefactor's identity, then I'll be able to determine the character behind his mask. Whether he's truly a friend, or my foe.*

*I go now to meet Silas, and together we'll learn the truth. For now, my hope is that you and I will meet again soon, so I may share with you what has been both grievous and joyful in my life. Until that day, know that I am—*

*Eternally yours,*
*Henry*

I bring the letter to my lips, testing the softness of the paper. My nose prickles with traces of turpentine and resin, his smell one of the things I'll miss most about him. When I wander into the library, it's still there. As time moves, the paint's essence will evaporate, but Henry's face in my mind never will.

It's a slivered moon under which Juliet fantasizes. Jewel-like and glistening, Henry's completed fresco seduces me to it. The colors are as bright as if he'd plucked them right from life and transferred them to his palette. Hesitating at her rose-wreathed balcony, Juliet faces away from Romeo, and he clasps her hand as if imploring her to turn, to face him and love him. She must be coaxed, for she knows better than to marry her heart to a stranger.

Juliet's eyes, I notice, are lapis. Like mine.

She's beautiful. As is Romeo, who's been painted to resemble—not Gaston as I thought he would be—but Henry. A dangerous risk, declaring to the world what sleeps inside his heart, dreaming of its awakening.

The fresco triggers in me an erratic sensation, a sort of swirling galaxy of desire and dysphoria, need and despair.

I'm split, half given to want and the other to fear. A paradoxical goddess, bestowing both. My shoulders hang with that deep-boned fatigue, a depressed exhaustion that, when I breathe, fills my lungs with a yawn that stretches on for days. I miss Gaston and Henry both with my whole body, creaky pains in the crooks of my bones.

I crawl onto the settee by the bookshelves, curling into a child's pose with the key in my fist. Its bow is heart-shaped, teeth jagged and smiling. The skeleton metal throbs with a singular heat—yellow, blue, then white, searing through my skin. Whispers slither into my ear, twisting around my heart.

*Look inside....*

I pull my legs closer to my chest.

"You don't look well, mistress." Alice has come into the library with a tray of tea. She pours the hot water over the tea-steep, aromatic bitterness crimping my nose. There's a meaty, metallic tang in the air I shrivel against, tightening my belly.

"Take that away, please, Miss Whipple. I don't want it."

"But 'tis Earl Grey, your favorite." The pot wavers in her hand like she doesn't know what to do with it.

"Even so." I slide myself into a sitting position, head aching. "I don't think I could stomach it today." Alice starts to leave, but I stop her. "Please, sit with me. I'm feeling off, and I don't want to be alone."

She plants herself stiffly on the edge of the couch,

tugging at the ends of her bronze hair, much like Anna does. Regret meanders through me, and dread. Gaston never told me what he did with Mr. Haskell, or if he was still alive when he left him.

"Here, let me serve you." Alice takes the tea I give her without debate, blowing on it before taking a sip. "How long have you been a servant here?"

"About five years, mistress. When I was fifteen, me mum birthed her tenth, my sister Lizzie, and as there was no more room in the house, I was sent to live with my uncle, Mr. Crawley."

"Indeed? Do you like it here?"

"Yes, ma'am, but sometimes—" She presses her lips together, hesitant to gossip.

I nudge her knee with mine. "Sometimes what?"

"Sometimes, I don't quite feel easy." She drops her tone, leaning in. "The house," she says, eyes shifting to the corners of the room, "it whispers. And the master—"

I twitch with impatience. "Well?"

"He changes." There's a cadence of terror in her voice. "Like there's somethin' inside him. Somethin'...beastly."

A shiver rolling down my back, I readjust myself on the sofa. How astute she is. I wonder what other things she's noticed.

"Did he give you that?" She nods to my necklace. "The key."

*Look inside.*

I cover it. "He did. He told me to keep it safe for him."

"He gave it to the mistress before you, Mistress Lenore. She wore it on a rosary, next to her cross of Jesus."

I frown. "Did she tell you why?"

"She said nothin' to me, mistress. Only—I did overhear him tell her never to use it. Strange, isn't it? Why keep it otherwise? It's like he was testing her."

The key feels hot—an impossible, corporeal heat I'm afraid will burn through the front of my dress. The chain bites into my neck, slick with perspiration, the key dipping down, weighted by that cunning voice.

*Look inside.*

Alice finishes her tea. I pour her another cup to keep her seated. "What was your former mistress like? Was she kind to you?"

"Mistress Lenore did her best to be kind, ma'am. Though, she liked to keep the house in proper order and I oft tested her patience."

"How gloomy the house must have been upon her death."

Alice gulps down a breath, her unfettered personality leaking through. Another mouthpiece for juicy rumor. "Actually, mistress, if I'm to be honest, we were each caught quite unawares. At least the servants were. Her death was sudden, like a storm had gathered above her bed and snatched her up in the middle of the night. No one but the master was allowed to see the body. Us servants were sent away, as occasions often be." A faraway look glazes her eyes and she stops mid-word. She jolts from the settee, her teacup bouncing to the floor, shattering.

I rise with her, rattled. “What is it, Alice?”

She moves as if caught in the thrall of some mystic, puppeted by strings. I have to take double-steps to keep up with her as she twists through the house, halting at the entrance to the dark wing. Her toes edge the line of the forbidden, reason warring with urge beneath her pale features. I reach out to touch her, but a warning tolls.

*This is not Alice.*

“Who are you?”

Her mouth cracks open, a mass of voices sliding out in unison. “We are Madame Dumas. We are the key.”

The necklace lifts at my throat, the key hovering in the air beyond my nose, pointing to the path I must follow.

*This can’t be real.*

“This isn’t real!” I rip the key from the air and spin Alice around, her speech returning to where it was before her possession.

“But the master, he did grieve, for a week or two.” She stumbles against the wall, nearly tumbling into the Mongolian suit. “How did we get here?”

“This isn’t real, Alice.” I grip her shoulders with curved fingers, needing to believe it’s not real, that she wasn’t just possessed by the spirits of Gaston’s dead wives.

“He will kill us!” she cries, her confusion leaping into

panic. She struggles, but I grip tighter, forcing her to listen to me.

"It's just a test, Alice!"

The maid sobs under my restraints. I let her go, and as she slides down the wall, the image is the same: me, cowering below Gaston's wolf. Only now, the wolf is me.

I'm the one who's cursed.

I stare at my hands, red with the flow of blood beneath my skin. And against my raging heart burns my lover's key.

## CHAPTER 32
# ALONE WITH HIM AGAIN

I trace my finger along the key's body, over the hills of its bow and down its teeth, its mischievous grin. Testing me. I thought I'd gained his trust, but Gaston is testing me as if I'm no different from his other wives. All ghosts, they haunt me with their susurrant temptations to unlock the chamber door, to join them in their betrayal of the husband we've each shared. I won't do it. I'll sit with this misery for as long as it takes to mend my life again.

I cradle my head in the crook of my arm as I lie on the divan, staring sideways at Henry's fresco. Vivid color sings with his name—Romeo's mouth, Juliet's eyes, the rose-tangled balcony. Each painted detail is a piece of his soul, the transparency of Henry's world fleshed open.

*My heart only has room for you, and until my love for you seeks to remove itself, I will forever remain in love with you.*

I press my face to the cushions and weep until tendrils of coral sunset stream across the walnut floor, bending up the furniture to warm my face, to dry those tears to salt beds. “I’m sorry, Henry,” I say after a time.

Gaston has been gone for two days. For two days, I’ve resisted the enticements of his ghost-wives to open the chamber door. The key is magic, and will show me more than abandoned canes and insect corpses. My necklace grasps at my hair, pinching, the key flaring with hellfire. It wants to be used. Like a mortal with a soul, it has a purpose, a role to fulfill. The key belongs to the lock, and always it will seek this union.

For two days I’ve resisted. I’ll resist for a hundred more.

My belly cramps with the slightest of pains, of womanly stirrings. I force myself to sip the willow bark tea Alice brewed for me. The bitter liquid seiches down my throat, and though its purpose is to ease the menses, my gut is left unsettled. I feel imbalanced. Seasick.

I hear my name called from somewhere in the house, and I swell with hope. I run to him, nearly dancing in my elation to tell him I’ve succeeded. I’ve passed his test, and he'll love me for it. He'll forget all about his other wives—how they failed him each in turn—and he'll only see me.

*Me.*

Not Parvati.

"Gaston!" I dash into the entrance hall, my foot catching on a board. I fly into arms that are freckled and strong. "You're home."

Henry's dappled brow crimps with misery. "I'm not him," he says, and he steps away from me. "Sorry to have disappointed you."

My tongue hits my teeth to tell him no—no, I'm not disappointed. Your arms are the ones I'd hoped to fall into. But when I search inside myself for the love I know is there, I find only panic. "You shouldn't be here," I say.

He bites his cheek, fighting for a gentleman's civility. "There's no need for whispering, Beatrice. It appears all your servants have quit the house. I saw myself in."

Alone with him again.

I use the ticking of the grandfather clock to sedate my manic heart. "Gaston isn't here."

"He's away, then." Relief. But then, "I'd hoped to speak with him."

My eyes narrow, suspicious. "What of?"

Henry hesitates, swallowing whatever bitter taste offends his mouth. "I wish to negotiate the terms of repayment for my education at the Royal Academy." He says this flatly, hardly an emotion in his eyes.

Comprehension comes as a breath held far too long.

"Gaston is your benefactor."

"Was. I no longer require his patronage. And as I've finished the work he commissioned me to do, his contract has no more legal standing. I'm free of his bonds." So cold and indifferent. Henry has lost his only dream; in searching for his benefactor, he thought he'd find a father, but instead he found an adversary. A rival for my love.

The silence between us stretches into oblivion.

"Speak to me," I beg, but he cloaks his pain with a shrug of indifference.

"I can say nothing you're no doubt sick of hearing."

I blink back the spate of tears, deserving of his disdain. I've given him no guarantee of my love for the future, and now I could lose that future altogether. I could lose *him*—my first and only friend.

Light shining through the stained-glass windows paints a mosaic on Henry's face. A pageantry of golds and reds and blues, glimmering on his skin. He's more than an artist. He's art itself. And I'm losing him.

No fate could be worse than never knowing the depth, the breadth, and the rhapsody of Henry's love for me.

Two steps are all my body will allow me. Two steps more and I could be in his arms, knowing that rhapsody. The beauty of his eyes, not looking at me, not drinking me in as I drink him. I say his name, and he relinquishes his grief.

Turning from me, he goes to the staircase to sit on its steps, and takes his head in his hands. I sit beside him, maintaining a most painful distance. "Beatrice, this promise I've made to you—it feels impossible. When I learned Gaston was my benefactor, I refused to believe it. I accused Silas of a tasteless joke and demanded he search again. I..." I take his hand. No thought, no pause, just take it. It's where my hand belongs, at least for the moment. He covers it with his other. "I hate him. I hate him for having you first."

Despite our solitude, I speak in undertones. "If you'd been a suitor come to court me, I would have been yours. Please, believe me. I wanted you before I ever wanted Gaston."

"But you *do* want him. Even now, you want him. It was his name you called."

Yes. It was. Gaston's name.

I take my hand back. "I can't explain it. From the very beginning, I told myself I wouldn't love him. That I couldn't because it was impossible. But something happened."

"What?"

"I looked at him. *Truly* looked at him. I saw he was a man with a broken heart, with a past he wanted to change, to relive. I thought, somehow, I could save him."

"And have you?"

"I don't know yet."

A minute's worth of ticks and tocks from the grandfather clock.

"What is this key you handle?"

Tick and tock and tick and burn, burn, burn.

"It unlocks a chamber in a wing near the back of the house. You followed me there, the night of the ball."

"I remember. The air felt strange. And your mouth..." His fingers hover in my breath. "It was like a charm, enticing me toward it."

And his mouth. Then. Now. Enticing.

"I'm forbidden from opening the door, but I've seen Gaston come and go. He gave me the key as a test, to see if I'll obey him."

"What will happen if you look inside?"

"Great sorrow, I am told."

Henry scoffs—*the inanity of such a test.* "He treats you like an acquisition," he fumes. "A bedmate. The way he's hurt you...it angers me to murder."

My eyes snap to his. "But you wouldn't think to carry it through."

Affixed to mine, there's no jest in Henry's eyes. "If I thought I could succeed, I would."

The key sizzles hot, white-hot. I push off the stairs, steeling myself to a window where humidity condenses on the panes. I gave no thought to whether I would succeed in killing Haskell. I simply struck, acting out my passionate hatred for him. I didn't think of the consequences.

"A mortal warrants mercy," I mutter.

Henry's voice is cutting in its strain. "Has he won you so thoroughly that you don't see his villainy? The way he's manipulated every person around him like a tyrant—all for his own gain?"

My eyes burn, stinging and watering like there's dust in them. I spin on Henry, a torrent of rage clambering up my throat. "If it weren't for Gaston, you'd still be a beggar on the street!" My voice, and *not* my voice. An echo over an echo.

Henry pulls back, watching me. Seeing me. But not seeing me. "Who are you?"

My sight loses focus, and I zone into a stupor. Something moves in me, a gliding out, a tearing away. And once within, I am without, floating above myself. "We are Madame Dumas."

I fall back against the steps, grasping at Henry for balance. My mind flitters and screams, the key slipping into my bodice and scorching my skin.

Henry at my side, in my mind: *Beatrice! Beatrice! What's wrong? What's happening?*

I'm sick. I'm frightfully sick. The curse has taken me, and I slip into him, into him, into him. *Gaston*, I say.

I WAKE up in his arms. In Henry's arms. His skin terrified, his cheek to my cheek, chafing, waking me up. He carried me to the library and laid me down but didn't let go. He'll never let me go.

*Unnngh.*

"Beatrice, what happened to you?" His eyes are glossy wet.

"The key." It swelters and blisters. "Don't use it."

Don't use it. Don't use it.

"Ah!" he cries. "It's hot."

"I won't open it. I won't look inside."

"Beatrice, listen to me." He holds my shoulders, holding me up. "No man who keeps his secrets locked behind a door could be a good man. I will prove this to you."

The chain snaps, loud and deafening like bones breaking, and his heart is wrenched away, brutally torn from my chest where I've kept it safe for so long. The ruby skitters somewhere to the floor, and Henry runs from the room.

"NO!"

Like plunging into a winter pond, I waken. I chase after Henry, his shoes buffeting the floor as he lurches into the forbidden wing to the chamber door. We wrestle for the key. I bite him, and he yells, but he jams the key into the lock and twists. The wards click, releasing the bolt.

Spinning myself around, I shut my eyes because I don't want to look. I don't want to betray Gaston.

The door rasps out an awful, gut-curdling sound. There's the strike of metal on wood—the key, dropping. And an odd splash.

All is like a graveyard.

Henry screams.

## CHAPTER 33
# CHEATING FATE

The hall mirror shows everything: Henry's fear-wracked shoulders. His shock-white face. And shapes, swinging back and forth behind the door. He pushes it open, filling the room with light as the rotted tang of putrescence breaches our noses. Inside the chamber, bodies sway in a placid breeze, middles roped and strung from the rafters. A head, detached, floats incomprehensibly next to each of their waists. I count them all:

One wife.

Two wives.

Three wives.

*Four* wives.

And one man.

Each as fresh, and gorgeous, and gory as on the day they were slaughtered.

My blood has ceased moving, the truth stopping time in its tracks. He killed them. Gaston killed his wives—even Parvati, whom he loved. He killed her for betraying him with Benjamin. Then he offered up his heart-key to test each successive wife, to see whether they'd betray him, too. They discovered the darkness that lies inside him, and he killed them each in turn.

Now, Gaston will kill me.

But he will kill Henry first.

Each wife's ghastly, open-mouthed expression stabs me with fear for my own life. But it's the man's expression—Benjamin's—clenching my heart. His eyes remain open, pleading to be spared. They're brown. Brown like Henry's eyes are brown. Henry's eyes.

I have to get him out of here.

The key fell into a sticky pool of congealed blood. I pick it up, scarlet strings clinging to it like fluttering cobwebs. Pulling Henry from the room, I draw the door and lock it.

He's rigid, petrified with shock. I smack his face. "Wake up!" Henry rubs his cheek, blood coursing back to him. "You have to leave." I drag him through the corridors, a plan forming in my mind as fast as my thoughts will fly. He mustn't go out the front; he could be seen. I take him to the kitchen, to the servants' door.

"I won't go without you," he says, stubbornly planting his feet at the threshold. "I won't abandon you to face that monster alone. Come with me—we'll escape together."

"Henry, if I run, he'll know. He'll come after me. He'll kill us." Gnawing on my lip, I taste blood. I shake my head furiously. "He won't find out. I'll scrub the key and pretend nothing happened. He won't know I betrayed him."

"Betrayed him how? By unlocking his chamber of death?"

"No." I look at Henry like it's obvious—as if my feelings for him were a glaring fact of the situation—but he doesn't know how I care for him. He doesn't know because I've never told him. "By falling in love with you."

The kitchen sighs, floured air and tottering pots disturbed by our presence.

His smile radiant, Henry takes my hand to kiss it. But even after my confession, I can't fight the impulse to pull back. Through fear and shame, I've trained myself to resist him—resist *us*. I love him, which is why he must flee. My love only puts him in danger. "Henry, run as far away from here as you can and don't stop, don't look back."

"Beatrice, come with me."

"I can't. I need time—I have to think—"

"But why?"

"Because I love him, too."

Whether by my own choice or through the dark influence of a curse, I'm in love with Gaston. And it kills me.

Now that I know what he is—the lies he's told and the people he's murdered—I can't stay with him without inevitably becoming his next victim. Yet, he'll be on our trail the second I run. All his life, he's hunted treasure, and I'm his greatest prize. If I bide my time with him, it's possible he won't see my escape coming.

"But you, Henry"—I touch his chest to feel his heartbeat, to keep from shattering—"*you* are my heart. I have to protect you. Please, let me protect you."

His mouth. All that pining, and enticing, and *pull* of his mouth. The temptation to kiss him has never been stronger, but if I do, I'll never let him go. The surest way to keep Henry safe is to release him from my net.

"Go," I beg.

"I love you," he says.

The air grows cold where he stood.

I DUNK the bloodied key into a kettle of soapy water and set it on the stove to boil. I've already tried to scrub out the unhallowed stains but they refuse to shift. They flare with a passionate red, auguries of my fate.

I think Gaston aims to arrive home today, because the servants aren't here. He doesn't like them in the house when he enters his chamber, and he'll want to tonight, having been so long apart from it.

Previously masked by some spell, the bodies now

reek, the scent clinging to my clothes and soiling my aura with death. My dress smells like rotted meat, its hem bloodied. I tear at it, squirm, cut the laces with sheers and wriggle out of it. I shove it into the rubbish bin with the vegetable tops.

The kettle cries. I sieve the water through a colander and scrub at the key once more. "Out, damned spot! Out!" I say, but it won't come off, and I slam the key onto the counter.

My only hope is to hide it and play ignorant when Gaston asks for its return. If I can't convince him of my innocence, he'll kill me with or without the evidence.

I tug at my hair, struggling to retain my sobs. Did he ever, even once, feel true love for me?

Scouring the house for a nook or embrasure, I find the Mongol, slipping the key into his leather girdle.

His ship sails into the harbor, guided by the lighthouse. Not long after, carriage wheels thunder up the drive, and I run out to meet him. The evening suffocates, sweltry and humid. Barefoot in my nightgown, I'm an actress in an opera, tears cascading down my face as I seize Gaston's coat. "Oh, husband! The key! I've lost it!"

"*Quoi?*" The word cuts through the murk, and he forces me back. Hand open, I show him the broken chain.

"The key must have been too heavy for it. I searched

the house, but it was hours before I realized it was missing. I'm sorry. I'm so sorry, Gaston. Please, forgive me!"

It is a violent search. Gaston tears through every room, kicking rugs and furniture and even his precious artifacts, oblivious to their snapping and breaking. The masks lie torn upon the floor amidst fragments of jade and glass and gems. In our bedchamber, he rips apart our bed with homicidal passion. I dodge a pillow as it knocks my portrait from the wall, puncturing the canvas on a table ledge. Henry's beautiful work, wounded.

Convulsing with terror, my legs no longer bear me up, and I fall to the floor, bawling into the carpets.

His tirade quells. Gaston picks me up with all the care of a parent for a distraught child, placing me on the mattress of our upended bed.

"I didn't open it," I blubber. "I didn't use the key."

He wipes my eyes, kissing them lightly. "I believe you. Ah, Beatrice, I knew you would not fail me. And for that, I love you." A look of surprise transcends his face, something akin to bliss. He replays the words—*I love you*—feeling them in his throat.

He shoots to his feet. "*La calamità!*"

I stare up at him, rising to my elbows.

With brash laughter, Gaston claps his hands, kissing them and raising his palms to the ceiling in some prayer of gratitude. "The curse," he declares, and he falls back to his knees before me. He kisses me quickly, baffling me.

"I'm redeemed. *Redeemed*, do you hear? You have done it! You."

*You.*

Me.

I shake my head wildly, not believing it. Because Fate is a liar. And love is a curse. "How could I have done that?"

"You obeyed." He sweeps the tangle of hair from my face. "I gave you the key, and you did not use it. I brought Monsieur Swain into our home—left you alone with him for nye on to three months—and you never betrayed me with him, never devised to leave me. And finally,"—he cups my face, bringing me close—"you loved me freely as your own. Beatrice, you have surpassed my every trial."

Each part of me numbs with his confession. Henry was a test. I'd suspected Gaston was watching me with him—deliberately, critically watching. But never once did I think he was bait set for a trap. That Gaston *expected* to catch us in the entwine of vice.

He never trusted me. Not even once.

Gaston believes I've passed all his tests, but the reality is I've failed every one. I never used the key, but I saw the truth inside the chamber. I never bedded Henry, but I told him I loved him. I almost kissed him. And as for Gaston, it's true, I gave myself to him, loved him freely as my own. But I was misled, duped into his romance by a kismet he controlled.

Am I now convinced? This world is dominated by gods and curses and tempted fates. It's a world of good men and bad men. Of villains and mortals and everything in between. Gaston, kneeling before me and overjoyed with his triumph, believes I've rent his irons, freed him of his paw-trap. He believes the wolf has left him, that he's been reborn. But he's wrong—I haven't broken his curse. I've only taken it on as my own.

Gaston's eyes overspill with tears, rolling into his beard. He lays his head in my lap and weeps into the white folds of my nightgown.

## CHAPTER 34

# GREAT SORROW

The wind croons to the sky, smothered by an incoming storm. Gaston lies next to me in the bed, his snores soft lion-purrs. His blue-gray mane catches the strands of moonlight drifting ethereally in from the window.

If I've broken his curse, why is his beard still blue?

A great gust blows the draperies inward, flapping against the walls. I draw deeper under the blankets when I should arise and close the window, but my childish fear of the sea and its circling eye of winds tightens my limbs, so that I can't act bravely. Lightning cracks and moments later the night bellows, pain deep in the sky's bowels. And through it all, Gaston slumbers. The violence of a storm can't arouse him from the rest of his raptures.

I allowed him to bed me tonight for the second time. A part of me astonished at the easiness of it, the inveterate flow of one touch into a deeper, more conscious caress. Yet in the curves of such pleasures my heart beat a sorrow such as I've never experienced before, one that I can only describe as Great.

It felt like dying.

His hands, his kisses, they were killing me. And I welcomed that death, as if it could cure me of this pain. This curse.

My stomach heaves, working itself into a dire snit. I sneak from Gaston's arms to the chamber pot behind the dressing screen, and bowing down to it on the floor, I let my head just hang. Saliva floods my mouth, and I vomit, my insides turned outside, emptied of everything but emptiness.

Roused to panic, Gaston worries at the screen. "You're ill."

"I'm fine."

"I'll send for the doctor."

I grasp the hem of his nightshirt. "It has passed." I drag in a breath, wiping my mouth.

The storm blasting through the windows pulls Gaston's attention, and he closes it, drawing the curtains.

"Take me to the bed," I say, and he does, drawing the blankets closely around us. He returns to holding me tightly, fearfully, as if I'll leave and not come back. But he knows, as well as I do, that's not possible. We're tied together, his heart to mine.

He nuzzles his face into my hair.

I close my eyes.

I attempt to sleep.

I STRETCH and coo like a collared dove.

Rancid mouth.

Rancid breath.

"Drink this." Gaston brings the tea to my lips, and I can tell he prepared it himself, strong and caustically bitter. I drink it all. He sits on the edge of the bed, putting his hand on my stomach, and stares, pensively, at it.

"You spoke your dreams last night."

I blink at him, feeling nothing. "What did I say?"

"A name."

"Yours?"

"No."

Henry's. I said Henry's name.

"It was just a dream," I whisper, and I weave my fingers with his, knotted together, as we are.

"Do you love me?"

I don't answer him. Just kiss him, pulling him with me into the bed.

He whistles through the house, jauntily swinging his cane over his shoulder like the picture in his study. It rains, dribbling from the hoary timbers of the house.

Plop.

Plop.

Plop.

Blood on stone.

"You're like ice." Gaston removes his coat, wrapping it around me. "This weather pales you like it paled Parvati. She preferred the sun and all its bright brutality."

We loaf on a couch in the library, thigh to thigh, watching the wind toss the ocean, the rain beat the panes. "I am like the rain," I say, mentally absent from the room. My thoughts are numb, everything I say and do lacking emotion. I'm a ghost trapped on the wrong side of the veil, with nothing to do but haunt the house like his other wives.

Gaston continues to whistle. A French tune. Lively, verbose, like him. "Do you know what *karma* is, Beatrice?" I've heard the word from Ami Rose, but I didn't understand it. I shake my head. "The Brahmans of India say our deeds in this life slate our happiness, or suffering, for the next."

"Heaven or Hell, you mean."

"I mean here, again, on Earth. You lived before, as another being, another heartbeat. In your previous life, you could have been a butterfly in the field—puffing along in the breeze—or one of the trees in your orchard, blossoming sweet with fruit." He laughs breathily. "I can tell by your smirk—there, in your mouth's corner—you do not believe me. But believe me, Beatrice, when I tell you I have loved you before."

"As whom?" I say, though already I know. He touches his thumb to the space of skin between my eyebrows.

"You were my first wife."

I have been possessed, as surely as Gaston's soul has been reborn. If reincarnation exists, then it's like the metaphysic transfer of the ghost: the body dies, but the soul seeks a new one. Parvati's soul displacing mine.

But I am not a goddess reincarnate. I'm the purveyor of Gaston's madness.

His arm slithers around my waist. "Touch me," he says.

I smooth his shirtfront.

"Kiss me."

I do.

He stands at the fresco, studying it with a critic's eyes. I wonder what he thinks of his beneficiary's hand. Henry told me of his association with a group of painters, bonded as brothers, who call themselves the Pre-Raphaelites. They've met the public with both rancorous scorn and buoyant accolades. Where does Gaston's opinion fall? Is he proud, like a father?

"Juliet," he says. "She has your aspect."

"Yes. Mr. Swain requested I model for her." Cool-headed. Uncaring. I hide Henry well. So long as I obey, never resisting, he'll be safe.

"*Magnifique.* He captured you almost as well as I have." Gaston grins. I smile. My blood moves a little slower in my veins. "It's just as I imagine the moonlit exchange."

His joy has blinded him. He doesn't see how Juliet is angled reluctantly *away* from Romeo. Or that Romeo's features are more like Henry's than his own.

"The rain has ceased," he says suddenly. A cool sunset streams in through the windows, highlighting the amber grains of the floor. "I wager the orchard is resplendent. Shall we go see?" He's not asking but telling. With greedy gestures, Gaston tows me from the windows to the door. "It will be muddy; you'll need to change into your habit. An enterprise which I should satisfy to help"—a crunch underfoot, he lifts up his boot—"you with."

A scattering of jewel dust and crushed scarlet. *My ruby.* Or rather, a crystal cut and pawned as a precious gem. The jeweler and his shop boy sold us a fake. But that's not what astounds Gaston.

"If the jewel be found here, why is the key not in its vicinity?" He turns to me. "Would you not have heard it drop on this floor?"

All at once, what it means to be emotive comes swinging back to me. My blood quickens, upsetting my stuporous, barely-living rhythm. "How strange," I say. "I can't explain it." I proceed to lead Gaston into the hall and up the stairs.

He prevents my ascension.

"What are you hiding?" His mood has gone black.

I feel my skin peeling from my bones in bare vulnerability. "I hide nothing."

I breathe.

*He must believe me.*

I ascend the first step.

The second.

On the third, his hand stiffens around my arm, and he yanks me back. My ankle rolls, and I pitch backwards into the Mongol, the armor clanging to the floor and fracturing joint from joint. The key shoots from the girdle, sliding fatally, fatefully, to Gaston's feet.

He picks up the bloodstained key, a beet flush moving across his face as he studies it. "How came this blood upon the key?"

He sees it all: the blood, my shaking, my spring of tears. All tells of my evident guilt. He sees, and now he understands my betrayal.

It transfigures him.

Gaston crushes the key in his hand, slinging it across the room where it gashes the wall. He rounds on me, broken on the floor like the faux-gem. I was supposed to be the one.

I'm just a girl.

I scuffle backwards, my ankle inflamed and dragged along, throbbing with a double beat. My back smacks the other wall. Trapped.

His azure beard aflame with vengeance, Gaston howls like the wolf that he is. "Did you open that door?"

"No," but it's a feeble word, stressed and half-spoken.

He kicks the Mongol's tufted helm, spinning it violently across the room. He wrenches me up by the arms, my feet dangling over the marble, and I feel the sparks of flame from his beard. Stray embers spitting, searing, branding my face. "I wanted you to be the one," he says, a dejected, hoarse whisper. He weeps, but the tears aren't for me. They're for himself and his life that must forever be accursed.

His hands press and bruise and hurt. I whimper. "Please, be merciful."

"Mercy," he spits. "What has Fate shown *me* of mercy?"

There's a moment where I think he'll forget himself and his vengeance, that he'll lay aside his choler and his cruelty and kiss me, the wolf's passion for violence conquered by a passion for other things. But when he does kiss me, it's grasping, rough, and cold, so incredibly cold that I feel his breath turn to ice in my mouth. It's the kiss of a soulless man, who does not love, but devours.

Breaking the kiss, he throws me onto the stairs. He goes to the scimitar mounted on the wall and takes it down. "Kneel."

"Please—"

"I said kneel!" He pushes me down.

"Wait! Kill me if you must, and you must"—*for I would rather die than live the rest of my life in such great sorrow*. I cling to his leg, driveling plaintively for more time. "I was untrue to you. But perhaps in my next life I'll be granted to try again. Please"—*please please please*—"allow me a final prayer."

Hot air blows from his nose. My failure is worse than that of the previous wives, because he loved me. Even as he holds me down, brandishing his weapon, I see in his eyes that he loves me, that it kills him to kill me. But he's compelled to do it. Compelled by a curse.

His jaw hardens, and I utter one final *please*.

"Quickly." Gaston lets go, and I face the stairs, kneeling on the bottom step. I clasp together my prayer hands, though I don't know if that's right. I've never prayed this way before.

"*Nīlakantha*," I start. "To Shiva, blue-throated one." My voice bounces and breaks, pebbles on an enchanted road. "Dancer of *Tandava*, primordial. Subdue my heart. Absolve my sins." Gaston glares down at me, and I see his soul escaping his eye through a teardrop on its rim. It splashes into his beard, hissing steam. "And bless my husband."

"Are you finished?"

"Amen." He grabs my hair, holding it off my neck. "I'm sorry, Gaston."

"Your sorrow does not excuse your sins."

"No," I say. "But it might absolve you of yours."

He tips back my head, exposing my throat, and I feel every particle of my body pump and slow, pump and slow, slow, slow. And calm. Absolute. Calm.

I'm not afraid to die. Like Papa, I'm ready. Ready to join the other wives behind the chamber door.

Gaston sets the scimitar to my throat, and I feel the ice-smile of its sinister blade. He pulls it back to swing. I shut my eyes. I listen to the sound of slicing air.

## CHAPTER 35
# ONE LAST SACRIFICE

Death is louder than I expected.

The front door crashes in, and Henry barrels over the threshold and behind him—

Behind him is my brother, Byron.

"Byron!"

Still wearing his uniform of cavalry black and yellow, he relies on a crutch. His gait limps painfully, but he stands uprightly, heroically, his shoulders square and his rapier pointed fully upon Gaston. "Step back from my sister, fiend. Or you'll have the pleasure to treat with my blade."

"Treat." Gaston releases me, rising to his full colossal height. Undaunted, Byron curls his lip in malice. "The treat will be yours."

Gaston tracks the floor in front of Byron, stepping casually, coolly. Back and forth, feeling my brother's size and his stance. He stabs left—Byron deflecting easily, hopping backward on his good leg.

My brother carries his strength in his chest and his arms—an even opponent—but his crutch makes his stepping hobbled and awkward and dangerously unsteady. A disadvantage Gaston will exploit. He paces the floor, patient, a falcon circling prey. Watching. Counting. Calculating.

Henry rushes to me, embracing the wall to clear the melee. "Are you hurt?"

"My ankle." It has purpled and swelled, but I don't think it's broken. "How did my brother get here?"

"He had his leg blasted in a street riot—said Simon pushed him out of the way of a musket that was aimed by one of their own soldiers. They discharged him to come home, and a woman found him days later in a tavern, anguishing over Simon's death. She claimed she knew Gaston, and that you were in danger." Rushed in his speech, Henry swipes the sweat from his brow.

"A woman," I say, panting. "What was her name?"

"Indira. They're lovers now, apparently."

Byron, still a rogue in every sense of the word. Gratitude blossoms in my heart for Indira—my clandestine savior—but my joy is short-lived. Henry grips my hand, the pistol in his other juddering violently. If he mis-aims, he could hit Byron. By the way he holds it—grip tight, afraid of the trigger—I gather he's never used a weapon before in his life.

Having learned his foe, Gaston fights viciously and swift. He feints a jab on Byron's left, forcing him to step with his injury, and thrusts center for a fatal dice and carve. Byron yells, taking the pain of his leg and embracing it, digesting its power. He leaps with a howl, hammering back the assault. Their blades blitz and shriek, steel grinding steel, as Gaston's inhuman beard flares like blinding smith-fire.

Glancing another hit, Byron lunges—*smiling*—cracking his crutch on Gaston's knee to hinge it and slicing his rapier skyward. But that was his mistake: the lunge. He stepped with his right leg, his good leg, leaving his bad vulnerable to Gaston's bone-snapping kick.

Byron's scream issues blood to my ears and his name to my throat. Wrenching the crutch from him, Gaston rives it across his thigh and throws aside the splintered pieces. He lifts his blade to end my brother.

I get caught in that movement. That lifting and lifting and the room stretching vertically thin, and I can't lose my brother a second time.

"Henry, the pistol!"

But he's already aimed, already taken the shot. The bullet misses, ricocheting off the face of the grandfather clock and whizzing back to me. I throw my arms over my head as the bullet tears into the banister, a fusillade of splinters haling down. A substantial piece lodges into Henry's shoulder. Seeing it, seeing the sickening way it has lacerated his flesh, pales him white as bone.

It's easy for Gaston to slam the pistol from Henry's hand and throw him across the floor, a smear of blood marking his flight. His body wallops the ground like a limp kill, head bashed unconscious on the marble next to Byron.

With menacing calm, Gaston turns back to me, his black eyes slick and hard as river stones. "The letter," he says, and it takes me an eye-blink to remember. Henry's letter. His declaration of love. I failed to hide it. "Did you love him as you loved me?"

In this, at least, I needn't lie. "I did not." Using that wrecked banister, I pull myself to standing, pressing weight on my ankle. Like Byron, I'll use its pain to fuel me into strength, into action if I must. "But I loved him better."

My words are a puncture and a drain. Gaston's surging chest collapses with his shoulders, the scimitar sinking to his side. No words or withheld affection have ever hurt him more.

Save for this.

"It's me, Gaston." I take a cautionary, limping step toward him, my foot knocking Byron's rapier. "It's Parvati. I've returned to you."

The deception works, giving him pause. Gaston's stone-eyes shine with belief. With beautiful, tragic hope. "Why did you do it, Parvati?" he chokes. "Why did you break my heart?"

Channeling the spirit world, I ask her the same. *Why did you do it?*

The answer comes in an instant, my voice a mouthpiece for Parvati's ghost. "The gods toiled with my life, but I failed to take it back. I saw that you were cursed, and I knew I could not save you."

Miserable lines fold around his eyes. I know only the thoughts Gaston utters, those he shows through his touch, his desire. I show him my desire, stepping and reaching for him, but he pushes out his hand. *Stop. Keep away from me.* And I feel that hand like a strike to my heart. I may have loved Henry better, but I've loved Gaston *most.* I can't let him go.

"I believe your grandmother's words, Gaston. *I* am your hope. I can save you."

His beard simmers cool, a faint smolder of cloudy blue and coal gray. The curse is waning. *Lifting.* He's coming back to me.

Gaston's shoulders rise, his chin titling into determination. Into resistance. Into hate. "But can you save *him*?"

He swings the scimitar at Henry.

I scream. And in that scream a furious power seizes control of my body. My foot digs under the fuller of Byron's rapier and kicks it upward to my hand, which catches it—*catches it*—and thrusts, shoves, *pushes* the blade into Gaston's back. Right into his heart.

My ears fill with the blatant ticking of the grandfather clock, still beating out its defunct time despite its shattered face. The rapier retracts, and I cry out. I did that. I made that blossoming wound. My weapon, his weapon, they drop simultaneously, clattering to the floor. Only mine has blood. Only mine broke flesh.

Gaston turns around, tormentingly slow. On his chest, a rosebud blooms, redder than I've ever seen. Winched to his knees, he falls, and I catch his shoulders, laying his head in my skirts.

Life is a mere flicker in his eyes. He looks at me with love, and he tries to say it, *I love you*. He tries to say it, but his voice is dying into shallow breaths.

"I didn't mean to," I sob. "I wanted to save you, Gaston, to break your curse. I..."

*Dare I say it?*

I do. I dare.

"I love you." Gaston reaches for my face, my mouth. I kiss his fingers, and they're warm. They're warm like his eyes are warm. "I wish I could have saved you."

"You did." A strange sort of ecstasy eclipses his face. The blue lifts from his beard, an evanescence vaporing to the air, leaving only slate, and silver, and a whole shore of the lightest freckles.

## CHAPTER 36
# PARTING GIFTS

I do not bury him alone. Henry stands at my side, along with Anna and Ami Rose, Byron and his fiancée Indira—who is in every way as elegant and fiery as her sister—and even Silas Mitchell, Henry's friend and now mine, too. They bow their heads with me in prayer for the souls of my husband and his wives, placing gifts upon their coffins.

Each wife has her place next to Gaston, even Parvati. In accordance with Hindu custom, we wrapped her in red and cremated her, now burying her urn between Gaston and Ami Rose's brother, Benjamin. Whether their love was a curse or a wish, I felt their bodies should be near each other, their stories remembered through that nearness.

For Clarimond, who played the pianoforte, I had Anna

compose a theme, which I rolled up like a scroll and tied with silk ribbon. For Angelique, I commissioned a sculptor—one of Henry's schoolmates—to carve a little Papillon out of dogwood bark. (Henry smiled, thinking my pun was intentional.) And for Lenore, I made a rosary from the jade beads and rose quartz gems of Gaston's own collection. These women deserve my admiration. They were brave and cunning and curious. They broke the rules to reveal the truth, and I hope, if reincarnation is real, that in some faraway future they'll live second lives to break the rules all over again.

My parting gift to Gaston seems less personal than for the others, but I couldn't think of any other earthly possession he'd want with him in the afterlife, when his soul is being weighed against a feather. He'll need proof of Set's toiling, that duplicitous god of chaos. Its power vanquished, whispering no more, I had the lapis falcon inlaid into Gaston's casket. Reticent and cold, as it should be, the amulet is a stone once more.

My veil of black lace flutters with the breeze, and I imagine Gaston encircling me, thanking me.

Stepping back from the grave, I turn to Henry, the morning sun washing his face in peachy hues. The tenderness with which he takes my hand brings an ache to my heart, bittersweet in its affection. "I'm free," I say to him, "but I've never felt more lost."

He brings me into his arms as I weep.

Indira throws her arms around us both, her sari casting off the sweet smells of jasmine and curry. She is warmth embodied, and I'm so glad to know her, to call her my sister.

"Just because you feel lost does not mean that you are," she says, her accent lyrical and soft. "My sister knew that better than anyone. Parvati left her family, her country, because the world was bigger than what she knew, and she needed to explore it. In many ways, you are like her." She kisses my forehead, a laugh at her lips. "She also was stubborn."

I laugh, too, smiling wide. "What would she do now, having just buried the only life she ever knew?"

Taking my cheeks in her hands, Indira says, "She would search the Earth for a new one."

I turn, a new hand of comfort at my shoulder. Silas. "If I may, Beatrice, now might be an appropriate time to discuss the matter of your inheritance."

I blink at him, trying to absorb what he's said. "Inheritance?"

"Your husband placed his assets in a trust for you. Though, until you reach the age of majority, the account must have a trustee." Retrieving a document from his briefcase, Silas reads, "One 'Amelia Rose Moore' was selected for the role."

Ami Rose steps forward, as surprised as I am. "What does this mean?" she demands.

"It means that you may access the entirety of Mrs.

Dumas's assets on her behalf until her twenty-first birthday, at which time she will be granted full control. I won't bore you with the legal jargon—just know that you are the guardian of her estate. Together, you can do anything you like with it."

Ami Rose and I look to each other—bewildered—then burst into exhilarated laughter. I've been truly *liberated.* No one will ever control my security again because it will lie within *my* own means. To be independent has been my greatest dream—a restitution, a gift. The most cherished gift Gaston has ever given me.

"Is it truly everything, Silas?"

"Dumas's manor house, his ship—it's all yours."

"His ship! The crew included?"

Silas laughs, though I'm too overjoyed to feel sheepish for my lack of knowledge. "If their salaries are maintained, I imagine so. If it pleases you, I'll offer my services as your lawyer, to ensure your assets remain secure."

"Oh, it pleases me! I could think of no nobler man for the job." I grab Henry's hand. "Where shall we travel first?"

"Travel!"

"Corfu? Morocco? Maybe India!"

Byron jumps in. "The maharaja won't be able to contain you."

"He could not contain me, either," adds Indira, and my brother kisses her, grinning.

"I believe I first have a debt to pay." Henry sweeps

back my veil, seeing my pout of displeasure. "I made a vow to myself to repay the guarantor of the life I was given. Even though he has passed, my debt to him still holds." He skims his thumb along my cheek. "Just as he did, you have saved my life, Beatrice. Every brushstroke I make from now on will be in repayment—in homage—to you."

"But I want you with me."

"I'll be right here when you return. You deserve everything, Beatrice. I won't ever keep you from your dreams." For the first time, he kisses me, and into that kiss he pours every thought of me he's ever had, extending further than I could have ever imagined. He's fearless, not for a moment thinking I'll never return to him, because he trusts that I will. In love, this is the truest sense of freedom: Henry is the string to my kite, supporting my flight.

But no journey is ever taken alone. I'll need a guide, a companion. "Anna," I say, gesturing her close. Waiting in the background like a wallflower, she thought I had forgotten her. But I will never forget my sister, my pearl. "Will you take this journey with me, with Ami Rose?" Hand-in-hand, all three of us, we wait for her answer.

For the first time in her life, Anna doesn't hesitate, her patient dreams finally given a voice. "Can we go to Vienna? Where Mozart lived?"

I pull her close, loving her more than I ever have. "First stop, Vienna. And then, the world."

THERE'S SO much to prepare for my first voyage across the globe. I mustn't forget to pack my hatpins—and riding boots—and a folio for writing my letters to Henry. I've commissioned a few pairs of trousers to be made for Anna and myself, and have purchased a fur muff as a gift for Mamma when we visit her in Bavaria, after our stop in Vienna. I think she'll be pleased with the quality, and that I spared no expense for her.

I'm glad she's far away from the pernicious rumors circulating about her sinful daughter, the scheming seductress who had her husband murdered so she could steal his money and elope with her artist lover.

No one ever mentions, or has even noticed, the absence of my guardian Mr. Haskell, and I've never spared another thought for him.

The town's gossip rolls over me like water, but I won't drown. I hold my head high, thanking providence I'm alive.

Folio case in hand, I search for a spare pen nib to add to it. As I go to Gaston's study to look for one, my feet freeze at the threshold. I haven't entered this room since that hideous day, when I broke his curse. In the aftermath of his death, as Dr. Crane and the magistrate consulted the witnesses to the crime in hushed, important tones, I floated like the dead into this study, sinking down in the chair at his desk. His youthful portrait stared down at me without an ounce of ire or blame, and laid my head down to cry. The catharsis—the release of regret and sorrow, hope and love—poured out of me until my chest felt light and I could breathe again. The room was an overwhelming calm.

The storm had passed.

Stepping cautiously into the room, I find a letter on Gaston's desk. A letter I couldn't see before through all my tears. A letter addressed to me.

*Beatrice.*

*I will write to you in this moment of clarity, when Set's evil lies dormant. He is a cruel god, capricious, chaotic. He will seek to destroy you through his infection of me, as he has all the others. Under his influence, I've deceived you, threatened you, but still you have withstood. I am a broken man, but it is too selfish a demand to ask you to mend me.*

*Every story I've told you is true, save one: I chose you not because of the color of your eyes, or your youth, or even my belief that you could rend these chains of mine. I chose you because I fell in love with you, quickly and all at once.*

*To want something and have it denied you is agonizing, but to take it is worse. I took you, Beatrice. I took you greedily for my own, to fill my emptiness, and I am a wretch for it. I cared little for your freedom until I saw you enduring every pain and injustice to satisfy your selflessness—a detrimental sacrifice in every way imaginable. I should have released you then, to spare you everything. I should have hoisted my misery upon my shoulders where it belongs as my own responsibility.*

*I have gloried in your beauty, your spirit. You have returned the life to my body—intellect to my mind—joy to my heart! It is because of you I have fought against Set so furiously. And I make this promise to you, my dearest wife: for you, I will keep fighting until you know the goodness of the man I once was.*

*Gaston.*

There was no date, no way to know whether he wrote this before or after he gave me his heart in the shape of a key. I press his letter to my chest and imagine he's here, holding me after the storm, kissing me in its calm. Gaston showed me what love is and isn't, how it grows with a word or a touch, or diminishes by neglect. In his arms, I was a woman—a limitless creature of power and pleasure and potential. He taught me about the world and that I belong everywhere in it. For all his faults, his moods, his curses, Gaston was a man I could love. And love him, I did. There's no doubt of it, because when I broke his curse, the love remained.

As I know it always will.

# Acknowledgments

An enormous thank you to Amy Michelle Carpenter and the team at Monster Ivy Publishing, without whom this book would still be just a story on my hard drive. You're all rockstars and I can't wait to work with you again.

Thank you to the indomitable Dana LeCheminant, my first reader and French dictionary. You hustle *hard* and I'm constantly in awe of you.

A million thank-you's to the OG Writer's Night: Janessa, Missy, McKenna, and Dana. You cheered me on, kept me on track, and never failed to give it to me straight. You helped my writing shine, and for that I'm forever grateful. No matter where you're at in your own publishing journey, I'm here for you. You're talented and will make your dreams come true.

Supportive friends have gotten me through the rough days when I felt like quitting. Thank you, Christina, Emily, and Cheyenne, for loving me just the way I am—weirdness and all.

A resounding THANKS! to my family for not rolling their eyes when I told them I wanted to be an author instead of a social worker. "Real jobs" just weren't for me. I like this much better.

A big *MWUAH* to my hubs for waiting to read my book while I dealt with my insecurities. Like the dedication says, you can read it now. I love you, boo. (Gross!)

And finally, thank you to the person who sparked my dream: Michelle Smith, educator extraordinaire. You saw potential in me when I was a maudlin teen with a daydreaming problem. Thank you for waking me up.

# About the Author

M. P. Halliday adores ghost stories and period dramas, gothic ruins and thunderstorms. If she could live in a haunted house, she would, but has settled for the humid woods of northern Georgia. *SkyBlue* is her first novel.

# DISCUSSION QUESTIONS

1. There are moments in the beginning of the book where Beatrice reminisces about her father, giving us the sense she once idolized him. But as his past sins are gradually revealed, Beatrice realizes her and her siblings' lives have been upended and their safety threatened. Why do you think Charles Tilney kept his failures a secret from his family? How do secrets hurt families? How can we foster communication and problem solving during the times in our lives when we need help?

2. After their father's funeral, Beatrice's brother Simon chides her for stating their mother should mourn her loss with her children instead of alone. It is later implied Marjorie Tilney may be suffering with depression. Does Beatrice understand what her mother is going through, or does she resent it? What toll does untreated mental

illness take on families and individuals? How can we make space for others' mental health journeys as well as our own?

3. Beatrice differs from Gaston not just in age, but in maturity and life experience as well. Does she hold equal or less power in their marriage? When are age gap relationships appropriate versus inappropriate? When do these types of relationships become abusive?

4. Ami Rose's response to Anna's sexual assault is patience, a listening ear, and the understanding that healing from trauma takes time. What would you say to a survivor of rape or abuse? How would you show them you believe them?

5. George Lucas's character Indiana Jones famously said, "That belongs in a museum!" But Gaston would disagree. In the book, he derides his fellow archaeologists for plundering a country's history by selling artifacts to museums in England and Europe. Is there a way to explore a culture without exploiting it? What does cultural appropriation look like, and what could we do instead?

A Conversation with M. P. Halliday

**Q: When you pitched *SkyBlue* as a retelling of the Bluebeard fairytale, responses were mixed. Some people knew the story while others didn't. Could you give a brief synopsis of the original tale?**

A: Sure! "Bluebeard" is a French folktale jotted down by Charles Perrault and later the Grimm brothers. The gist is, a mysterious foreigner marries one unsuspecting girl after another, gifting her with a key to a locked chamber she's told never to open. When she inevitably does, she solves the gruesome mystery of her predecessors' fates: one by one the wives were murdered—and now she's next! Bluebeard is one of those dark stories with dozens of iterations, often allegorical of the Bible's Eve and her forbidden fruit of knowledge. In my retelling, the heroine is faced with the same choice the girl in the original tale was; she's given a key to terrible knowledge, but she's also up against her greatest fear: intimacy in an era that demands her innocence. *SkyBlue* is ultimately about a girl's self-discovery, her maturity, and her first love.

**Q: Why did you choose to retell this fairytale as opposed to more popular ones?**

A: Like his wives in the story, I was drawn to Bluebeard out of simple curiosity, but then quicky grew frustrated. You see, the original tale provides no motive for Bluebeard's murderous acts, and insensibly focuses on the "lesson" for all girls: do as you're told but nothing more. *No, no, no,* I thought. Women have always been smart, resilient, and above all *curious*. When I envisioned Beatrice Tilney, I wanted to draw out this dilemma the world has created in us girls—that we must be everything all at once—and show the turmoil it creates inside us when we want things we're told aren't for us, or are put in situations we're just not ready for.

**Q: Is Bluebeard still the villain in your retelling?**

A: Yes and no. Perrault's Bluebeard was a prototypical serial killer—violent, narcissistic, hated women. I'd like to think mine, Gaston Dumas, is more interesting. When I created him, I wanted to make sense of his motives, and I didn't want him to be a misogynist. He is still a man in a world run by men, with tendencies towards benevolent sexism. But ultimately, he is a human being with two masks: the one he wears for others, and his true face, the tormented man struggling against an ancient curse.

**Q: The characters Jane and Mr. Rochester from Charlotte Brontë's novel *Jane Eyre* feature prominently in Beatrice's self-exploration. Are there parallels between Jane and Beatrice?**

A: Definitely! Both girls are captivated by temperamental, haunted men (a staple of gothic literature) and both long for independent lives they're allowed to control. Popular media seeking to modernize *Jane Eyre* point out the novel's flaws—the gaslighting, the impropriety of falling for an older man, and his hypnotic sway over an iron mind like Jane's. While those issues certainly exist, what readers may overlook is Jane's commitment to her values; she leaves Rochester rather than live with him in iniquity, which teaches her to put herself first. They reunite in the end, but only after Jane has become emotionally self-reliant. A bit unromantic, but I think it teaches a lesson I certainly had to learn in my own life. Self-love is vital to a successful romance, and Beatrice undergoes a similar arc in *SkyBlue*.

**Q: Are there books or authors who inspired your writing?**

A: It's obvious I love the Brontë sisters and their moody, problematic leading men, but the books that inspired me to write *SkyBlue* came from writers like Lauren DeStefano (her Chemical Garden trilogy), Laini Taylor (*Daughter of Smoke and Bone*), Libba Bray (*A Great and Terrible Beauty*), and Leigh Bardugo (her Grishaverse). These writers have lush, poetic voices that helped me develop my own. I absolutely love them.

www.ingramcontent.com/pod-product-compliance
Lightning Source LLC
Chambersburg PA
CBHW060550310726
48982CB00008B/1079/J